CRIMINAL KINFOLK

DALE O. GARRETT

CRIMINAL KINFOLK

CRIMINAL KINFOLK

INTRODUCTION

Greetings, and thank you for delving into the pages of "Criminal Kinfolk." As the author, I bring forth a narrative rooted in true events and family secrets that remained concealed for many, many years.

A shadow of shame enveloped me for the better part of my life due to our family's well-guarded secret. Being a law enforcement officer alongside my two older brothers, I often felt the weight of our three half-siblings stained with the labels of bank robbery and murder, casting a dark cloud over our family name.

The inspiration to pen this book emerged when my brother Gary shared an old newspaper article on social media. The article chronicled a daring bank robbery and shoot-out involving our now deceased half-brothers, shedding light on their criminal exploits and subsequent arrests.

During my formative years and into adolescence, Malcolm, one of the half-brothers, made sporadic visits to our home while on the run from the law. These visits, though infrequent, revealed Malcolm's adeptness at evading the law, with prison escapes spanning from Florida to Tennessee to Indiana.

The catalyst for this book crystallized as Gary and I discussed our criminal half-brothers at length following the post of the newspaper article. Recognizing the amazing juxtaposition of their story against our law enforcement careers, we concluded that their tale, akin to a Hollywood movie, needed to be shared. And thus, the inception of this book took root.

Having delved into court documents, additional newspaper articles, and interviews with cousins and living relatives who were able to shed additional light on the outlaw trio, I now find myself honored to be the one selected to immortalize our family's saga - warts and all - in these pages.

This is the tale of law and order, crime and punishment, and, in one instance, a journey towards redemption. It's the chronicle of brothers who walked life's path on opposite sides of the badge.

I invite you now to turn the page and accompany me on this thrilling, captivating, and unforgettable journey.

Dale O. Garrett

DEDICATION

With the release of this book, I extend my deepest gratitude and love to the extraordinary woman who shaped my world—my mother, Delois Garrett, God rest her soul.

Her unwavering commitment, persistent concern, and meticulous evaluation of the company I kept were not merely acts of maternal duty, but were the vigilant threads that wove the fabric of my life. She steered me and my four elder brothers towards the righteous paths we tread today.

It is a testament to her influence that two of my brothers and I found our calling in the honorable field of law enforcement, dedicated to upholding justice and enforcing the law. Simultaneously, the twins among us chose the noble path of serving in the military and later transitioned into becoming respected journalists.

As I reflect on our collective journey, what sets our narrative apart is the stark contrast with my much older half-brothers, who, tragically, succumbed to a life of violent crime and prolonged incarceration. Their story, a reflection of their upbringing, lays bare the consequences of a childhood marked by the absence of guidance and discipline.

I place a lot of the blame squarely on them for it was their own choices that led to their downfall. But I also place much of the blame elsewhere. They were victims of circumstances shaped largely by their mother, Grace—an unfortunate soul trapped in a self-destructive cycle of promiscuity and alcoholism.

Often abandoned during their formative years, they were denied the parental guidance and discipline crucial for a healthy development of morals - leading to unfortunate yet predictable outcomes.

In this dedication, I want to honor not only the guidance and discipline my mother instilled in me but also her keen sense of protection. Her watchful eyes shielded me from negative influences, ensuring that the company I kept was a source of positivity.

Mom, thank you and Dad too for meticulously curating my environment, for being the shield against adverse influences, and for shaping me into the person I am today. Your efforts, both seen and unseen, are eternally cherished, and I shall carry the invaluable lessons you imparted with me until my final breath.

CONTENTS

ACKNOWLEDGMENTS

I extend my sincere gratitude to the individuals who played crucial roles in the creation of this book:

Foremost, my thanks go to God for guiding me through the entire writing journey. His divine inspiration was indispensable, and without it, completing this work would not have been possible. I am appreciative of His constant presence, the blessings bestowed upon me and my family, and for Him providing me the opportunity to share this story with others.

Special appreciation is reserved for Lynn Garrett, Renee Eckert, and Fred Moore. Their invaluable feedback and editing skills were instrumental in shaping the manuscript into its finest version.

I am deeply indebted to my brothers in blood and in law enforcement, Gary and Carl Garrett, whose contributions, especially the untold stories of our outlaw half-brothers, greatly enriched the content of this book.

Reluctantly, I acknowledge my deceased outlaw half-brothers, Malcolm, Jimmy, and Billy Ray Garrett. Their escapades, although unconventional, immoral, and criminal, served as the foundation for this book's existence.

Lastly, but certainly not least, my heartfelt thanks go to

my wife Lynn. Her unwavering support and encouragement were the pillars that sustained me throughout the writing process. She not only provided valuable plot ideas and story structure but also elevated the book beyond my initial imagination. Without her love and patience, this book would not have come to fruition.

Dale O. Garrett

PROLOGUE

Maryville, Tennessee - Monday January 1, 1973

It was 42 degrees. Malcolm sat fully dressed and wrapped in an old tattered quilt in a rocking chair. Sitting on the front porch of the run-down apartment he'd been living in for almost three months was one of his favorite things to do. The porch floor looked more like weathered barnwood than it did a porch. There were a few loose planks too, so Malcolm was always careful where he walked and where he put his weight down. The apartment was close to town – about a half mile - but would still be considered by most folks to be pretty rural.

The view down the hill Malcolm could see from his perch on the porch wasn't much to write home about. Just the back of a strip mall across the road and a few dumpsters. As he sipped on his morning coffee that he always drank black, an old rusty pick-up truck drove by and the friendly farmer behind the wheel honked his horn and waved hello to Malcolm.

Malcolm managed a two-finger wave in response, but recoiled a bit from the tinge of pain he felt in his head.

"Goddamn hangover," he thought to himself as he endured the repercussions from drinking way too much Jack Daniels Number 7 whiskey with Penny. Penny was a whore he had picked up the night before at Lucky's Place, a nearby hole-in-the-wall bar. She had followed him back to his place in her own car to celebrate New Year's Eve with him.

About that time, Penny came out onto the front porch with her purse in her hand while running her arm down into the sleeve of the same pea-green knee-length jacket she was wearing the night before. Her hair was still a bit tussled from all of the rolling around in the bed they had done.

Walking briskly and talking fast, "It's eleven o'clock, I gotta go sugar! I'm late for work at the diner!" said Penny as she rushed off of the porch and hopped into her black '64 Ford Fairlane.

"Well alright then. C'mon back when you can stay a while," was Malcolms only response as he raised his coffee cup a bit toward her as if he were toasting her departure. As he gestured with it, the coffee sloshed in the cup. A small wisp of steam rose from the still very hot beverage into the chilly morning air.

As Penny backed out of the gravel driveway onto the blacktop, Malcolm heard loud rock music coming from an approaching car. The car came into view from behind the kudzu. It was Malcolm's two brothers, Billy Ray and Jimmy Garrett in Billy Ray's two-door '69 baby blue Gran Torino. Malcolm could hear "Hello I Love You' by The Doors playing even with the car's windows rolled up.

4

In the car's back seat were two new fellas. William Mooney and Charles Fagin. They had done time with Jimmy in the Knox County lock-up. William and Jimmy had become pretty good friends. Billy Ray turned off the car's ignition and hopped out of the driver's seat. As if he could tell that Malcolm was nursing a bad hangover Billy Ray said loudly and cheerfully, "good mornin' sunshine!"

"Go fuck yourself," was Malcolm's muted response. "And fuck that hippy shit you call music too!" Billy Ray grinned broadly and chuckled at the rise he'd gotten out of Malcolm.

While Billy Ray was greeting Malcolm, Mooney and Fagin pushed the seat backs forward and climbed out of the back seat of the Gran Torino. They trailed behind Jimmy and Billy Ray as they all walked to the yard in front of the porch. Jimmy spoke up, "Malcolm, this is William and Charlie. These are the guys I was telling you about."

Malcolm toasted with his coffee cup again toward the two strangers and said, "mornin' boys."

In unison, they both replied, "howdy."

Billy Ray said, "Hey ladies! Can we all go inside? It's cold as a witch's tit out here!"

"Yeah, I reckon so," replied Malcolm as he shrugged off the quilt onto the rocking chair, rose to his feet, and led the way into his apartment.

The apartment was small and sparsely furnished. There was a tattered brown love seat and a mis-matched dark blue wing-back chair in the living room. Once everyone was inside the apartment, they sat down where they could. Dilly Ray and Charlie sat on the love seat and Malcolm sat down in his usual seat, the wing-backed chair. Jimmy slid two of Malcolm's worn-out wooden kitchen chairs from the kitchen into the edge of the living room so he and William would have a place to sit.

William spoke first. "Jimmy tells me you boys have a bank job up in Fairmount, Indiana you need help with."

"We don't really need any help to be honest with you." replied Malcolm. "We've been doing just fine with just the three of us."

Jimmy interrupted, "Hear them out Malcolm!"

William said, "Look, I'm from Fairmount. I know the streets and I know the people that work there. Fairmount is a bigger bank than that one y'all knocked over in Swayzee last year. There are also more cops on duty in Fairmount."

Malcolm scoffed, "Pffft! Fairmount is a one-horse town just like Swayzee – just like all the other jobs we've done! Hell, that's why we pick'em! They're small shitty banks in small shitty towns!"

"Yeah," said William, "but I'm telling you man, Fairmount has more cops."

"Well how many cops do you reckon they've got?" asked Malcolm.

William replied, "I know for a fact they've got three. Maybe four if the Chief's working and you count him. You guys need us because Charlie can cut the alarm and I can drive another car and distract the cops while you boys are doing your thing!"

Malcolm pondered a moment on what William had said and asked, "How do you know so much about alarm systems Charlie?"

"I don't know shit about alarm systems," replied Charlie. "I do know about electricity though. I do electrical work for a livin' – I mean - you know - when I'm not in the can!" Everyone chuckled.

Pivoting toward the kitchen where William was sitting, Malcolm asked, "and just how would you go about distracting Johnny Law?"

William replied, "Easy! I'm going to do some donuts in my 'Stang' on the opposite side of town in front of the cops!"

Billy Ray spoke up, "Why would you do that man? The cops are going to chase you and that'll just bring more cops!"

"No, they won't," said William. "I'm not going to run! While they're busy writing me a ticket, you boys will be doing your thing across town at the bank and there'll be one, maybe two less fuzz out there that could accidentally drive by at just the right time and pinch you guys!"

Billy Ray responded, "but you'll get a ticket man!"

William said, "So what!? They write me a $20 speeding ticket and later, I pay it with my take of the money!"

"Damn!" said Billy Ray, "That's pretty slick man!" This all sounds good to me! What do you think Malcolm?"

Malcolm took a sip of his coffee and replied, "You know what? I actually like it!" We're going to need some new wheels for the getaway though. Something fast!"

"Oh, don't worry about that big brother!" said Billy Ray. "I've already got that covered!"

Malcolm asked, "It's a four-door, right?"

Billy Ray replied, "Nope, it's a five door!"

"What the fuck are you talking about!?" asked Malcolm.

"It's an ambulance!" said Billy Ray.

With a quizzical look on his face, Malcolm responded, "I'm sorry, it sounded like you just said you got us a fucking ambulance for a getaway car."

Billy Ray grinned a big shit eating grin and said, "Yep! It's a '70 Cadillac, Miller-Meteor Life-liner Ambulance!"

"Are you outta your ever-loving mind?" asked Malcolm.

Jimmy interjected, "I don't know, it could work! Think about it! The cops ain't gonna stop no ambulance with its lights and siren goin' because they'll think it's on its way to an emergency or some shit!"

"BINGO!" exclaimed Billy Ray. "We'll be hiding in plain sight, right under their fucking noses! Clean getaway big brother!"

Malcolm pondered for a moment and said, "I hate to be the one to break the news to you, but they're going to be looking hard for a stolen damn ambulance. They probably already are!"

Billy Ray replied, "No they won't and no they ain't either! It ain't stolen! I bought it myself fair and square with cash money from the Swayzee job we did! Got it up there at the auction house in north Knoxville! It had a fucked-up fender, but I'm already working on that. I've gotta sand the Bondo down a little more and give it a shot coat of primer and a little paint and we'll be good to go!"

Malcolm thought a bit and rubbed his chin as though in deep thought. "Hmmm. Maybe. Just maybe," he said softly.

Charlie spoke up, "I think it's a great plan! So, are me and William in or what?"

Billy Ray replied, "I say you're in."

"I say you're in too," added Jimmy as he looked over toward Malcolm for his approval. "What say you brother?"

Malcolm paused for a second then smiled and replied, "Any friend of my baby brother is a friend of mine! You boys are in! We'll hit the bank on the 12th. That's a Friday," said Malcolm looking at the January 1973 page of the big calendar that was hanging on the wall beside him above the non working black and white TV set. "They're always ripe for the pickin' on Fridays!"

"Me and William are gonna need guns," remarked Charlie.

Malcolm replied, "I'll take care of that little detail myself!" Malcolm raised his coffee cup in the air in a final toast and continued, "we're gonna be rich boys!"

Billy Ray let out a loud whoop in excitement followed by a shout of "Hell yeah!" from Jimmy as he pumped his fist in the air.

The men all had big smiles on their faces thinking about the untold amount of money they were all about to come into in only eleven days. Little did any of them realize in that moment of elation that within a short time, one of them would soon draw their final breath.

CHAPTER 1
LITTLE HORSE THIEVES

Maryville, Tennessee - August 12, 1945

It was a hot humid August day in east Tennessee. Like much of the southeastern United States, Maryville is known for its warm and humid summers. Ten-year-old Malcolm and his brother Jimmy, three years his junior, were bored and needed a way to cool off. Initially, they talked about going swimming, but there wasn't an area in the creek deep enough and suitable for swimming. They decided to hike to the creek anyway and just wade in the water and maybe try to catch some crawdads.

Their favorite crawdad hole was about a mile and a half from their grandmother's house. The long hot walk to get there would be rewarded by the wonderful feeling of the cool 68-degree knee-deep creek water.

They didn't ask permission from their grandmother. They didn't really want or need her permission. Malcolm and Jimmy grew up like feral cats. They pretty much went where they wanted to go and did what they wanted to do.

Growing up, their carpenter father, Al Garret, was often times gone away from home and working on jobsites. Al was a hard-working man. He only had an 8th grade education, but he excelled at carpentry and used that sole skill to provide for his family. Sometimes the jobsites he worked at were two or more states away. He would be away from home a week, sometimes two weeks at a time.

Their mother, Grace, was a horrible mother. She stayed drunk most of the time and while she was supposed to be home raising the children, she would leave them and the baby, Billy Ray with their grandmother or a neighbor for days at a time.

While Al was away working, she would spend her time catching rides with truckers and other men she would meet at bars and truck stops and have sex with them. Sometimes the men would give her a little money, but making money wasn't her focus. She was just promiscuous and she enjoyed the company of men. Although Grace's husband Al suspected that she was being unfaithful to him, he tried his best to ignore all the signs of her infidelity.

When she WAS at home with the children in the small apartment they lived in, Grace would get on her drunken benders. The alcohol combined with her fiery temper caused the smallest things to set her off.

She once beat eight-year-old Malcolm almost to the point of unconsciousness when he had forgotten to change Billy Ray's diaper like he was supposed to. More often than not, either Malcolm or Jimmy would be wearing a black eye or bruises from the belt marks on their backs and buttocks from when she would beat them.

Malcolm and Billy Ray started their crawdad hunting adventure walking down the long, dusty, dirt road that ran in front of their grandma's house. As they walked along they started taking turns kicking an old tin can that they found lying in the weeds by the dirt road.

While kicking the rusty bent can that had a bullet hole through it, they chatted about the Lone Ranger radio show. They had both listened to several episodes of the show when Grace had left them with a neighbor during one of her own self-indulgent excursions.

"What do you think "Kemosabe" means?" asked Jimmy.

"I'm pretty sure it's Indian talk for 'friend'," came Malcolm's reply. "Tonto speaks good American, but sometimes, he slips back into his injun talk," explained Malcolm to his younger brother.

"Where do you think they live?" asked Jimmy.

"How the hell am I supposed to know that? They don't talk about their houses or nuthin' on the radio. Besides they're always too busy huntin' down bad guys and helpin' people," surmised Malcolm.

Jimmy replied, "I bet the Lone Ranger has a great big-ole ranch somewhere and Tonto probably has a tee-pee or maybe the Lone Ranger lets him sleep out in his barn."

Malcolm scoffed, "Tonto don't sleep in no barn you half-wit! He wouldn't be able to get no shut-eye smelling all that horse shit all night long! Besides, injuns don't need nuthin' soft like hay to sleep on. They can sleep on the ground or on rocks if'n they have to."

"I didn't even think about the horse shit," said Jimmy. "You're right, he probably has a tee-pee somewhere on the Lone Ranger's ranch or sumthin'."

"Yeah, he probably does," Malcolm acknowledged.

"Reckon how come he wears a mask?" asked Jimmy.

"I don't know," replied Malcolm. "I guess he just don't like people knowing who he is."

Jimmy responded, "Maybe he wears a mask in case he wants to rob somebody instead of helpin'em."

Malcolm, slightly annoyed at Jimmy's suggestion that the Lone Ranger would ever even entertain the thought of robbing someone, said, "The Lone Ranger ain't no crook! He's a good guy. Sure, he wears a mask, but he's still a good guy!"

Now satisfied with Malcolm's answer, their conversation trailed off as both boys continued walking down the dirt road kicking the can.

As they came to a meadow, they left the dirt road and walked through a downed section of a barbed wire fence. They walked about fifty yards through the meadow to the wood line. Entering the woods, Malcolm led the way down a trail he knew well through the woods. About fifty more yards through the thick, lush forest they came to the creek and their favorite crawdad hole. Pulling off their worn, black, lace-up shoes and rolling up the pant legs of their well-worn, faded and patched blue denim overalls, they waded into the cold refreshing water.

"Woo! This water feels nice!" said Malcolm. Jimmy was standing next to Malcolm, bending over and sucking in several swallows of the chilly water. Malcolm duplicated Jimmy's actions and took in big gulps of the sweet, tasty creek water. It was especially refreshing since the temperature was sweltering that day and they had worked up a thirst during their walk to get there.

They both started turning over rocks in the creek bed looking through the crystal-clear creek water for their crawdad prey. Jimmy was the first to find one. "I got one, I got one!" he exclaimed. "He's a fat one too!"

"Let me see him!" said Malcolm. Jimmy held the crawdad up for Malcolm to inspect. "He's a nice one! He's gonna make some good eatin.' Put him in the sack!" said Malcolm.

"Uh, Malcolm." said Jimmy.

"Yeah?" replied Malcolm.

Jimmy continued, "I didn't bring no sack. I thought you were bringing it!"

"You mean we walked all the way down here to go crawdad huntin' and ain't neither one of us got a sack to put'em in!?" asked Malcolm.

"I thought you were bringin' it," repeated Jimmy as he dejectedly sat down on a rock about the size of an average coffee table next to the creek. Malcolm waded through the knee-deep water and sat down on the big rock next to his brother. Jimmy could sense Malcolm's disappointment. He mumbled again quietly, "I thought you were bringin' it." He hated that he had disappointed his older brother.

"That's alright," said Malcolm, putting his hand on Jimmy's shoulder to comfort him. "I wasn't really in the mood to hunt crawdads anyhow," said Malcolm.

His mood brightening a bit, Jimmy asked, "Well, what do ya want to do now?"

"I don't know," replied Malcolm. And then an idea struck him. "Hey! Reckon where the water in this here creek comes from?"

Jimmy replied, "I don't know. Don't reckon I ever thought about it much. We ain't never explored much up the mountain."

"Well, let's find out where it comes from!" said Malcolm with renewed excitement as he stood up and waded over to where his shoes were on the bank of the creek. Jimmy followed suit and they both hurriedly got their shoes on. So began their new adventure to find the mysterious source of the water.

Following the creek upstream for almost 30 minutes, Malcolm and Jimmy pushed their way through thick underbrush and kudzu as they hiked along on their journey. Suddenly, Malcolm thought he heard something over the constant loud buzzing of the cicadas.

Malcolm stopped dead in his tracks and looking back at Jimmy, held up his index finger to his lips to alert Jimmy that something was happening and to be very quiet.

Jimmy froze and listened intently to hear what Malcolm had heard. Seconds later, they both heard the puzzling sound again. It was voices! It sounded like two people talking and they were ahead about fifty yards through the forest. Malcolm and Jimmy slowly and quietly crept through the bushes until they could clearly see the two men they had heard talking. They both dropped down to their bellies behind some bushes and intently watched the two men in the clearing.

They were tending a fire under a big copper pot. A pipe connected that pot to a thumper keg next to it and then that connected to a coiled copper "worm" tube which ran into another container being used as the condenser. Boxes of glass Mason jars sat on a tree stump about six feet from the condenser.

What the boys were looking at was an illegal moonshine still! It made sense that the two men had set their still up where they did. The location was deep in the foothills of the Smoky Mountains. It was isolated and the stream provided them with a constant supply of the purest, sweetest water in all of Tennessee. The creek was fed by a spring and the water produced by it had traveled to the surface via limestone caverns deep in the earth.

Malcolm knew immediately what it was. He had seen one once before when his father, Al, had taken him to visit a cousin on a farm. The boys also noticed that the two moonshiners hadn't hiked up to the still like they had just done. There were two old sway-back farm horses tied to a tree not too far from the still. One was brown and the other one was gray.

Malcolm and Jimmy remained motionless on their bellies for over an hour watching the two men sip from a shared Mason jar. It was obvious that the two men had become inebriated when one of them stood up and stumbled to the edge of the clearing to relieve himself in the bushes.

He sat the half-full jar of shine down on a log and began trying to undo the zipper of his overalls. As he fumbled with his zipper, he got over-balanced and fell over drunk, face-first into the bushes before he had even had a chance to pee.

The man remained face down passed out completely. His partner didn't seem much better off. He too had fallen asleep on the ground next to a rock he had been sitting on just a bit earlier. Malcolm whispered to his brother, "They're drunker than Cooter Brown!"

Jimmy nodded in agreement, although he didn't completely understand what Malcolm had just said. "I say we take those horses. They're sleeping. They don't need'em. I want the gray one!" said Malcolm. "He looks just like the Lone Ranger's horse, Silver."

"Malcolm, Silver is white and I ain't never rode no horse!" said Jimmy.

Ignoring Jimmy's correction about the color of the Lone Ranger's horse, Malcolm replied, "Well I ain't either," said Malcolm in a hushed tone. "But how hard could it be?

Cowboys do it all the time! You just jump on'em and kick'em in the ribs with your heels."

"OK," said Jimmy. "If you say so. I just hope them fellers don't wake up. They'll flip their wigs!"

"They ain't wakin' up Jimmy! They're sauced!" said Malcolm. "That one's asleep and that one over there is passed out drunk and probably pissed himself." The boys slowly stood up and began making their way toward the two horses. They made it to where the animals were secured to the tree and began to untie the horse's reins. The brown horse let out a loud whinny. Malcolm and Jimmy were startled by the unexpected noise and were scared the sound would wake up the two men, but it didn't. So far, so good!

Malcolm climbed up into the old, worn saddle of the gray horse and turned to look at Jimmy's progress. Jimmy was having trouble getting his foot high enough to put it in the stirrup. Without speaking a word, Malcolm climbed back down from his horse and boosted Jimmy up and into the saddle of the brown mare. The horse took a couple steps backward which frightened Jimmy a little bit. He held onto the saddle horn tightly.

While he was on the ground assisting Jimmy, Malcolm spotted something that gave him another idea. He tip-toed past the one man who was lying next to the rock and over near the man who had passed out in the bushes. Malcolm retrieved the single jar of corn-squeezings and quietly walked back over to where the horses were.

On his way, looking back toward the now loudly snoring man in the bushes, Malcolm accidentally bumped into the three-box high stack of Mason jars that were sitting on the stump. The top two boxes tipped over and crashed onto the rocky ground. Rousted by the loud sound of the breaking glass, the man that was next to the rock, raised his head to look toward the commotion.

Malcolm sprinted the rest of the way and like an Olympian, sprang from the ground, and landed on top of the horse. Juggling the reins of his own horse, Jimmy's horse, and the jar of liquor he yelled, "GIT-UP!" And gave the horse several sharp kicks in the ribs.

The two horses began to gallop away from the scene of the crime as fast as an old sway-back horse can gallop anyway. Now the one man had gotten to his feet and was yelling for his partner to wake up and come help him. The horses were in a full trot now crashing through the underbrush and the bushes as they made their escape. A gunshot rang out, but they kept going on the horses. Malcolm was driving them as fast as they would go! Jimmy was holding on for dear life!

"They're shootin' at us Malcolm!" screamed Jimmy. "They're shootin' at us!" Malcolm's only response was loud laughter. He seemed to find the whole experience exhilarating.

Bursting through the bushes, Malcolm noticed a path through the woods created by the repeated movement of wildlife through the forest that's commonly referred to as a "game trail."

He began directing his horse to follow the game trail. Eventually, after Malcolm was sure the two men were no longer chasing them, he slowed the horses down to a slow walk and circled back through the woods until he came to the creek again. Following the creek downstream they made their way to their crawdad hole and back through the woods to the meadow.

Once they got back to the dirt road. Malcolm decided that their grandma would be none too happy that they brought home a couple of horses. Besides, how would they explain how they came to be in possession of them.

The boys climbed down off the horses, pointed them in the opposite direction of their grandmother's house and Malcolm gave each of them a slap on the ass. Both horses took off trotting up the road. The boys got back to their grandmother's property, but before going inside, they hid their jar of hooch out in the barn behind the old wooden crates with hay in them that the hens use to lay their eggs in. They mutually decided to save it for another day and another adventure.

CHAPTER 2
TURKEY TALK

Frostproof, Florida - November 22, 1973

A brand new 1972 Plymouth Fury rolled silently down an alleyway in down town Frostproof, a tiny town in the southern-most part of Polk County, Florida. The car was creeping along at no more than three miles per hour.

The headlights of the vehicle were turned off which seemed a bit suspicious. The single occupant in the vehicle swiveled his head from side to side inspecting the alleyway doors to businesses. All the doors looked like they were closed tightly and secure, but the car's occupant decided he would stop the car and physically try some of the door knobs of the closed businesses.

The third door knob he put his hand on and turned, was unlocked. "BINGO!" He thought to himself. He quietly swung the business' door wide open and stepped inside. It was a furniture store and it was dimly lit. The man turned on his flashlight and began walking slowly and methodically through the store. The stillness of the night and the eerie silence inside the store made exploring it a bit nerve-wracking, but he continued to push forward.

As he rounded an aisle where the baby bassinets were on display, movement caught his eye. He raised his revolver quickly and pointed it and his flashlight in the direction of the sudden movement. With his pistol now trained on a full-length mirror and staring at his own reflection, young twenty-three-year-old rookie police officer Gary Garrett, lowered his gun and silently chuckled at himself for almost blasting a hole in the mirror with a bullet from his pistol.

He finished searching the building and when he returned to his patrol car, he radioed his dispatcher and asked her to contact the store's owner to see if he wanted to come down and secure the door. Gary would have done it for him, but the only lock on the back door was a key lock on both sides of the door. It would take a key-holder to lock it up and properly secure it.

After a few minutes, the police radio crackled back to life and the dispatcher told Gary that the owner wasn't interested in coming down to the business at 3:30 in the morning on a holiday. The owner requested that the officer just close the door and drive by and check on it periodically the rest of the night. Gary, having already pulled the door shut when he came back outside responded to the dispatcher, "OK. 10-4."

The rest of Gary's shift was uneventful unless you count Gary pausing around 6:45 AM to shoo a stray dog off of the front stoop of the police department building where it had decided to lay down and take a nap. "Go on, get outta here! GIT!" Gary said to the dog. The brown and black, lazy stray mutt stood to his feet and slowly sauntered away.

Gary went into the police department building and chatted with the oncoming officer and dispatcher who were already there and having their morning coffee and talking to Gary's midnight dispatcher. Gary briefed the dayshift officer about the back door of Weaver's Furniture Store. "Old man Weaver will be coming down later today to lock it up." said Gary.

"Alright, sounds good," said the oncoming officer, "I'll keep an eye on it."

"Well, I guess I'm gonna head to the barn," said Gary as he handed over the patrol car's keys. "I just filled it up about an hour ago for you, so you should be good through your shift."

"Alright, I appreciate it. Take it easy and hey, happy Thanksgiving!" said the other patrolman.

Gary replied, "Happy Thanksgiving to y'all too. "Y'all try not to eat too much later today!" he joked.

Gary opened the police department's front door to leave and that same brown and black stray dog was in the exact same spot on the building's front stoop again. Gary didn't even say anything to it this time. He just sighed, slowly shook his head, and stepped over it as he continued on his way to his own personal car.

He drove the mile or so to his apartment and once in his bedroom, immediately stripped off his gun belt and uniform and was asleep next to his wife Marcie within ten minutes of his head hitting his pillow. After all, he had to get back up in a few hours for Thanksgiving dinner at his parents' house in Lake Wales.

His four hours of sleep went by quickly. At eleven AM, Marcie was waking him up and telling him it was time to get in the shower. "Get up honey! Thanksgiving lunch is at one o'clock!" said Marcie. "We've got to get moving!" A quick shower, a hot cup of coffee and two Marlboro cigarettes later, he was ready to walk out the door.

His parents' house was about thirty minutes north of Frostproof in the slightly larger town of Lake Wales. He pulled into the grass driveway of their home next to several other vehicles and got out of the car. While Marcie retrieved a bowl of potato salad out of the back seat, Gary's nine-year-old baby brother, Dale ran from the front patio barefoot to hug Gary's neck and greet him. His father Al, his two younger twin brothers, Ronnie and Roger who were both wearing their Air Force uniforms, and his other younger brother Carl, were all sitting on the patio shooting the breeze.

Gary walked up and sat down in an empty folding chair with the group. Marcie joined Carl's wife, Kelly and Al's wife Delois in the kitchen where they all were busy preparing dishes, setting the table, and putting the finishing touches on Thanksgiving dinner.

"It's about time you got here young man!" said Al, Gary's father.

"Yeah," smiled Roger, "if you can't get here on time, just get here when you can!"

"Hey!" responded Gary, "I'll have you all know that I worked all night last night! I didn't get but maybe four hours of sleep!"

"Oh, boo-hoo!" said Carl jokingly.

Nine-year-old Dale was always fascinated with the idea of his big brother being a police officer. He looked up to him a great deal. Interrupting, Dale asked Gary excitedly, "Did you arrest any bad guys last night brother?"

Gary tussled Dale's hair and said, "as a matter of fact I almost had to arrest a four-legged stranger earlier this morning!"

"No you didn't! Strangers don't have four legs!" Dale responded incredulously.

"It was a 'stranger dog.' I didn't say it was a 'stranger people!'" laughed Gary.

Al spoke up, "Dale, go in the house and ask your mother to send me out another cup of coffee, will you?"

"Yes sir." replied Dale as he dutifully trotted into the house to get the coffee for his father.

Al leaned forward in his chair and lowered his voice. Addressing his four eldest sons, Al said, "Don't mention this to your mother boys, but I got a call from your uncle Hayden yesterday. He said Malcolm has done escaped from prison again."

"Again!? What is this, like four or five times now!?"" asked Roger.

"You don't think he's going to show up here again, do you?" asked Ronnie.

"I have no idea where he'll go. He might turn up here or he might not," said Al. "But like I said, don't mention any of this to your mother. She'll be worried about it for days or until he's captured again. You boys know how much she doesn't want him around y'all, and truth is, I don't either for that matter!"

"He's a dangerous man," added Roger.

"Yeah," said Carl, "but he wouldn't do anything to hurt us."

"I know he wouldn't hurt any family either, but where wanted men go, men with badges and guns go looking for them. Y'all know your mother's a worry-wart and she's always imagining some big 'shoot-out' and you boys getting caught in the cross-fire if he comes around here," said Al. "And y'all know that could actually be a possibility after what happened up in Maryville!"

"Well, If he shows up in Frostproof, I guess I'll be the first officer at Frostproof Police Department to have to arrest his own half-brother!" said Gary, only half joking.

Al cleared his throat and said, "When Dale was just a little fella, I was about to leave to take him to his Cub Scout meeting. Malcolm had busted out and showed up on our doorstep. Your mother was at work and I let him ride with me and Dale to the scout meeting and afterward, when we came back here, y'all's mother about had a conniption fit! She had gotten home from the citrus plant and she was fit-to-be-tied when she found out that I had driven him and Dale in the same truck to the..."

"Who did you drive in the truck Daddy?" asked Dale returning with his father's cup of coffee.

"Nobody boy," replied Al. "How are those women in there doing on dinner!? My belly's growling like an ole bear!"

"Mine is too! Now that you mention it! I haven't even had breakfast yet!" said Carl.

Addressing Gary, Dale asked, "Can I see your badge again brother?"

Gary said, "Not right now 'D,' maybe a little later alright?"

"Ok! After dinner maybe?" asked Dale.

"We'll see," replied Gary.

About that time, Delois, the boys mother, poked her head out of the front door and announced to everyone that it was time for dinner. "Y'all get in here and worsh up. Everythings ready and we're putting it on the table now."

Al and the five brothers all stood up and shuffled into the house. Carl and the twins rough-housed a little bit on their way inside and play-fought with each other about which one of the three would get to use the bathroom sink first to wash their hands.

The family sat down around the large custom-made dining room table that Al had built himself by hand - using his amazing carpentry skills and some wooden bowling lanes he had salvaged from a bowling alley he helped to remodel. It was a wonderful meal and one of the last ones that Dale and all of his older brothers were gathered in the same place at the same time for a Thanksgiving holiday.

Sure enough, on the following Tuesday at about 7:00 PM, there was a knock at the door. It was Malcolm. Delois told him that he could stay for an hour to visit with his father, but after that, he had to go. She also said to him, "And you know

I'm gonna call the law on you when you leave, right?"

"Yes Ma'am," replied Malcolm. "All I ask is that you give me a thirty-minute head-start."

"I can do that," replied Delois as she turned and went back to the kitchen to give her husband an opportunity to talk to his misguided son alone.

At the end of the hour, it all played out exactly as Delois had intended. Malcolm said his good-byes and thirty minutes later, just as she told him she would do, she called the sheriff's office to report that Malcolm was an escaped prisoner and had been at her house.

Two sheriff's deputies responded, but it was too late. Malcolm was nowhere in the area. Nobody ever knew how he was able to just disappear from the authorities like that. But he was like a ghost. Malcolm was always a master at not only escaping from custody, but avoiding detection while he was on the run from the law.

CHAPTER 3
DIAMOND GRILL MARKS

Knoxville, Tennessee – June 15, 1953

A giant sizzling Porterhouse steak cooked medium rare with some of those fancy diamond shaped grill marks on both sides of it, a big ole baked potato with cheese, a bowl of fresh pole beans, a soft butter slathered dinner roll, and some ice-cold beer to wash it all down!

That's what Malcolm decided that he wanted to eat for supper tonight to celebrate his eighteenth birthday. And he didn't want just any ole truck-stop steak. He wanted a meal from that fancy restaurant called "Vincent's" in downtown Knoxville that he had heard about.

Turning eighteen Malcolm considered it a milestone in his life. He was now of legal age and the special occasion called for this special meal. After all, Malcolm thought to himself, "I'm a good person, I deserve the finer things in life."

'You Don't Have Love' by singer Little Jimmy Dickens playing quietly on the radio in his boarding house room was unfortunately making Malcolm feel a little blue though. Malcolm didn't have a girl or anybody else for that matter to join him during his birthday celebration tonight.

Billy Ray was only ten years old and was staying with their grandmother most of the time.

Fifteen-year-old Jimmy was in juvenile lock-up over in Oakridge because he had gotten caught by the police in a stolen copper colored, Ford Customline Club Coupe and then decided to run from them. He had given Malcolm a ride in it a few days before he got busted with it.

That car had a flathead V-8 in it and it ran like a scalded hound dog! Jimmy would have easily gotten away from the cops in it if he hadn't lost control on a sharp curve hauling ass back toward Maryville. He crashed it into a fully mature Southern Red Oak tree and that was all she wrote for that car. Jimmy got out with only a few cuts, bumps, and bruises. Most of Jimmy's minor injuries were caused by the vehicle crash, but a few of them may have been added by the pissed-off arresting officers as they were dragging him out of the crashed car's broken window.

Malcolm's father Al, was down in Florida again, working at a construction site down there somewhere.

His mother Grace… Lord knows where Grace was at the time. Even if she had been home, Malcolm wouldn't have wanted to spend this momentous occasion celebrating with her! Malcolm thought to himself, "I guess I'm on my own tonight."

There were two small issues that Malcolm had to overcome though. He didn't have a car and he didn't have any money. But he wasn't going to let minor details like those stand in his way of a good time.

Those fancy restaurants, like Vincents, that cook those diamond grill marks into their steaks weren't cheap. He needed to get a car and make some quick money so that he'd be able to pay his supper bill.

Oh sure, he could have just eaten the steak meal and then bolted out of the restaurant without paying - like he had done dozens and dozens of times before at other greasy-

spoons and juke-joints - but since it was his birthday, he
wanted to pay for his food with cash and feel like all those
rich big-shots who could afford to eat there whenever they
wanted to.

Malcolm hastily devised a plan to get a car and some cash.
He would walk from McSpadden's boarding house where he
was staying to a close-by liquor store that he had spotted
from the dusty Greyhound bus window as it was pulling into
town from Maryville. He would put his hand in his pocket
like he was holding a pistol, and demand the liquor store
clerk turn over his car keys and the money in the cash
register.

About an hour later, he put his plan into motion. He left the
boarding house and walked the fifteen blocks through
downtown Knoxville. He would stop along the way, every
once in a while, to stare up at the tall buildings. "They sure
don't have anything like this back in Maryville," Malcolm
thought to himself as he marveled at the towering structures
– some of which were up to ten or twelve stories tall!

Soon, the liquor store came into view. Malcolm leaned up
against a coin-operated newspaper box for a while watching
the heavyset clerk with greying hair go about his duties in
the store. The clerk was an older man, "probably in his

fifties." Malcolm silently thought to himself, "He'll be a push-over. If he does chase me, he ain't gonna be able to keep up," he silently chuckled to himself.

It was go-time! Malcolm entered the older mom and pop liquor store and pretended to be shopping. The older clerk spoke up, "Afternoon! Anything I can help you find?" Malcom replied, "No sir, I'm just browsing."

"Well alright," replied the clerk. "We've got a real good sale going on Blatz Beer if you're interested." Malcom nodded toward the clerk, smiled, and continued his shopping ruse.

Eventually, Malcolm wandered back up to the front of the store and asked for a pack of Lucky Strikes that were displayed on the wall behind the counter. When the clerk turned around to retrieve them, Malcolm slid his hand into his trouser pocket and shouted, "This is a hold-up old man! Gimme your car keys and the money in the drawer!" Stunned, the man spun around to look at Malcolm. He saw Malcolm's concealed hand and assumed he had a gun. "Hurry up! Money and Keys! NOW!" shouted Malcolm.

The clerk reached in his own pants pocket and removed his car keys, placing them on the countertop. He then punched a few keys on the old decorative yet tarnished brass cash register that had ornate scrollwork and engravings all over it.

The drawer rolled open with a loud "DING." Nervously, he put the money on the counter. As he did so, Malcolm scooped it up and stuffed it in to his front pants pocket while continuing to keep his index finger pointing like a gun at the clerk through the fabric of his opposite pocket.

Malcolm told the man "Lay down on the floor!" The man complied, placing his hands behind his head. "You wait ten minutes before you get up. You hear me old man!?" shouted Malcolm. The man didn't reply.

Malcolm ran from the store to the street and suddenly realized that he had no idea which car belonged to the liquor store clerk. Now in full panic mode, he paced a few steps back and forth on the sidewalk.

In a frenzy, he started to turn to go back into the store when he heard the store's ringing alarm start going off. He turned again and began a full sprint down the sidewalk when he heard a voice shout, "HEY! YOU! STOP!" It was the law. There were two Knoxville police officers on the sidewalk only fifteen yards from where Malcolm was standing. They both had their pistols trained on him! Malcolm froze in his tracks.

The two officers handcuffed him with his hands behind his back and led him back to the liquor store where the ringing alarm was still blaring. The clerk fumbled with the alarm button behind the counter and turned off the deafening, annoying alarm. Pointing at Malcolm, the clerk said "That's him officers! That's the sorry son of a bitch that just robbed me! How did y'all get here so fast anyhow!?"

"We were just leaving the dry cleaners two doors down and saw this guy running and heard the alarm," said the first officer.

"We figured it out pretty quick after that" added the second officer, holding Malcolm's bicep in case he was tempted to make a break for it.

The officers booked Malcolm into the Knoxville jail on strong armed robbery charges since he didn't actually have a gun in his possession during the crime. He spent the remainder of his eighteenth birthday sitting in a ten-foot by ten-foot jail cell and eating a bologna sandwich made with bread that was well on its way to going stale for supper. No steak with the diamond shaped grill marks on it for him tonight like he had hoped for.

Malcom was there for about three days. By watching the guards and learning the daily routine, Malcolm's wheels began to turn. He figured out that the secured area part of the jail and the visitors lobby were separated by a thick wall, but connected by a common drop ceiling.

Being ever observant, he also had noticed that when the janitor would take his lunch breaks, he would take off his coveralls and leave them in his mop and supply closet.

One day as the prisoners were let out of their cells to file into the lunch area, Malcolm hung back so that he was last in line. When the guards were distracted, he ducked unseen into the custodian's mop closet.

Inside the closet, he quickly took off his jail uniform consisting of a light grey shirt and slightly darker grey pants. Then, he slipped on the janitor's dark blue coveralls. Once the guards had shut the heavy metal door that separated the hallway where the cells were located and the dining area of the facility, Malcolm made his move.

He climbed up a step-ladder that was in the closet, removed the ceiling tile and climbed into the ceiling. Fifteen feet was all he had to crawl to be above the empty visitor's lobby.

Once over the lobby, he moved the second ceiling tile out of his way enough to drop out of the ceiling and into the unattended, vacant lobby. Then, he just simply walked out of the front door of the police department to freedom. And like a magician, he disappeared on the streets of Knoxville.

Although he was recaptured a few weeks later, this incident at the Knoxville Jail marked the first of many brazen escapes that Malcolm would successfully perpetrate over the rest of his long-lasting criminal career.

CHAPTER 4
GARRETTS GALORE

June 7, 1982 - Lake Wales, Florida

Dale Garrett had a huge smile on his face as he crossed the stage to receive his high school diploma from the Lake Wales High School Principal. His smile couldn't have been bigger however than two particular people in the audience watching their son's graduation ceremony. Al and Delois were witnessing their youngest son complete his high school education.

Neither one of them ever completed high school. Delois made it to the tenth grade, but Al only had an eighth-grade education. When they were young, times were tough. Growing up, both of their families needed them to work and help contribute financially to their separate family's income.

But today was all about their youngest son Dale achieving the goal they had set for him and each of Dale's older brothers. A goal that they themselves never achieved. The goal of getting an education and receiving a high school diploma.

Al was especially proud on this day because his sons Billy Ray, Jimmy, and Malcolm from his previous marriage to Grace - had all rejected the concept of education - barely ever attending school at all. All of them had elected street smarts over book smarts and living as criminals over living right.

After the graduation ceremony, Al and Delois took Dale to the Black Forest Restaurant on Highway 27 south of town for his big celebratory graduation dinner. They told him that he could have anything on the menu he wanted. He ordered a whole steamed lobster. They were joined at the restaurant by their other son, Carl and his wife Kelly and their two young sons, Chris and Curtis. Gary's son, Alan, who had also been in attendance at Dale's ceremony was there as well.

Dale being his normal self was cracking jokes and making his family laugh. Even people sitting at nearby tables started paying attention to him and his comical antics. After dinner, Dale picked up the shell carcass of the lobster he had just devoured and was manipulating it as though it was a puppet and making it dance on the tabletop.

He sang 'Tea For Two' and used his fingers to move the lobster's tail as though it were the legs of a high-kicking Radio City Rockette dancer. Everyone at the table laughed and guffawed. Dale's mother, Delois, laughed too, but her face also turned beet red with embarrassment as she noticed the diners at the other tables watching her son's impromptu musical puppet show.

It was natural for Dale to be the center of attention. He loved making people laugh from the time he was old enough to understand what a joke was. At seven years old, he got interested in magic tricks when his cousin David in Tennessee taught him a few simple tricks he had learned in Vietnam from another soldier. Dale's interest was more than a passing hobby though. He studied magic books in his school library like a scientist would study physics.

He began performing magic shows for civic clubs and organizations. His mom would work the phone to book shows for him and his father would drive him to his "gigs." His show continued to grow and become more and more polished.

Al was a master carpenter and built Dale a number of large

stage illusions from building plans Dale mail ordered from Abbott's Magic Company in Colon, Michigan. Al and Delois both would always beam with pride when they would watch their youngest son perform on stages all over central Florida.

After all the joking around had died down around the table, Al asked his son a serious question. "Well, now that high school is behind you, have you decided on what you want to do for a living?" Everyone at the table got quiet and looked at Dale in anticipation of his answer.

Dale, who had been working at Burger King since he was fifteen years old, replied, "Well, things are going pretty good at the restaurant right now and they're talking about me maybe becoming an assistant manager." He continued, "But y'all know I really would like to be a police officer too. So, I imagine it'll be one of those two things. I'll probably be a police officer though."

His father smiled and responded, "Well, at least you have a plan. That's good!"

All of Dale's talk about becoming a police officer sparked his brother Carl's interest in perhaps following that same career path. Carl had ridden with their older brother Gary when

Gary was a police officer down in Frostproof. He enjoyed the excitement of the job, but hadn't thought about pursuing it himself. Carl had gone to vocational school after he had finished high school and was making pretty good money working as an electrician.

Still, all this talk from his little brother about going into law enforcement piqued his curiosity and he was considering a career change. Both he and Dale joined the Auxiliary at the Winter Haven Police Department after attending Auxiliary Police Standards at Polk College. They would both ride with full time officers once or twice per week at night as their full-time job schedules would permit.

Dale was already focused on police work, but that time in the Auxiliary sealed the deal for Carl. They both applied at the Winter Haven Police Department for full time police officer positions.

Carl was hired! But Dale received bad news and good news. He was told that because of a nepotism policy, two family members couldn't be hired at the department. However, the department agreed to sponsor and pay for both brothers to attend the police academy since they were established auxiliary police officers already.

At the time, there were two police academies running at the same time. One at night which ran for four hours and one during the daytime that ran eight hours per day. Carl elected to attend the nighttime classes so that he could still do electrical work to bring in money since he had two kids to support. Dale went to the daytime class. The nighttime class started three months before the daytime class so it worked out that Dale and Carl graduated the police academy on the exact same day.

While attending the police academy, Dale was still working at the restaurant but had also put in a job application with the Polk County Sheriff's Office since the Winter Haven Police Department wouldn't hire him because of the nepotism policy. Dale was hired by the Sheriff's Office and after graduating the police academy, began his career in law enforcement.

He spent his first seven months working in communications as a complaint taker and occasionally he worked on the radio as a dispatcher. After those seven months, he was sworn in as a full-time deputy sheriff and was assigned to "the ridge," an area of Polk County that encompassed the town he grew up in – Lake Wales. He was also tapped to work undercover in narcotics for a short while because of his youthful appearance.

Dale met his wife Lynn at the sheriff's office in 1985. He had stopped in to communications after booking a prisoner into the jail on a warrant. It was only Lynn's second day on the job. Within about six months, they were married in a church wedding in Lynn's home town of Fort Meade, Florida.

Eventually, Lynn left the Sheriff's Office and went to work at the Winter Haven Police Department. Apparently, the nepotism policy at that agency had been relaxed as she joined Carl who was of course already working there.

A few years after that, Dale left the Sheriff's Office and also started at the Winter Haven Police Department. Now there were THREE Garretts all at the same law enforcement agency.

A few years later, Gary, now divorced and re-married a few times, most recently to his wife Lindy, moved back to Florida from Maryville, Tennessee where he and Lindy had been operating their own successful private investigation business.

Gary applied at the Winter Haven Police Department too and

was hired. Kelly, Carl's wife, joined the department next as a Community Service Officer. Finally, Lindy came onboard at the department as a sworn officer. Now, there were SIX Garretts all working at the same police department – three brothers and all of their wives! Their co-workers joked about the novelty of so many members of one family working at one agency with some saying that the department should be re-named, "Garrett P.D."

Even though it had obviously eluded Billy Ray, Jimmy, and Malcolm, there may have been something in Dale, Carl, and Gary's DNA that caused them to be drawn to law enforcement. Their distant relative was none other than Sheriff Pat Garrett, the legendary lawmen from the old west that finally killed the infamous outlaw, Henry McCarty, AKA, William Bonney, better known by his nickname "Billy The Kid" way back in 1881.

The three brothers, Gary, Carl, and Dale, all of course started in the patrol division. Dale eventually transferred to the Community Policing Unit as a DARE officer and taught the anti-drug message in all of the elementary schools within the city's jurisdiction. His position as a DARE officer allowed him to utilize his skills as a magician to wrap entertainment around the serious lessons about avoiding drugs. The children of the community of course loved their magical DARE officer and excitedly looked forward to his visits to their classrooms every week.

Carl became a motorcycle officer and traffic homicide investigator. His duties also included marine patrol in the chain of lakes that covered the city. Eventually due to an injury he received in an accident on the police motorcycle, he worked in the detective division investigating property crimes.

Gary loved the patrol division and remained there throughout his career. He was certified as a Field Training Officer and taught newly hired rookie officers how to do the job. He retired from the department as he had begun his career in Frostproof those many years ago – as a street cop.

The administration made a concerted effort to spread the family out on different shifts back when they were all in the patrol division. However, there was one incident other than city parade details that brought the three brothers together. It was a fight with a prisoner.

Dale was working midnight shift and was just coming on duty at eleven PM. Carl had worked evening shift and was just getting off at eleven PM. Because the department was shorthanded, Gary was working an overlapping shift.

"Hey, I had Kelly drop me off at work because my car is in the shop. Can you give me a lift home?" Carl asked Dale.

"Sure!" Dale replied as he loaded his equipment into the patrol car to begin his shift.

After Dale had transferred his briefcase and gear bags to his patrol car, he asked Carl, "you ready to go?"

Carl who was standing a few patrol cars down and was chatting with another officer, looked over at Dale and said, "Yep. Let's go." He ended the conversation with the other officer he had been chatting with and walked over to Dale's unit. He opened the passenger side door and sat down.

As Carl was buckling his seatbelt, Dale was telling the dispatcher that he was now in service and available for calls. Almost immediately, the dispatcher called Dale and dispatched him to a disturbance call regarding a man beating his grandmother.

"Well, I guess you're going to a disturbance call with me

before I take you home" Dale said to Carl.

"That's alright," replied Carl. "I'm in no hurry."

Dale drove to the address he had been given. He and Carl both stepped out of the patrol car and could immediately hear a man angrily yelling and screaming. They quickened their pace as they walked toward the front door of the residence. Just before they got to the steps, a man burst out of the front door. When he saw Dale and Carl, he began cussing at them and moving toward them with his fists clenched in a threatening manner.

While they were attempting to get the drunken, irate man to calm down and talk to them, he swung at one of them. It was on then! Dale and Carl both wrestled the man to the ground. Although the man was drunk, he was very strong and was difficult to restrain and control as he resisted arrest. After a lengthy scuffle, they managed to get him handcuffed and wrestled him into the back seat of the patrol car.

Breathing heavy from the fight, Dale radioed the dispatcher and informed her that he had a prisoner in custody and was on his way back to the department. Dale glanced over at Carl during the drive and said, "Well, I guess you're going to be delayed further in going home."

Carl chuckled and said, "yeah, looks like it."

Once at the police department, they wrestled the alcohol crazed man out of the back seat, into the building, and down the long hall, past the squad room, to the holding cell area. Dale managed to reach in the man's back pocket and remove his wallet in order to obtain his identity. The man was still struggling with them and cussing at them at the top of his lungs as they removed his handcuffs and pushed him into the holding cell, quickly locking the cell door before the man had a chance to turn around and fight them again.

As Dale and Carl looked at the man's driver's license and caught their breath in the adjoining ID room where prisoners were fingerprinted and photographed, Dale realized they had not taken the man's belt and shoe laces per the department's policy. This was a policy put in place to prevent prisoners from possessing the means to commit suicide in the holding cell while in police custody. "Crap!" said Dale. "Guess we need to get those from him."

They both walked back into the holding cell area and addressed the still belligerent, angry man behind the bars.

"Brian, we need your belt and shoe laces."

"Fuck you!" came Brian's reply.

"C'mon Brian, hand us your belt and shoelaces through the bars," demanded Carl.

"If you motherfuckers want'em, you're gonna have to come in here and take'em!" responded the man.

Dale and Carl looked at each other and sighed as Dale stepped around the corner to retrieve the cell's door key. As soon as the cell door was unlocked, the prisoner shoved the door open and bolted out to fight the officers again.

Carl managed to get behind the man and intended to grab him in a bear-hug from behind. But the man raised his arms and Carl bear-hugged the man's torso instead. Dale made his attack from the front which was not the safest direction to approach from as Carl's hold on him left the man's wildly swinging arms free to punch and strike and his legs and feet free to kick Dale as he approached.

Dale came in to try to grab the prisoner and the man swung, striking Dale in the left jaw. Dale shook off the punch and again came in to help his brother control the prisoner. Again, the man swung and hit Dale a second time in the same jaw. Dale looked past the prisoner's face at Carl.

Carl was chuckling at the fact Dale had been hit twice in the jaw. For some twisted reason, he thought it was funny. It was as though the drunk man was a puppet being controlled from the rear by Carl. Not seeing any humor in the situation at all, and tired of being used as a punching bag, Dale said to himself, "No more! Not again!" He lowered his jaw and ran full force into the prisoner knocking both him and Carl backward to the ground.

While on the ground struggling with the prisoner, Dale got a hand free and managed to put out a radio call, "Officers need help in the holding cell!" Coincidentally, Gary was just pulling into the parking lot returning to the police department on a completely unrelated matter. When he heard the distress call, he didn't hear who the officer was who had called for help. He only knew that a fellow officer was in a fight and needed assistance pronto!

He ran down the long hallway, took a right, and ran past the squad room into the holding cell area and was surprised to see it was his own two brothers who were fighting with a prisoner. The only part of the prisoner sticking out and not covered by either Dale or Carl was the man's upper bicep.

Like a professional wrestler, Gary came down full force on the man's bicep with his knee. Carl still had one of the man's arms stretched upward leaving his ribcage exposed. Dale pounded the man several times in the ribcage trying to regain control and end the fight.

With three Garrett's on him, the man eventually ran out of gas and they managed to remove his belt and shoelaces and get him back into the holding cell. The next morning, the man was surely sore in places on his body that he didn't even know he had.

The following weekend during a family cookout, Gary brought up the fight again. "You know guys, I know it wasn't planned like it all played out, and everything we did was justifiable, but some people might question how three brothers came to all be all over one prisoner at the same time." They all chuckled.

One year later – almost to the exact day – Carl needed another ride home after dropping off his police motorcycle for maintenance. Dale was there for him again. Half way between the department's motor-pool and Carl's home, Dale received another call for service. It was in regards to a man wishing to report that he and his girlfriend had been involved in a verbal argument. Dale and Carl immediately recognized the address as the one they had gone to a year ago on that call with "Drunk Brian."

Dale looked over at Carl and said, "Uh-oh. Here we go again." When they arrived at the house, Brian came out in a much less agitated, much more subdued state than he was during their first encounter with him. Dale spoke to him as he and Carl walked toward him on the sidewalk. "You're not going to cause any problems for us this time, are you?"

The man clearly did not recognize or remember Dale or Carl. He looked back at them and said, "Hell no man! The last time I messed around with the Winter Haven P.D. a year ago, eight Winter Haven cops beat my ass!"

The brothers glanced at each other and smiled about Brian's miscalculation of how many officers he fought with a year ago. Dale took the report from the man and continued to drive Carl to his house. They chuckled the whole way about Brian's partial memory of the incident. "It probably SEEMED like eight cops were beating his ass!" joked Carl.

Dale chuckled and replied, "Yep, you're probably right!"

Even after they all retired, the story of "Drunk Brian" vs. "The Brothers Garrett" would still occasionally come up in conversations between Dale, Carl, and Gary. That memory lasted their lifetimes...

CHAPTER 5
THEIR FIRST DANCE

Maryville, Tennessee - May 3, 1947

Al drove through Maryville in his 1944 Chevrolet AK series pickup on his way to his apartment to see his family. He had been working for six weeks straight at a construction site up in Elkhart, Indiana. He was tired and looking forward to some down time before beginning on a new construction job closer to home up in Gatlinburg, Tennessee.

When he drove up to his apartment around five PM, he discovered that Grace and his three sons weren't there. He walked out in the yard and saw a neighbor who he didn't know by name. The man was cutting his grass with a reel lawn mower. He walked over near the fence and spoke to the man. "Excuse me sir, do you happen to know where the lady and kids are that live here?"

The neighbor stopped pushing his mower and removed a red

bandana from the back pocket of his blue faded overalls to wipe the sweat from his brow. "No sir, I ain't seen hide nor hair of anyone over there in a couple weeks."

Having a second thought, the neighbor continued, "Wait a minute. Ya know, I did see the lady of the house five or six days ago come to think of it. I was sitting over yonder on my front porch drinking some buttermilk and seen her pull up in the yard with her husband. They went inside for a few minutes and then they came out and left."

"I'm her husband." Muttered Al under his breath.

"How's that?" asked the neighbor not quite hearing what Al had said.

"Did she say where she was going by any chance?" asked Al, ignoring the man's question.

The neighbor, now wiping the back of his neck with his bandana replied, "No sir. I didn't speak to them a'tall. She had a suitcase in her hand though. Figured they were heading out on a trip someplace."

Al was convinced more than ever that Grace was running around on him and not tending to their three children when he was out of town. He had heard from his oldest boy, Malcolm, that strange men were always in and out of the house and that Grace would go on road trips with some of these strangers.

Al thanked the neighbor who gave him a wave and continued his yard mowing. Al went in to his empty house. Upset about his wife's behavior and exhausted from his long drive from Elkhart, he fell into the bed fully dressed and quickly fell asleep.

The next day around seven AM, a sun beam streaming through a crack in the curtain shined in Al's eyes, rousting him from his fourteen-hour slumber. Needing some coffee and feeling hungry, Al got out of bed and stumbled to the bathroom to relieve himself and then to the kitchen. Opening the Frigidaire, Al noticed it was almost completely empty. There was certainly not enough of anything in there to make a decent breakfast with.

Al started the percolator brewing his morning coffee. "At least there's coffee in the house," he thought to himself. He sat down at the kitchen table and smoked an unfiltered Camel cigarette. When the coffee was ready, he lit up a second one.

Contemplating what he should do about his marital situation, which he pretty much knew was over at this point, he decided to drive over to his brother Hayden's place to talk to him about it.

Al drove out in to the country where Hayden's house was and parked in the front yard underneath the shade of a big dogwood tree. He could see that Hayden was sitting up next to his house at a little makeshift table working on something. Hayden was also a fine carpenter but he also had an artistic touch. He was always picking up junk other people would throw away and fixing it up to sell it.

"Howdy brother!" Hayden yelled as Al exited his pick-up truck.

"What in the world are you doing?" asked Al as he looked down at Hayden's table that was covered in small rocks. Hayden was using another rock to chip away at the one rock he was working on that was lying on the table in front of him.

"I'm making Indian arrowheads," came Hayden's reply as he reached down beside him and picked up a small burlap sack. He dumped the sack onto the table to show Al fifteen to twenty Indian arrowheads he had made.

Al picked up one of the arrowheads and carefully examined it. "Boy howdy!" said Al, "they look like the real deal!"

"You best believe they do!" said Hayden.

"Well what are you planning to do with all these arrowheads anyhow? Go buffalo huntin'?"

"Naw," smiled Hayden. "I'm gonna sell'em to people!"

"Who's going to buy fake Indian arrowheads?" asked Al.

"Well, lots of folks," replied Hayden, "I've been talkin' to a lady at the Smithsonian in Washington D.C. about her buying some and I've already sold a big batch to the University of Knoxville! Made a nice wooden and glass display case for'em and everything."

"They knew you made them?" asked Al.

"Nope. I told'em I found'em in a fresh tilled field." said Hayden.

"So you fibbed?" asked Al.

"I didn't tell no lie." retorted Hayden. "I found every one of these rocks out yonder in that field."

Al just chuckled and shook his head at his brothers somewhat shady ingenuity. "So, what brings you 'round?" asked Hayden.

For the next several hours, Al told Hayden everything that had been going on with Grace and discussed what his next moves should be. Hayden encouraged him to get a divorce and rid himself of the whole matter. After their long talk, Al agreed and said that the next morning, he would go to check with the courthouse about how to file for divorce.

A bit later, Al said his goodbyes and told Hayden he had to stop by the grocery store because there wasn't a thing to eat at his house. Hayden invited Al to stay and have supper there, but Al politely refused and drove back toward town.

When he got there, Al pulled into the parking lot of 'Happy Jack's Grocery Store.' He went inside and gathered up some ham, bacon, a dozen eggs, some fresh green beans, a loaf of bread, a bottle of milk, a pack of pork chops and some Spam. As he was standing in line to pay for his items, he noticed that the cashier was a beautiful girl. As he was cashing out, he asked her name. "Delois," came her reply.

She was a vision of loveliness and Al gave his best effort flirting with the young girl. "There's definitely a spark there," Al thought to himself as he paid her for his groceries. For Delois, the feeling was mutual as she thought Al was one of the most handsome men she had ever met. She couldn't help but notice his strong muscles and his dark tan - both of which were the result of working long hours in construction - outdoors much of the time.

Al continued to go back to the store almost every afternoon to buy things. He eventually had fully stocked his Frigidaire and his pantry, but started dipping into his secret cash he kept hidden in the bottom of one of his tool boxes so that he could keep going back to make more purchases just to talk to Delois.

Before his job in Gatlinburg was due to start, Al got the ball rolling on his divorce from Grace. After she was finally tracked down staying at a motel/truck stop in Chattanooga, they subpoenaed her to come in for a deposition about her infidelity. During the deposition, she freely admitted that she was frequently having sex with other men while being married to Al. The divorce came pretty quickly after that.

On one Friday afternoon, Al left work a little early and drove the hour back to Maryville from Gatlinburg. He made a now familiar detour by Happy Jack's before heading home. When she saw her beau walk in the door, Delois called another cashier up to the front to take care of customers saying, "Julie, I'm gonna go take my break now! Watch the register please." Julie obliged.

Al and Delois walked down the side walk in front of the store chatting about nothing in particular. Then Delois spoke up, "You know... There's a dance tomorrow night up at the Music Barn."

"Is that so?" remarked Al.

There was a pause in their conversation and finally Delois said, "well ain't you gonna ask me?"

"Ask you what?" replied Al cluelessly.

"To go to the dance at the Music Barn tomorrow night silly!" she said.

"I don't know how to dance," replied Al.

"Well, I don't either," said Delois, "but we could at least go and listen to the music!"

Al excitedly agreed and asked, "Would you like to go to the barn dance with me tomorrow night ma'am?"

Delois batted her eyes, curtsied and replied in an exaggerated southern belle accent, "Why, I would be delighted to accompany you Mr. Garrett!" They both chuckled and made plans for Al to pick her up at her family's farm at five o'clock the next evening. By five thirty, they both walked into the music venue where a live country western band was already playing on stage.

They sat down at a table and for the next three hours listened to music, sipped on lemonade, and talked each other's ears off. When the evening was coming to a close and the band started winding down by playing slow songs, Al and Delois got up to leave.

As they were crossing the dance floor headed toward the door, the band was playing 'Rainbow At Midnight' by Ernest Tubb. Al unexpectedly grabbed Delois' hand and pulled her close to him.

They stared into each other's eyes and began swaying back and forth with each other – slow dancing like they had seen the other couples at the Music Barn do throughout the night. They both felt like they were the only ones on that dance floor. In fact, in that moment, they both felt like they were the only two people on Earth.

Their love sparked during that chance meeting at Happy

Jacks continued to grow and with Al's divorce from Grace finally finalized and Grace receiving custody of Billy Ray, Jimmy, and Malcolm - Al and Delois were happily married on June 14, 1948.

A year later in 1949, Delois gave birth to Gary. Less than a year later in '50, Delois delivered the twins, Roger and Ronnie. In 1953, Carl entered the world. Al and Delois thought that their family was now complete, but fate had other plans for them. A happy little accident occurred eleven years later in 1964 and they named him Dale. Five sons were definitely enough. They were done.

CHAPTER 6
THE JOHNSON CITY JOB

Johnson City, Tennessee – March 21, 1958

It was 2:00 PM and chilly outside – 36 degrees and snow piled up on the ground, especially in the shade of buildings and trees.

Malcolm sat alone in Doc's Diner in a booth next to the front window listening to 'A White Sport Coat' by Marty Robbins as it played on the jukebox in the background.

At two o'clock in the afternoon, the diner's lunch rush was over. Malcolm was practically the only one left in the place. He sat there alone and sipped on his cup of black coffee as he focused his gaze on the comings and goings of the people across the street at the First National Bank of Johnson City.

Johnson City was a good 120 miles from Maryville which in

Malcolm's mind made it a great place to rob. Nobody in this town knew him and he had become a firm believer in not shitting where you eat.

The foot traffic in and out of the bank had slowed a bit since all of the people who had bank business and had taken their lunch hour to stop by had now come and gone. At about 2:05 PM, Malcolm decided it was time to go to work.

He paid for his coffee and walked out of the diner toward the bank. He thought to himself, "this coat is cumbersome." He reached into the right pocket of the heavy black wool coat he was wearing to wrap his hand around the grip of the Colt snub nose five-shot revolver he had concealed there.

He stepped up onto the sidewalk and took a few more steps toward the glass doors of the bank. Just then, two businessmen exited the bank chatting with each other. Malcolm spun around as if he had momentarily changed his mind about robbing the bank.

He nervously ran his fingers through his dark hair and thought about how much more severe the consequences of robbing a bank were compared to other places like the liquor store he knocked over on his eighteenth birthday or the L and K Grocery store he robbed in Maryville a year and a half later.

"This is federal. If they get me for this one, it's gonna mean more than a slap on the wrist. I'll be lookin' at some serious time!" he thought to himself. "Still, banks are where the money is. Bigger risks equal bigger rewards," he rationalized. Convincing himself it was a good idea to carry out his plan, he turned and walked into the bank.

There were only two elderly customers standing at the teller's window making a transaction when he entered. Pulling his revolver into view and holding it toward the ceiling, he pulled the trigger firing a deafening shot! "This is a robbery!" he announced. "Give me all the money!" he said leveling the barrel of the pistol at the two tellers.

Hurriedly, they removed the money from their teller drawers and placed it on the counter. Realizing in that moment that he had forgotten to bring any type of container to carry the loot away in, he told them, "Put it in a bag!" They complied scooping up the money from the counter and stuffing it into a white canvas bank bag that had the name of the bank printed prominently in black ink on the side of it.

Taking his focus off of the cashiers momentarily, he noticed that the elderly couple who had been at the teller's window when he came in and had backed up several feet to give him a wide berth, were both trembling in abject fear. The elderly man was holding his wallet outstretched in his shaking hand toward Malcolm.

Malcolm looked at the old man and asked, "Is that your money in that there wallet mister?"

The man fearfully responded, "Yes sir."

"You keep that," said Malcolm. "I'm only here for the bank's money!"

By then, the tellers had put all the money into the canvas bag. Malcolm grabbed the bag off of the counter, tipped his grey wool flat cap to the old couple and hastily made his exit with the bag of cash in his left hand and the gun in his right. When he got to the sidewalk, he put the pistol back in his jacket pocket and stuffed the bag into the front of his jacket which created a huge bulge.

Quickly he walked down the sidewalk toward the side street

where he had parked his stolen 1955 blue and white Packard Clipper with white wall tires. Jumping in the driver's seat, he could hear the bank's alarm bell starting to ring. He leaned over and stuffed the bag and its contents underneath the passenger side seat and drove away quickly from the area heading down State Road 321 back to Maryville.

As he entered the small town of Greenville's city limits, Malcolm noticed that the gas level was getting low. He pulled into a service station. The service stations bell rang twice as the Packard Clipper drove over the rubber hose by the pumps. The clerk came out and asked Malcolm, "Fill'er up sir?"

"Yes sir, if you don't mind." Malcolm decided that he was far enough away from Johnson City that he could relax a bit. He opened the car door and stood up to stretch. When he stood, he realized he needed to relieve himself. He asked the attendant, "y'all got a can I can use?"

Yes sir," replied the service man, "it's to the left there on the side of the building."

Malcolm thanked him and joked, "It's a long drive to Maryville."

The attendant chuckled and replied, "Yes sir. Sure is."
Malcolm walked over to the side of the building and went
into the men's washroom to take a leak.

While he was in there, the gas station attendant started
cleaning the windshield of the car. As the attendant was
scrubbing an especially stubborn spot of bug guts from the
windshield, his gaze refocused on the floorboard of the
Packard. He saw the bank bag sticking partially out from
under the seat. He could clearly see enough of the printing
on the bag to tell it read, "First National Bank of Johnson
City." Several bills of various denomination were lying on
the floorboard, spilling from the bag.

The attendant's suspicion was now on high alert. He had the
presence of mind however, to keep his cool. He walked to
the back of the car. He removed an ink pen from his uniform
shirt pocket and wrote the car's tag number down on the
palm of his hand. He had barely made it back to the side of
the car to remove the gas nozzle when Malcolm returned
from the bathroom. "Need the oil checked sir" asked the
young man.

"Naw, that ain't necessary." replied Malcolm.

"That'll be $5.80." said the attendant.

Malcolm sat back down in the car and leaned over to the passenger side. Picking up a twenty-dollar bill from the floorboard, he shoved the open bag and rest of the spilled cash further under the seat. He handed the attendant the twenty-dollar bill and said, keep the change buddy!"

The attended took the twenty and said, "Thankya mister!"

Malcolm drove away, continuing his journey back toward Maryville. The clerk waited until Malcolm was out of sight and picked up the phone to report what he had seen to the police. He told them about seeing the bank bag, the cash on the floorboard, the tag number he had written down on his hand and the fact that Malcolm had mentioned that he was heading to Maryville. He intentionally however, left out the part about Malcolm giving him a twenty-dollar bill for six bucks worth of gas.

The police in Greenville contacted the police in Johnson City who in turn contacted the police in Maryville. The police in Maryville joined by two Tennessee Highway patrolmen and by Deputy Marshal Thomas Kelly Jr. who just happened to be in Maryville on official business, set up a road block on State Road 411 and State Road 321 – the two most likely paths that the robber they were looking for would approach from as he came into Maryville.

They had barely gotten their road block set up when one of the State Troopers and Deputy Marshal Kelly spotted Malcolm's blue and white Packard approaching on State Road 411. Malcolm hit the brakes and skidded to a stop when he realized that he was driving straight into their trap.

He did a U-turn to head the opposite direction. The car's white-walled back tires kicked up a rooster tail of gravel, grass, and snow from the side of the road as Malcolm completed his U-turn and accelerated away at a high rate of speed.

The State Trooper and Deputy Marshal Kelly gave chase. As he was fleeing the lawmen, Malcolm hung a sharp right onto Charles Road and lost control in the turn because of the icy road. The Packard rolled three times coming to rest on its roof in the edge of the woods. Dazed from the accident, Malcolm crawled out of the driver's side window of the car. He dropped to his belly momentarily in the snow to get his bearings. He could visibly see his warm breath every time he exhaled into the cold air. He assessed his injuries which seemed to be limited to a small cut on the top of his left hand and a slightly sore right knee.

By this time, the State Trooper and Deputy Marshal Kelly had screeched up to the scene in their patrol cars and jumped out with their weapons drawn. They ordered Malcolm to come out with his hands up. Malcolm popped into view around the trunk area of the overturned vehicle and instead of complying with their orders to surrender, he fired two shots in the direction of the lawmen! The two law enforcement officers returned fire and bullet holes began to appear in the right rear fender and side of the trunk area of the Packard.

When the frequency of their shots had died down, Malcolm on his knees behind the Packard, peeked around the trunk area again and fired two more shots. He would have shot more rounds, but on the third pull of the trigger, all of the gun's five cartridges had been fired – one at the bank into the ceiling and the rest at the lawmen.

The last two shots that he fired however, had found their target. Deputy Marshal Kelly was hit once in the right chest and once in the center of his abdomen. He fell to the ground bleeding and writhing in agony while the State Trooper radioed for help. The trooper held his position of cover behind his patrol car – not knowing whether Malcolm would fire in his direction again.

With his pistol ammunition all spent, Malcolm tossed his gun down in the snow and fled into the woods – crashing through briars and bushes like he and Jimmy had done on horseback when they were running away from the moonshiners back when they were kids. Like back then, Malcolm again seemed to be enjoying the adrenaline rush that he was feeling in the moment. The trooper's view was obscured by the overturned Packard and he did not see Malcolm's escape. He continued to hold his position and attempted to render medical aid to Deputy Marshal Kelly.

A massive man-hunt immediately went into effect with more than eight Maryville police officers, about ten state Troopers, a dozen Blount County deputies, four Agents from the Knoxville field office of the F.B.I., and several more lawmen from surrounding small towns all responding to the scene.

Night fell but the lawmen were sure they had Malcolm contained somewhere in the wooded area. Policemen were set up on a perimeter surrounding the woods. By sunrise, Malcolm was found shivering from the cold and hiding under a partially hollowed log about four hundred yards deep in the forest and taken into custody.

Deputy Marshal Kelly was admitted to the hospital in Maryville in critical condition. After a few days, he stabilized enough to transfer to the larger, better equipped Knoxville Hospital where he underwent a risky surgery to remove one of the bullets that had lodged dangerously close to his spine. After spending almost three months in the hospital, Kelly made a full recovery and returned to active duty. About three months later, after his return to work, Kelly testified at Malcolm's bank robbery trial.

For the car theft, bank robbery in Johnson City, and the critical wounding of Deputy Marshal Kelly, Malcolm was sentenced to thirty years in prison with his sentence to be served at the Brushy Mountain State Prison in Morgan County, Tennessee. When Judge Reginald Quarels read Malcolm's sentence, Malcolm dropped his head and looked down at the floor in front of him. Quietly under his breath, the only thing he said was, "well shit."

CHAPTER 7
DOING RUBY WRONG

Petros, Tennessee - April 1, 1961

The Alcatraz of the south. That's what many called the Brushy Mountain State Penitentiary in the community of Petros in Morgan County, Tennessee. Originally built as a wooden structure in 1896, It was replaced in the 1920s with an imposing building constructed from stone mined by prisoners from a quarry on the sprawling eighty-six-acre property.

A rock fortress tucked in the woods of the Appalachian Mountains, the prison was almost completely encircled by rugged, wooded, mountainous terrain in a remote section of the Cumberland Plateau.

Escape attempts were almost always unsuccessful. Even if an inmate were able to somehow scale the 18-foot stone wall topped with razor wire, they would have to survive the harsh topography surrounding the prison.

Before he was eventually paroled from Brushy Mountain Penitentiary, Malcolm would spend his time looking at pictures in magazines in his cell and exercising. For three months, his cell happened to be four cells down from Brushy Mountain's most notable inmate, James Earl Ray, the convicted assassin of Martin Luther King Jr. Malcolm didn't become close friends with Ray, but was cordial with him when they would see each other in the chow line. Malcolm could never understand why someone would kill another man just because he was a different ethnicity.

It's surprising that Malcolm even received parole status at all in late 1969. His escape from the facility in 1961, three years after the bank robbery in Johnson City would in most people's minds, have eliminated him for being considered for parole. The overcrowding problem at the prison was certainly a factor - coupled with Malcolm being a model prisoner after his recapture.

He began formulating a plan two and a half years into his sentence on how he would escape. The plan involved a young twenty-three-year-old girl name Ruby Alexander. She was an attractive young lady with shoulder-length strawberry blonde hair and a figure like Marilyn Monroe.

Although naïve in some ways, she was wise beyond her years in others.

Malcolm had met Ruby a few months before the Johnson City bank robbery. In fact, one of the main reasons he had for robbing the bank in the first place was to play big-shot and take Ruby on a trip to Cuba or maybe Las Vegas.

He met Ruby at her job as a nursing assistant at the Maryville Hospital. Malcolm had cut his hand helping his uncle Hayden rip some lumber. The cut wasn't too bad but required a few stitches to close the wound. Malcolm made small talk with Ruby while waiting for the doctor to come in and sew up his hand.

The emergency room chatting evolved into some dates. They had gone out only a few times. Usually just dinner out at a drive-in diner or a movie at the theater up at the Midland Mall. Malcolm liked Ruby but thought she was young and impressionable.

Once Malcolm was arrested, he was almost sure she wasn't going to have much to do with him as the story of him robbing the bank in Johnson City and shooting Deputy Marshal Kelly was all over the newspapers, radio and TV, but he decided to take a chance. He wrote to Ruby from Brushy Mountain c/o the Maryville Hospital and somehow, the letter made it to her.

Over the next few months, they exchanged letters back and forth. Nothing particularly romantic. Malcolm would write about life in the prison and witnessing an inmate get beat-up or shanked. Ruby would write to him about exciting things that happened at the emergency room at the hospital while she was working.

Ruby was infatuated with Malcolm. He was a tall, handsome, dark-haired man. Ruby was charmed not only by his smile and smooth talk, but was intrigued because he was "a little dangerous." She seemed magnetically drawn to him just because he was what modern society would call a "bad boy." She embraced his criminal past instead of being repelled by it. She was falling in love.

Ruby's feelings about Malcolm were however not mutual. Malcolm thought she was fun to go out with and he certainly entertained the thought of getting into her panties, but that's about as far as it went. He had no real intention of allowing the relationship to blossom.

To Malcolm, Ruby was a creature of convenience. She was someone to write letters to in order to pass the time. But lying on his bunk alone in his cell one night, he began to think about how he could potentially use Ruby to aid him in escaping Brushy Mountain. He thought to himself, "maybe I will take her with me on the run." Then he thought better of it, saying to himself, "naw, that's probably not a good idea. She would just slow me down."

Malcolm's correspondences with Ruby became more and more romantic in nature. In one of his letters to Ruby, he suggested that she drive the hour from Maryville to Petros to visit him in prison on the first of the month, the one and only day per month visitors were allowed. He knew he couldn't pitch his escape plan in a letter because there was always a possibility that letters could be intercepted, opened, and read by the guards. Ruby eagerly agreed to come and visit him.

A week or so later on visiting day, Ruby drove up to the foreboding walls of the Brushy Mountain Penitentiary. Just seeing the high castle-like walls, razor wire, and guards in towers holding rifles made her a bit uneasy. She persevered though because she was there to see a man that she had daydreamed about who one day, might be her husband and the father of her children.

After showing her driver's license at the main gate and at a secondary check-point, she pulled up in the visitor's parking lot of the prison. She saw other families, even some with small children, get out of their cars and walk toward the visitor's entrance. Ruby thought to herself, "they've obviously been here before. I guess I'll just follow them." And that's what she did.

Inside the visitor's lobby, she waited in line behind the family that she had just followed through the parking lot and into the building. Once they had checked in with the guards at the window the family sat down in the busy waiting room. They then waited for the inmate they were there to see to be brought down to the visitor's area from lock-up and for their visitor's stickers.

Ruby, lost in her thoughts, looked around at the bars on the windows of the visitor's lobby and at the intimidating steel door that led to the general visitation area. She felt a nervousness in her stomach.

"Next!" said the guard authoritatively. Ruby, still lost in thought and not paying attention didn't move. "Ma'am?" said the guard again to get Ruby's attention. Still no reaction from Ruby. This time, the guard raised his voice and loudly said again, "Ma'am! Step up to the window please!"

Snapping back into the here and now, Ruby apprehensively spoke up, "Oh, I'm sorry. Yes sir." Ruby said as she stepped up to the window.

"Name?" said the guard.

"My name or the person I'm here to see?" asked Ruby innocently.

"Let's start with your name honey." the guard replied.

"I'm Ruby. Ruby Alexander." she said.

"I need to see your ID please." the guard said. As Ruby fumbled through her small purse, the guard looked inside of it to make sure there were no weapons. Ruby handed the guard her driver's license.

"And which inmate are you here to visit ma'am?" asked the guard.

"Malcolm Garrett," Ruby replied.

"Are you his wife?" asked the guard while writing her information down on a clipboard.

"No sir," replied Ruby. I'm his girlf- uh, I'm his friend."

The guard filled in her name on the visitor sticker. "Wear this at all times while you're visiting and return it when you leave." the guard said sternly. "Have a seat right over there and we'll call you when inmate Garrett has been brought down."

"Yes sir," said Ruby. "Thank you, sir." Ruby walked across the dirty floor of the crowded lobby and sat down in one of the well-worn, paint-chipped metal waiting room chairs. She stared at the ugly, mint green, paint-chipped walls and at some graffiti that someone had scratched into the wall's paint trying to make out what it said.

In about twenty minutes, the guard, looking at his clipboard shouted, "Ruby Alexander!"

Ruby stood and said, "Yes sir, that's me."

The guard told her, "Step up to the yellow line on the floor and when the door buzzes and opens, walk in and stand on the line in front of the second door. When the second door buzzes open, you may enter the visiting room. You have one hour."

Ruby understood the instructions and stepped up to the line. The door buzzed and automatically opened. Clutching her small black purse with both hands in front of her, she stepped in and saw the second steel door. She walked a few steps and stood on the second yellow line painted on the floor. The first door automatically closed behind her. A moment later, the second door buzzed open and she stepped inside.

Walking into the room, she saw a lot of families visiting with their incarcerated loved ones. They were all sitting around individual steel tables that looked like picnic tables. The steel benches at each table were bolted to the floor just like all the tables were.

She looked around and spotted Malcolm sitting alone at one of the tables on the opposite side of the room. She waved and quickly walked over to him. They shared an embrace. "It is so good to see you, Ruby!" said Malcolm.

"You too Malcolm! I had almost forgotten what you looked like!" joked Ruby. For the next 30 minutes, they talked about some of the same things that they would discuss in their letters back and forth to each other.

"Listen Ruby," said Malcolm. "I miss you so much and I've been thinking about a way to get outta here so that we can be together forever. But I'm going to need your help." Ruby remained silent and intently listened to the plan as Malcolm laid it out for her. He explained, "We can't say anything about this in letters to each other because the guards snoop in the mail sometimes."

Ruby nodded that she understood. A guard circulating around the room holding a clipboard walked past their table and said, "Five more minutes Garrett!" With their hour almost over, Malcolm went back over the plan summarizing the details.

"I love you baby! I can't wait for us to start our life together!" lied Malcolm.

They embraced again and Ruby replied, "Me too Malcolm. I love you too!"

The guard circulating the large room came by again and said "Times up Garrett. Time to go."

Malcolm gave Ruby one more hug and a kiss and said, "I'll see you one month from today sweetheart!"

"I love you baby!" said Ruby as she watched the guard escort Malcolm through another one of those steel doors close to where they had been sitting. Ruby started crying as she walked back toward the doors that led to the visitor's lobby where she'd come in. It broke her heart to leave her beau in that awful place. Ruby was buzzed through both doors and returned her visitor's sticker to the guard at the window in the lobby.

Over the next month, Malcolm and Ruby exchanged several letters, both being careful not to mention any of their impending plans, but saying things to each other about being together in a way that someone reading the letter wouldn't understand what they were planning.

Petros, Tennessee – May 1, 1961

Visiting day was here again. Malcolm woke up in his cell earlier than usual, his anticipation and anxiety about today's impending escape attempt was of course forefront in his mind. He stood in front of his small mirror shaving his face over and over again. He didn't want a single sprig of facial hair to be present when Ruby arrived later that morning. He had already painstakingly shaved his arms, legs, and chest hair the night before.

Sitting on the edge of his bunk with his hands on his knees and his right knee bouncing up and down in anticipation, Malcolm waited. Glancing again and again at the big clock mounted on the wall across from his cell, Malcolm was clearly impatient. Ruby was supposed to have been there at 10:00 AM and it was already 10:22 AM. He worried to himself that Ruby had gotten cold feet and abandoned her plan to help him.

Suddenly a guard walked down Malcolm's cell block and shouted, "Garrett! You've got a visitor!"

Malcolm sprang to his feet and stood in front of his cell door waiting for the guard to open it. The guard led Malcolm down the long row of cells. Malcolm glanced in each cell as he walked by. Some inmates were lying on their bunks reading, some were doing sit-ups or push-ups to exercise. One inmate was on his knees next to his bunk praying. "I hope he's praying for my success today," Malcolm smiled to himself.

Malcolm and the guard turned the corner and walked together down a long hallway. During their walk, they had to be buzzed through several heavy steel doors. Finally, the last door buzzed open and Malcolm stepped through it into the visitation room. Malcolm took a seat and in just a few moments, he immediately spotted Ruby wearing a white top and a plaid skirt and wearing over-sized dark sunglasses. She walked toward Malcolm as she removed the glasses and hugged Malcolm's neck and kissed his lips.

They both sat down at one of the steel tables near the doors to the bathrooms that were meant for both the inmates and the public during visitation time. "Did you bring everything?" asked Malcolm in a lowered voice.

"Yes, I brought it all. It's all in there," she said, gesturing with her eyes toward her larger, over-sized purse sitting on the steel bench next to her.

"Good! Good!" replied Malcolm. "Did the guards give you any trouble?"

"Not really," replied Ruby. "He looked in the purse for guns or knives and saw the clothes rolled up and raised his eyebrow. I told him that I was having some incontinence and carried the extra set of clothing in case I wet myself. He didn't ask me anything else after that!"

"Oh, baby that was perfect! You did great!" said Malcolm.

"I gave my notice at the hospital so that's all taken care of. I rented the motel in Lenoir City and have you a change of clothes laid out on the bed there like we talked about," stated Ruby.

"What a girl!" replied Malcolm.

"So where are we going? Did you decide? Las Vegas? Cuba?

Somewhere else?" asked Ruby excitedly.

"Which one would you like to go to baby?" asked Malcolm.

"I've always wanted to see California." said Ruby.

"Then, California here we come!" laughed Malcolm. Ruby giggled with anticipation.

They sat and chatted a while longer. One of the newer guards assigned to the visitor's room area that day came by and announced, "Fifteen minutes Mister Garrett."

"OK boss-man." Malcolm replied. As the guard left, Malcolm told Ruby to hand him the stuff. She reached in her purse and removed the bundle of tightly wrapped clothes and other items and handed it and a small zippered make-up bag to Malcolm. Malcolm quickly stuffed the items under his prison shirt. He stood up and looking at Ruby said, "Just like we planned baby."

Ruby nodded and replied, "Just like we planned" and peeled the visitor's sticker from her top and handed it to him.

Malcolm stuck it to the inside of his prison shirt.

Malcolm made his way to the men's restroom just off of the visitor's room. He closed the door behind him and latched it. Quickly he removed his blue prison shirt and grey prison pants and donned the white top and plaid skirt that Ruby had brought for him. The low-heeled shoes she had brought were a tight fit, but Malcolm forced his feet into them and made it work.

Using the make-up in the small zippered make-up bag, Malcolm applied rouge to his closely shaven cheeks and red lipstick to his lips. He pulled the wig down tightly on his head and wrapped a scarf around the faux hair just as Ruby had worn when she came in. After putting on an identical pair of over-sized sunglasses and sticking Ruby's visitor's sticker on his white top, Malcolm unlatched the restroom door and peeked out at Ruby.

Ruby held her hand up as to say wait a moment. Malcolm waited and watched from the cracked door. A few seconds later, a larger group with several women in it were walking toward the exit door. Ruby gave Malcolm the high-sign and he walked back into the visitor's room carrying a canvas bag that had also been rolled up with the other items. He fell in line behind the group that was leaving.

Ruby went in to the ladies' room and sat down on a toilet in one of the stalls nervously waiting and watching the time on her watch. She heard the first exit door buzz. Then, she heard the second one buzz. Five minutes later, she came out of the ladies' room and headed swiftly to the steel exit door.

The guards buzzed her through both doors and she stepped up to the window and said, "I think my sticker must have fell off. It wasn't sticking very well to this fabric when you first gave it to me." While she had been in the ladies' room, she had unbuttoned the two top buttons of her blouse revealing a good portion of her ample bosom.

The guard tried to surreptitiously peer down her blouse and said, "That's ok Ma'am. You have a nice day now." said the guard. Once outside, she walked with purpose to her baby blue 1958 Chevrolet Biscayne. Her hips swayed back and forth as she made her way through the parking lot.

Malcolm, still wearing his convincing disguise, was already sitting in the passenger seat watching her wiggle as she approached in the rear-view mirror that he had adjusted so he could see the prison's exit doors behind him.

Meanwhile, back in the visitor's room, the guard came back by to return Malcolm to his cell. Of course, Malcolm was gone and so was his visitor. The guard should have told his superior or put the place on lock-down, but he didn't. Being a young, inexperienced rookie guard, he just assumed that another guard had escorted Malcolm back to his cell. He didn't even bother to confirm it.

Back outside, Ruby pulled up to the first guard check point. The guard asked to look in her trunk. She turned off the ignition and handed him the keys. The guard made sure no one was hiding in the trunk, returned her keys and sent her on her way. At the second exit checkpoint and main gate, a guard walked out of his guard shack and asked, "Did you ladies have a nice visit today?"

Ruby responded "Oh it was lovely."

"How about you ma'am?" directing his attention to Malcolm who was holding a handkerchief to his face as if he were crying.

"She's a little emotional," said Ruby.

"I understand," said the guard, "We see that all the time here." Tipping his uniform cap at Malcolm and Ruby, the guard said, "You ladies have a nice day."

"You too sir," replied Ruby.

The two of them drove straight to the motel in Lenoir City. Malcolm washed the make-up from his face in the shower. His hair and face covered with soap and water and his eyes closed as he rinsed it all away, he heard the shower curtain slide open.

Ruby had disrobed and joined him in the shower. They passionately kissed and embraced each other and eventually moved their love-making to the motel room's bed. They shared a sensual night of love-making. The next morning, Ruby got redressed and Malcolm put on the men's clothes Ruby had bought for him. "Let's get outta here baby," said Malcolm, picking up her keys off of the motel nightstand. "I'll drive from here on out."

Malcolm opened the door for Ruby and then walked around the Chevrolet and sat down in the driver's seat of Ruby's car. He put the keys in the ignition and then said, "Damn it! I forgot that wig and shit. We need to toss that in a dumpster on our way outta here. Can you go back in and get it sweetie?"

Ruby said, "Sure baby," as she exited the car and stepped back in the motel room. When Ruby came back out with the ladies clothing, wig, and shoes, her car and Malcolm were gone! She knew in that moment that she had been used by Malcolm to get what he wanted - freedom. She sat down on the curb in front of their motel room and cried for over two hours.

For her role in the escape, Ruby Alexander was sentenced to three years in prison in the women's wing of the Tennessee State Penitentiary near Nashville. With good behavior she was released early after twenty-two months of incarceration.

Malcolm remained a free man for a total of four months and two days. Robbing gas stations and small mom-and-pop grocery stores along the way for spending money, he had made a brief hour and a half stop in Lake Wales, Florida to visit his father. Following the visit with his father, Malcolm was pulled over by the Florida Highway Patrol for speeding just east of Tampa. He was still driving Ruby's car.

He was re-arrested and brought back to Brushy Mountain to

serve out the rest of his original sentence plus five more additional years for the escape. Due to his good behavior and the prison overcrowding problems, Malcolm was paroled on December 20, 1969. He was a free man again, but that wouldn't last long.

For the rest of his days, Malcolm often thought about Ruby. In breaking her heart, he unwittingly had broken his own as well. Before he died. He talked about his life of crime to a nurse at the hospital he was in at the time.

Malcolm spoke of all the people he had robbed, the cars and money he had stolen. The people that he had physically injured. The lives of people he had shattered or negatively affected with his actions. He talked about all of the days, months, and years he had spent locked in cages. But he lamented that one of his biggest regrets in life was doing Ruby so wrong.

CHAPTER 8
THE HAT

Frostproof, Florida, March 9, 1972

"Let me tell y'all something," said Chief Jessie Masters as he addressed his four patrolmen in his office at the Frostproof Police Department. "I want you boys lookin' spiffy and professional for the public. We've got an image to project. So, if you boys get out of your car, I want you wearing these new hats. They're part of your uniforms now. No if's ands or buts about it. Y'all hear!?"

"Yes sir," replied the four officers.

Chief Masters removed four brand new grey straw Stetson cowboy style hats each still wrapped in plastic from a cardboard box that had been shipped to the department straight from the John B. Stetson Hat Company in Philadelphia.

He passed one to each of his patrolmen including his newest officer, Gary Garrett who had only been working there for right at six months. "Oh, and y'all take damn good care of these lids too now," the Chief sternly warned, "they weren't cheap."

Two days later on Saturday, March 11th around 7:00 PM, Gary was patrolling the north city limits of the town when a light green '68 Ford Mustang came barreling toward town around Lake Moody on Highway 17 and drifted into the lane of oncoming traffic. Gary jerked the steering wheel of his Plymouth Fury patrol car really hard to avoid a head-on collision with the Mustang.

Doing a quick U-turn, Gary turned on the patrol car's blue lights and siren and began pursuing the car. It wasn't going that fast, but it wasn't stopping either. The car took a right onto Swingle Street and immediately pulled into the front yard of a house.

Gary exited his unit, remembering to put on his new Stetson, and approached the driver's side of the Mustang. The driver was already getting out of the car and Gary could tell right away that the short, stocky, muscular man had been drinking by the way he stumbled as he stood up out of the car.

The man, forty-year-old Clayton Carter, immediately met Gary with a belligerent attitude. He was uncooperative and tried to walk away from Gary toward the house. Gary told Clayton that he needed to stay there a minute and talk to him. Clayton aggressively snatched his elbow away from Gary's grasp. Gary made the decision in that moment to go ahead and arrest Clayton for driving under the influence.

Clayton was having none of it, and the fight was on! Both men began to tussle with each other in the front yard between the patrol car and the Mustang. The fight became more and more intense as Clayton ripped Gary's uniform shirt open during the violent, knock-down-drag-out brawl.

Gary was starting to run out of gas. He shoved Clayton backward to give himself time to reach back to his back pocket for his impact weapon. It was called a "Black Jack." It was basically a sixteen-ounce piece of rounded lead with a spring handle which was all sewn in between slabs of tough leather. It was a common tool used by law enforcement officers on resisting suspects.

Clayton charged at Gary again and Gary swung the Black Jack, rapping it hard against Claytons head just above his right ear. Almost immediately, Clayton began to bleed profusely from the wound. Blood covered his shirt and flowed down a foot below his waistline, soaking his pants.

Clayton touched his hand to the side of his head and then pulled it away to look at the blood. Then, he looked at Gary and said, "You hit me!" Then he turned and ran toward the house. The front door was standing open. Gary pursued on foot and just after they cleared the small front porch of the house, Gary tackled him in the edge of the living room and straddled him on the floor as Clayton continued to struggle and fight.

Hearing all the commotion, Clayton's fourteen-year-old daughter and Clayton's seventy-seven-year-old father came in from a back room using his cane for support. The elder man exclaimed, "What the hell is going on out here!?" With one hand, the old man picked Gary up by the scruff of the neck and threw him off of Clayton.

Up until that moment, Gary's straw Stetson hat had somehow miraculously remained on his head the whole time. But when the strong old man, a bricklayer like his son, had tossed him off of Clayton, the hat finally came off and rolled into the middle of the living room floor.

As soon as she saw that, Clayton's fourteen-year-old daughter started jumping up and down on the hat. She kicked it and marched in place on top of the hat flattening it and putting creases in it that were beyond repair. She continued to jump up and down on it for what seemed like a full minute, intentionally destroying the hat of the man who was fighting with her daddy.

Clayton managed to get to his feet and ran toward the back bed room stating "I'm getting the gun!" Hearing that statement, Gary wisely decided it would be in his own best interest to retreat to the yard behind his patrol car and radio for back-up.

Fifteen minutes went by. While waiting for his back-up to arrive, Gary saw a now calmed down Clayton come to the porch and could clearly see that he wasn't armed. Clayton continued to walk out to the patrol car and leaned against it with his arms crossed while carrying on a surprisingly civil conversation with Gary. In that short amount of time, for some reason, Clayton had calmed down and was being much more rational.

Clayton's daddy hobbled out to the yard using his cane for

support and started interrupting the conversation and re-heating tensions. Gary pointed at the house and said, "The best thing you can do old man, is go back in that house over there while we're talking." While Gary was pointing, the old man swung his cane at Gary's arm striking his wristwatch and breaking it.

Just then, Gary's back up arrived. The old man went back into the house. The back-up was a Polk County deputy named Gerald Powers. Deputy Powers for lack of a better description was shaped like the capitol letter "V."

He was a muscle-bound man and stood a towering six and a half feet tall. His slim waist accentuated his huge broad shoulders and the fabric on his uniform shirt sleeve strained to contain his bulging biceps. Gerald got out of his patrol car and surveyed the scene. He looked at Gary and his ripped up uniform shirt and he looked at Clayton and the blood that had streamed down his shirt and pants.

Gerald also noticed the divots in the yard where Gary and Clayton had scrambled around for toe holds during their fight. Gerald remarked in his deep country drawl, "It looks like a damn herd of cattle came through here." Redirecting his attention toward Clayton he asked, "Boy, are you causing this officer trouble out here tonight?"

Clayton looked up at the skyscraper of a man and replied, "no sir."

Gesturing toward Gary's unit, Gerald said, "Well then, you best go over there and get in the back of that car."

Clayton responded like a guilty, scared boy caught stealing cookies from the cookie jar. He lowered his head and said, "Yes sir." With that, Clayton walked over to Gary's patrol car, opened the back door, sat down, and then closed the door.

Gary joked with Gerald, "Well hell, why didn't he do that for me when I asked him?" Gerald chuckled and said, "I guess you just don't have the magic touch, Gary." Both men laughed. "Anybody else here need to go to jail tonight?"

Gary replied, "No, the old man broke my watch, but I'll just do an affidavit on him for battery on a LEO and pick him up later."

"Well alright," said Gerald. "If you don't need me for

anything else then, I guess I best be getting back up toward Lake Wales."

"I think I'm good now. Appreciate the assist." said Gary.

"No problem. Anytime." said Gerald as he got back in his unit and backed out of the yard.

Gary transported Clayton to jail and decided to start the paperwork on Clayton's daddy the following day. After booking the prisoner in at the Polk County Jail in Bartow and getting back to Frostproof, Gary swung by his apartment and changed uniform shirts. Then, he drove to the police department to get a cup of coffee and a few forms he needed to finish up his report and do the affidavit on Clayton's daddy.

When he walked into the police department, Chief Masters was standing in the lobby leaning on the counter and talking to the dispatcher. He had stopped in just to check on things. He looked over at Gary and said, "Anne here tells me you've had a busy night."

"She ain't wrong about that!" replied Gary. He went on to

describe the encounter with Clayton Carter. He told the Chief about Clayton crossing the center-line and almost hitting his patrol car head on.

He explained the initial encounter with Clayton and the fight in the yard. He shared how Clayton had practically ripped his uniform shirt completely off of him and how he had to smack Clayton up-side his head with the Black Jack to try to get him under control.

He told him about Clayton's bloody wound and chasing him into the house where he tackled him and the secondary fight happened. He mentioned Clayton's daddy and how he had struck him with his cane and broken his wristwatch. And about Clayton saying something about a gun and Gerald having to respond as back-up.

Chief Masters, staring at the top of Gary's head the whole time while he was listening to the story finally spoke up at the end of Gary's recounting of the tale and in his heavy southern accent asked, "Say, where's your hat boy?"

Gary sighed deeply and said, "Uh, yeah, Chief, about the hat..."

CHAPTER 9
OLE SALLY

Maryville, Tennessee - July 15, 1952

Billy Ray was the most sheltered of the original three Garrett boys. With his mother's constant drinking and whoring around and his father Al constantly away from home working on construction jobs, he grew up finding interesting ways to entertain himself. He spent most of his youth living with Grace's mother.

His grandmother was older and had a difficult time keeping an eye on Billy Ray in order to keep him out of trouble. He wouldn't mind her when she told him to do his chores and he was starting to skip school on a pretty regular basis when it was in session.

Billy Ray took advantage of his grandmother's kindness. She took him in and he repaid her by stealing money from her purse starting when he was just seven years old because he wanted a soda-pop from the little country store that was about a half mile from her house and farm.

By nine years old, Billy Ray was becoming ungovernable by his grandmother. He was being heavily influenced by his older brothers Jimmy and especially Malcolm who were both committing crimes and getting away with them. He saw them doing whatever they wanted to do with no one holding them responsible for their actions. He thought to himself, even at his young age, "Why play by the rules if I can get what I want by breaking them?"

It was a hot humid mid-July day in Maryville. At 10:00 AM, it was already 85 degrees outside and the high would top out that day around a steamy 94 degrees. With Jimmy and Malcolm gone who knows where, Billy Ray was bored. He needed an activity to occupy his mind.

Walking down the dusty dirt road from his grandmother's farm to the little general store to get another RC Cola to cool off with, Billy Ray took in the beauty of the surrounding mountains. He stood for five minutes watching two squirrels chase each other around and around a tree. He was impressed by how they quickly anticipated each other's moves and would run and scamper around the tree to avoid each other. "Damn!" Billy Ray thought to himself, "those little bastards are fast!"

Once he got to the country store, he noticed the clerk busy helping a customer. Billy Ray seized the opportunity to slip an Almond Joy candy bar and a pack of Topps baseball cards with bubblegum into his faded overall's pocket. He left the store after only paying for the soda-pop.

As Billy Ray walked back toward his grandmother's house, he ripped open the package of Topps baseball cards and crammed the entire piece of bubblegum into his mouth – chewing it like a cow working a cud.

Thumbing through the baseball cards, he saw Mickey

Mantle's rookie card. Removing it from the stack of five trading cards, he wadded it up and tossed it unceremoniously into the weeds next to the road. He hated the New York Yankee team that much! Of course, Billy Ray had no way of knowing at the time that the now crumpled, discarded Mickey Mantle card would have someday been worth upwards of 12.6 million dollars!

Billy Ray continued along the dry dusty road and noticed a shiny new red Farmall Super M tractor parked in a field on a neighbor's farm. The farm was about half-way in between his grandmother's place and the general store. The man who owned the property had left the farm equipment parked there while he took a break from the heat on his front porch and drank a lemonade. Billy Ray climbed through the barbed wire fence to get a better look at the fancy bright red tractor.

Mr. Jackson was the man who owned the place and the tractor. He lived there on the farm alone. He was a kind, older gentleman and was a widower. His one and only child was now grown and had moved away long ago.

Mr. Jackson watched Billy Ray circle around and admire the Farmall and was enjoying seeing his youthful fascination with the piece of machinery. Jackson set his empty glass down, adjusted his worn tan colored straw hat with a hole in the brim on his head, and stepped down from his porch. As he walked toward Billy Ray still staring wide-eyed at the brand-new tractor, Mr. Jackson said, "Howdy son!"

Billy Ray replied, "Hey mister. This sure is a purty tractor! It's so shiny!"

Mr. Jackson replied, "Well, it ought to be! I just bought Ole Sally brand new four days ago!"

"Ole Sally?" asked Billy Ray.

"That's what I named her," replied Jackson. "She's a beauty ain't she?"

"She sure is! Does she go fast?" asked Billy Ray, spitting out his bubblegum to make it easier to talk.

"Well, she's a four cylinder and has a forty-four-horsepower motor. I don't reckon I rightly know how fast she'll go, but I know she'll get the farmin' done around here a lot faster from now on!" Mr. Jackson continued, "Ain't you one of them Garrett boys from up the road yonder?"

"Yes sir, I'm Billy Ray. I'm staying with my grandmother over there," said Billy Ray gesturing with his head toward his grandmother's farm.

"I thought so," said Jackson. "Me and your grandpappy used to go rabbit and squirrel huntin' in them woods right over there. Fact is, we used to hunt all over these here mountains when we were knee-high to a grasshopper. Probably 'bout your age."

"My grandpa died a few years ago. I never knew him much," said Billy Ray.

"Yeah, I know he did son. I know he did. I sure was sad to hear that. He was a good man," said Jackson pensively.

Billy Ray, turning his attention back toward the tractor asked Mr. Jackson, "You reckon I could sit up on this here tractor?"

"I'll tell you what son, I'll do ya one better than that! If'n you want, I'll ride you on it all the way around the field!"

"That would be a gas mister!" came Billy Ray's reply.

Mr. Jackson climbed up on the tractor and took his seat behind the wheel. Patting the tractor's giant rear tire, he said, "Climb on up here boy."

Billy Ray crawled up the side of the tractor and stood on the deck next to Mr. Jackson's seat. Mr. Jackson pointed out to Billy Ray all of the levers, pedals, and controls and explained what each one was for. Billy Ray listened and watched in awe, soaking it all in. Billy Ray wasn't book-smart, but he had a special fascination with all things mechanical and took a keen interest as Mr. Jackson talked.

Jackson cranked up the noisy tractor and Billy Ray smiled with joy as Mr. Jackson revved the motor a few times. Billy Ray watched with glee as the grey/black exhaust smoke shot into the air from the large silver exhaust pipe sticking up from the front of the tractor.

Jackson put it into gear and off they went, driving around Jackson's entire field and all the way around his barn not once but twice! He came back to roughly the same spot where it had been parked before and shut off the engine.

"Well, that's the end of the line son. I reckon I need to get back to work," said Jackson.

"Gee mister, that was swell! Thanks for the ride!" said Billy Ray leaping down from the tractor.

"You're mighty welcome son. Come on back another day and maybe I'll give you another ride on Ole Sally here," smiled Jackson, patting the steering wheel.

"Alright, that'll be great!" said Billy Ray excitedly as he walked away, climbed back through the barbed wire, and happily headed back to his grandmother's farm.

Nine-year-old Billy Ray couldn't stop thinking about Ole Sally. He regretted Mr. Jackson not flooring it in the field to show him how fast it would go. It was about this time that the wheels in Billy Ray's head began to turn. "I betcha I could drive Ole Sally myself," thought Billy Ray.

The more he thought about sitting in the driver's seat of that tractor and flooring it to see how fast it would go and feel the cool wind in his hair, the more the idea of stealing it appealed to him.

Waiting until nightfall, Billy Ray crawled out of the second story bedroom window of his grandmother's farmhouse and jumped from the roof to a tree branch that was close to the house. He shimmied down the tree and down the road he went on his mission to drive Ole Sally.

He got to Mr. Jackson's property and even though there was just a little light coming from the waning crescent moon, he could see that the tractor was no longer parked in the same spot. He climbed through the barbed wire fence and walked further onto the property straining to look through the darkness trying to spot the tractor. It was nowhere to be found.

Billy Ray thought to himself, "There's only one other place Ole Sally could be. In Mr. Jackson's barn!" He made his way through the field to the old faded red barn and turned the well-worn piece of wood that latched the walk-through barn door shut. Once inside, Billy Ray saw the object of his desire. He unlatched the two big barn doors and pushed them both wide open. They creaked loudly and Billy Ray was scared that the noise might alert Mr. Jackson, but it didn't. Then he climbed up on the tractor and sat down on the driver's seat.

When he cranked up Ole Sally, Mr. Jackson's Labrador Retriever started barking from somewhere over by the house. "Too late dog!" thought Billy Ray. He strained to reach the tractor's pedals and slipped the tractor into gear. He floored the gas and the exhaust smoke once again rolled from the front-mounted pipe on the tractor. The tractor accelerated and by this time, one of the big barn doors had swung back partially closed. The tractor collided with the door with such force that it ripped it from its hinges and it fell with a huge thud to the ground.

Continuing, Billy Ray drove the tractor into the field and right through the barbed wire fence tearing a large section of it down. He looked over his shoulder at Mr. Jackson running after him from the porch of the house while pulling his suspenders up onto his shoulders. The elderly Jackson couldn't keep up and Billy Ray was soon out of sight.

Billy Ray continued down the dirt road and was at the closed country store in no time. He hung a left onto Montvale Road. As Billy Ray rolled along, he thought to himself, "Maryville ain't that far. I think I'll drive down town!"

He chugged along toward Maryville but about three miles out of town, the tractor started sputtering and bucking. Ole Sally was out of gas. Billy Ray managed to get it pulled over on the side of the road as it was running out of fuel, but he didn't realize that there was a deep ditch that ran alongside the road. The big rear tire slipped down into the ditch and the tractor fell over - coming to rest on its side and doing quite a bit of damage to the side of the tractor.

Mr. Jackson's benevolence toward Billy Ray had run its course. He was angry! The next day, when the police had located Ole Sally, he signed an affidavit against Billy Ray for the theft of the machinery and damage to the tractor, his barn and the fence.

Billy Ray was arrested and remanded by the judge to The State Reformatory School for Boys - a facility for wayward boys and troubled youth. Two months later, he stole one of the counselors' cars from the facility and took two other boys on a joy-ride through downtown Maryville. He was re-arrested for that offense and several other times for car theft.

Getting arrested and incarcerated was never a deterrent for Billy Ray. He got a huge thrill from stealing cars and driving fast – especially when the law got behind him. If you think about it, Billy Ray's past experience with stolen cars and his love of high-speed driving was the perfect resume' for being the wheel-man a few years later for his older brother Malcolm's bank robberies.

CHAPTER 10
FRIENDLY FIRE

Winter Haven, Florida – May 29, 1986

Mutual Aid. That's what it's called when one law enforcement agency assists another agency with law enforcement duties. The majority of the time, the two agencies work closely together during pre-operation meetings in the event of search warrants or drug raids. Each officer on the detail knows his or her role in the overall operation.

With proper pre-planning, most events like this go off without a hitch. The public is kept safe. All officers involved go home that night. And all the bad guys go to jail. That's how it's supposed to work in a perfect world. But we don't live in a perfect world. Sometimes things can become so chaotic that they become what the military and many in law enforcement simply refer to as "a clusterfuck."

This was the case on the evening of May 29, 1986. Under-cover narcotics deputies, Wayne Allerton and Steve Clarke were putting together a case against a drug dealer who resided in an upstairs room of a wooden, rickety old two-story boarding house in a run-down area in the northeast part of Winter Haven. On the bottom floor of the boarding house, the owner operated an illegal bar.

Deputy Allerton had a confidential informant make a drug buy of crack cocaine from the bad guy who lived upstairs several days before. The confidential informant told Deputy Allerton that the drug dealer may well have a firearm in his possession and advised caution if he goes into the room to arrest him. Allerton and Clarke met with Winter Haven Police officers, Tim Close, Daryl Curland, and Carl Garrett at 8:00 PM at the Winter Haven Police Department in the squad room to go over the plan in detail.

Deputies Allerton and Clarke along with Carl would enter through the front of the boarding house. Winter Haven officers Close and Curland would enter from the back. Both the front and the back had exterior staircases going up to the second floor.

As it happened, Carl was in the patrol division and was in service and available for calls – as were Curland and Close.

All of them had planned to advise the dispatcher that they were going to be unavailable for calls at 10:30 when the raid was scheduled to happen.

Around 10:00 PM, Carl got a call for an accident that happened on Havendale Boulevard on the northwest side of town. One woman involved in the minor accident was nine months pregnant and the excitement and anxiety of the traffic crash brought on contractions. Carl was almost sure that he was going to have to deliver the baby right there on the side of the road.

Fortunately, the ambulance arrived before that happened, but it delayed Carl in getting to the staging area of the drug raid that he was assisting on. The other officers had waited for him as long as they could, but decided to go ahead and perform the raid minus one officer.

Carl heard the deputies and the officers on the special tactical radio channel announce that the greenlight for the raid had been given. He was racing to get there to assist. Carl was flying across town on Havendale Boulevard to make it to the boarding house. When he crossed the intersection of Hwy 17, he hit the huge dip in the roadway. For a moment the road noise from the tires went completely and eerily silent.

He was airborne! BOOM came the sound of the '85 Ford
Crown Victoria patrol car as it crashed back to Earth. Right at
that second, Carl glanced in his rear-view mirror and saw a
huge fireball of sparks explode behind him from where the
undercarriage of the car had landed hard on the roadway.

The force was so great that the shock absorbers did little to
soften the impact. Even with such a hard landing, the car
was still perfectly operational. Those Crown Vics were tough
cars! That's one of the reasons many police agencies from
around the nation used them in their fleets.

When it was go-time, Close and Curland entered the back
stairs as planned and plain-clothes deputies Allerton and
Clarke started climbing the stairs in the front of the building.
Carl came skidding up to the front of the building just after
the illegal bar operator and boarding house owner had
caught a glimpse of the plain clothes deputies carrying guns
going up the front stairs. Thinking they were there to rob his
friend, the drug dealer upstairs, the boarding house owner
bent down behind the counter and retrieved a silver H&R .38
caliber revolver and fired it into the ceiling to scare what he
thought were the robbers away and to warn his drug dealing
friend.

By this time, Carl had made it to the base of the staircase in front of the building. Hearing the gunshot from inside the first floor, he diverted from the staircase and entered the first floor – the illegal bar area - of the boarding house. He saw the man who was later identified as Willie Johnson Jr. still holding the gun in his hand. Carl shouted at him, "Drop the gun! Get on the floor!"

Surprised by the sudden appearance of someone else carrying a gun and not noting that Carl was a uniformed police officer, Johnson raised the gun in his direction. Carl fired toward Johnson one time but the shot missed. Suddenly realizing that Carl was in fact a real police officer, Johnson tossed his gun to the ground and threw his hands into the air. "I didn't know you were a cop! I didn't know you were a cop!" Johnson repeated multiple times.

Carl shouted authoritatively to Johnson, "Get on the ground motherfucker!" Johnson complied and dropped to his belly on the floor. Carl quickly closed the distance between them and jumped on him straddling him while re-holstering his firearm. He handcuffed Johnson's hands behind his back.

Meanwhile, the drug dealer up-stairs heard Johnson's initial gunshot and the gunshot fired by Carl and picked up a table leg that he kept in his room to use as a weapon. He opened his room door and stepped out into the dimly lit hallway. "What the fuck is going on out here!?" shouted the drug dealer. Deputy Allerton who also had heard the shots but didn't know exactly where they had come from saw the black colored table leg in the drug dealer's hand.

In the dimly lit hallway, Allerton thought the drug dealer was holding a rifle or shotgun. Deputy Allerton fired two shots in quick succession at the drug dealer who had ducked back into his room after being hit in the shoulder by one of Allerton's rounds. Meanwhile, Winter Haven P.D. officers, Close and Curland were entering the up-stairs hallway from the back stairwell. Officer Close had come in first just in time to see Allerton's muzzle flashes from the other end of the dark hallway.

Believing that he was being fired upon by a bad guy, officer Close fired one blast from his department issued Mossberg 12-gauge shotgun toward the muzzle flashes at the other end of the dark shadowy hallway. The blast struck Deputy Allerton's head and upper chest area.

Initially, it was unclear just who shot who because of the chaotic scene both downstairs with the shooting incident Carl was involved in and the craziness that transpired upstairs with Deputy Allerton, the drug dealer, and Officer

Close. But eventually, all the facts and details were figured out. Deputy Allerton had been hit by "friendly fire." After two surgeries, Deputy Allerton survived his injuries.

Several months after the raid, Allerton returned to work and resumed his duties at the sheriff's department. Less than a year later, on March 15, 1987, thirty-seven-year-old Allerton was fishing in a boat with another off-duty deputy when he fell into the water and died. The cause of death was determined by the medical examiner to be cardiac arrest caused by a brain lesion that had resulted from the gunshot wound Allerton received when Close fired his shotgun down the hall of the boarding house.

Because of those circumstances, Allerton's death was and is considered an "in the line of duty" death. His name appears at The National Law Enforcement Officers Memorial in Washington, DC. It is carved into one of the two curving, 304-foot-long blue-gray limestone walls along with the names of more than 23,000 other officers who died in the line of duty throughout U.S. history - dating back to the first known death in 1786.

Carl, of course, was placed on administrative leave following the incident while the whole fiasco was under investigation. He was later fully cleared for his role in the raid and for the discharging of his firearm and returned to active duty.

Of all the Garrett brothers, Carl was the only one during his law enforcement career to be forced to fire his weapon on duty. He understands that what happened to Allerton was all a terrible mistake, but he still thanks God every day that it wasn't HIS bullet that killed a fellow officer. Still, it was an incident that would stick in his memory for the rest of his life.

CHAPTER 11
CAJUN WEED

Nashville Tennessee – June 3, 1963

Twenty-year-old Jimmy Garrett was arrested and charged
with aggravated battery on a man during a drunken bar fight
at a honky-tonk in Knoxville in early 1963. He had cut the
man with a knife across his face pretty badly, leaving a
permanent scar. It wasn't really a surprise to him when the
judge threw the book at him sentencing him to four years in
the Tennessee State Prison.

The prison was a massive Gothic, fortress-like structure and a
formidable correctional facility located six miles west of
downtown Nashville, Tennessee. Like his brother Malcolm,
Jimmy had considered attempting to escape, but never made
it to the planning stage. For Jimmy, escaping was just a fun
fantasy to think about to pass the time. Besides, with every
day that ticked by on the calendar, he was one day closer to
being released.

What made his stay in The Tennessee State Prison more tolerable was the great friendship he shared with his cellmate, Jean-Claude Pierre Devereaux, or "J.C." as everyone called him. J.C. was a good ole boy from Lafayette, Louisiana who was doing time in the Tennessee State Prison on drug trafficking charges. J.C. was caught in Chattanooga with fifty pounds of marijuana in the trunk of his car during a traffic stop.

J.C.'s friendly, out-going demeanor coupled with his charming, yet thick native Louisiana accent made him instantly likable. He was only a year younger than Jimmy and they were both scheduled to be released roughly about the same time. J.C. and Jimmy spent many hours talking about their very different childhoods.

Jimmy told him about his past of robbery and theft and hunting in the beautiful mountains of Tennessee and J.C. shared his history of using shrimp boats out of Grand Isle to import marijuana and wrestling alligators down on the Bayou. The two of them got along famously.

Sitting in their cell, Jimmy asked, "What do you reckon you're gonna do when you get out J.C."

"Ooooh-weee! Dat dere's a fine question my friend!" responded J.C. I'm gonna go back to Lafayette, find me the biggest bowl'o gumbo what you ever did see and a plate just brimmin' with étouffée!"

Jimmy, ignoring J.C.'s reply mainly because he had no idea what étouffée even was, said, "No, I mean whatcha gonna do for bread man?"

"I'll gets me a big ole basket'o hush puppies or a baguette I reckon!"

"No, ya Cajun dumbass!" Jimmy said, "money! Whatchu gonna do for money!"

J.C. fell back on his bunk laughing and holding his belly. Through his laughter, he replied, "I knew what'chu meant ya dumbass hillbilly!" joked J.C. Both men chuckled.

"In all seriousness doh, I think I'll go back to bringin' in d'devil's lettuce on dem shrimp'n boats. Can't beat d'money sho'nuff!"

"Where do you get it from?" asked Jimmy.

I knows an ole Mexican boy, a sho'nuff couillion, down in Tampico dat gets me all dat I can buy. Cheap too!" replied J.C. "All's I gots to do is pick it up in Mexico and ride it real easy like 'long d'coastline back to Grande Isle in Louzianne."

Over the next few hours, J.C. and Jimmy talked about marijuana and how lucrative it was to sell it. After they were done talking and it was lights out. Jimmy stretched out on his bunk, silently thinking about how he would go about selling marijuana in and around Maryville if he were able to get it in large quantities from J.C. He fell asleep pondering the huge amount of wealth he could build and never have to commit another dangerous grocery store or bank robbery for the rest of his days.

The days, weeks and months passed by. Jimmy and J.C. had many more conversations about the marijuana business and working together once they got out. Jimmy was released on April 10, 1967 and J.C. was released toward the end of that same month. J.C. went back to Louisiana just like he always said he would and Jimmy returned to Maryville, Tennessee.

On March 1, 1968, the phone at Jimmy's grandmother's

house rang. She picked it up and talked to the man on the other end of the line. Between her difficulty hearing and the man's strange accent, she wasn't able to understand much. What she did get was that the man wanted to talk to Jimmy and a phone number where he could be reached.

A few days later, Jimmy dropped by his grandmother's house for a visit and to get a piece of her delicious apple pie. She gave Jimmy the scrap of paper that she had written down the information on and he called J.C. long distance from his grandmother's phone.

J.C. answered his phone and Jimmy said, "Hey you Cajun ass convict! What'chu doin'?"

J.C. recognized Jimmy's voice immediately and said, "Ooooh-weee! Dat dere's a voice I been waitin' to hear from, I garontee!" said J.C. excitedly. J.C. shared with Jimmy what a hard time he had tracking down a phone number to contact him. The two friends chatted for a while and J.C. asked Jimmy if he was still interested in buying a load of grass.

Money had been pretty tight for Jimmy since getting released from prison and Jimmy responded with an enthusiastic, "Hell yeah, I'm still interested!" J.C. told him the amount he was thinking about bringing in from Mexico and the amount of cash he would need from Jimmy to purchase it. The two of them talked a bit more and J.C. told Jimmy that he needed to make some phone calls and would call him back with more details once he gets them. Jimmy gave J.C. the phone number to the motel where he was living in Maryville so that J.C. wouldn't have to call his grandmother's house again.

Within a week, J.C. called Jimmy at the motel and told him everything was a go! They made arrangements to meet up with each other in Memphis, Tennessee, roughly the halfway point between Maryville and Lafayette on April, 4th to make the exchange. Jimmy went to work immediately raising the money for J.C. Jimmy robbed two grocery stores in Oakridge, a liquor store in Alcoa, and a small bank branch in Knoxville to put together the buy money.

On the morning of April 3rd, the day before the scheduled meet in Memphis, Jimmy woke up with chest pains. He figured it was just anxiety from the robberies and the stress about the impending drug buy but in the back of his mind, he couldn't help but worry that it was something more. He was told that he had been born with a leaky heart valve and throughout his lifetime growing up would have periodic heart palpitations.

Even while in the Tennessee State Prison with J.C., he found himself in the prison hospital several times for the same chest pain issues. He was concerned about it, but never went to a doctor on the outside as an adult to address the issue. He threw back some Bayer aspirin like he always did and chased it with a beer before starting out on the seven-hour drive from Maryville to Memphis to meet J.C.

Jimmy checked in by himself to a Howard Johnson's Motor Lodge in Memphis and once in his room, hid his suitcase full of cash under the bed. He had a nice steak dinner in their restaurant that night. Tomorrow was going to be a big day. He had arranged to meet J.C. in the parking lot of an A & P grocery store off of Highway 78 at 8:00 PM.

He woke up in his hotel room at 9:00 AM that morning and had breakfast at the hotel's restaurant where he had eaten dinner the night before. He decided to go for a drive and see the sights to kill time. So, he lugged his heavy suitcase out into the parking lot and put it in the trunk of the car.

He drove down Beal Street. He looked and marveled at all the jazz bars and clubs that lined the street that was well known for its music and partying into the wee hours of the night. He wished he had more time to visit them, but he had an important meeting that night.

He also drove down a street in the Whitehaven neighborhood and saw Graceland mansion, the home of Elvis Presley. He thought he saw Elvis out in the yard with a shovel and drove around the block to get a second look. It turned out not to be Elvis, but rather a gardener working on the property that had a remarkable resemblance to The King.

He stopped in for a late lunch around 2:00 PM at one of the many BBQ joints that peppered the area. Jimmy glanced at his watch while having lunch and thought to himself, "Only six hours to go before I have me a trunk load of grass!" He finished up his meal and stood to leave the restaurant. Just after exiting the door is when it happened. Jimmy had an intense pain shoot through his chest and down his left arm. He stopped and leaned against some newspaper boxes just outside the door clutching his chest and breathing heavily. Then, everything went black. Jimmy fell to the ground in the parking lot unconscious.

People from the restaurant rushed outside and gathered around him. Somone called an ambulance and Jimmy's next memory was waking up in a hospital bed with an IV attached to his arm. A little groggy, he caught the attention of a nurse walking by his hospital room. "Nurse!" he called out to her.

The nurse stopped and turned around and came into Jimmy's room. "You're finally awake I see!" said the nurse cheerfully.

"What the hell happened?" asked Jimmy.

"You've had a heart attack young man. You're in Saint Joseph's Hospital," responded the nurse and then seized the opportunity to check his vital signs.

"How long was I out?" asked Jimmy.

"About four or five hours." replied the nurse.

"FOUR OR FIVE HOURS!? Oh shit!" said Jimmy sitting up in the hospital bed and looking down at his wrist which was now missing his watch. "Where's my watch!? What time is it right now!?"

The nurse looked at her watch. "Your clothes and belongings are right over there in that little closet. It's 7:05 right now," said the nurse.

"I've got to get out of here!" Jimmy said in a panic.

"Mr. Garrett, you need to just lay back down and take it easy. We're still waiting for some of your tests to come back!"

"You don't understand! I've got a meeting to be at! I've got to go! Where's my car?" inquired Jimmy.

"I have no idea sir. I was told that they brought you in by ambulance," replied the nurse. "Tell you what, I'll go find the doctor and have him come in to talk to you."

Jimmy said "OK, OK, Please hurry!"

The nurse had no more than left the room when Jimmy jerked the IV from his arm and jumped out of bed to get dressed. He quickly pulled on his pants and shirt. Then he sat down and put his socks and shoes on faster than he ever had before.

Walking briskly out of his room, he took a left but could see the nurse's station up ahead and did an about face. He found an elevator that took him down to the emergency room.

As soon as the elevator doors opened, all Jimmy could see was wall-to-wall people. Wall-to-wall black people to be more precise. He pushed his way through the crowd to the exit door and started looking for a payphone to call a taxi cab to take him to the A & P. When he saw the payphones, there was a long line of black people waiting to use the phone. Some had angry expressions, some were wailing and crying.

Jimmy saw a white ambulance driver walking quickly out of the emergency room toward his waiting ambulance. "Hey mister, what's going on!? How come there's so many colored folks here running around like chickens with their head's cutoff?" asked Jimmy.

"You haven't heard!?" asked the ambulance driver without even slowing his pace. "Somebody shot Martin Luther King Jr. and he just died in the emergency room!"

"Holy shit!" said Jimmy. "At this hospital?"

The ambulance driver said, "Yeah, just a few minutes ago!"

Jimmy didn't make it to the rendezvous with J.C. He later found out that J.C. didn't make it to the meeting either. On Highway 51 just north of Jackson, Mississippi, J.C. got pulled over by the Mississippi State Patrol. During the stop, they found the 200 pounds of marijuana in the back of the moving truck J.C. had rented. At trial, J.C. was convicted and sentenced to twenty years in the Mississippi State Penitentiary in Parchman, Mississippi.

Jimmy eventually was able to get a taxi back to the BBQ joint where he had left his car. Unfortunately, the car and the suitcase of money in the trunk were gone! It went against his grain to ask the police for help, but he did call them and reported his car stolen. He intentionally left out the part about the copious amount of money that was in the trunk. The car and its contents were never recovered.

Jimmy used what little money he had left on him to catch a bus back to Maryville - with absolutely nothing to show for his efforts but a bad memory.

CHAPTER 12

THE BUMOLOGIST

Winter Haven, Florida – September 12, 1989

Bumologist

(noun)

[bum-olo-jist]

A law enforcement officer who while on duty, befriends, researches, and studies; bums, winos, hobos, beggars, vagrants, tramps, boozehounds, pan-handlers, vagabonds, drifters, nomads, transients, and other homeless people and their various relationships and interactions with law enforcement and the general public and their environment within the officer's jurisdiction.

You will not find the above definition of a "bumologist" as an official entry in any known English dictionary. However, the term was jokingly used by his co workers to describe Officer Dale Garrett.

Dale's interest in mingling and fraternizing with the type of people listed in the description above was well known in the department. If any officer wanted to know something about a homeless individual or the identity of same, all they had to do was ask their co-worker, Dale. When a new vagabond arrived in town, one of the first people he (or she) was likely to meet was "Officer Dale" as most of the street people called him.

Dale's fascination with street people came about in an unusual way. He was patrolling behind a closed strip mall at about 3:00 AM on the foggy morning of September 12, 1989. He was checking for burglaries and suspicious activity.

Shining his patrol car's spotlight through the fog on every rear door and occasional window, everything looked secure. Suddenly he noticed some movement out of the corner of his eye near the dumpster. He exited his marked Ford Crown Victoria patrol car to investigate further.

As he walked up to the dumpster and the concrete wall that surrounded it on three sides, he could see someone crouched down behind the dumpster and ordered the man to step out from behind it with his hands raised. A dirty disheveled man came into view with his arms outstretched showing his hands to be empty. His face was partially obscured by shadows. Dale ordered him to put his hands on the dumpster and searched the suspicious subject for any weapons he might be carrying. He was clean.

"I didn't mean no harm sir. I was just looking for cans," said the man.

"Why were you hiding from me?" asked Dale, noting the bag of cans on the ground by the dumpster.

"I didn't want no trouble sir," came Frank's reply.

"Turn around," ordered Dale. When Frank turned to face Dale to talk to him, Dale was taken aback by the man's appearance. Not the fact that he was dirty and shabbily dressed, but his actual physical appearance and facial features shocked Dale.

Dale thought he looked exactly like his own father, Al Garrett, who had passed away five years before. The fact that it was only a month till Halloween, the spookiness of the fog, and the appearance of this man who looked incredibly like his deceased father, made Dale feel uneasy and as though he was living in a scary movie. The hair on the back of his neck stood up.

Shaking off the uneasy feeling, Dale mentally reminded himself that this is NOT his deceased father. This is not a horror movie. And the fog was just a naturally occurring weather phenomena. He mentally smiled and reminded himself that he was a police officer and was there to do a job.

He asked the man for his identification in order to perform a wanted persons check on him. In just a matter of moments, the dispatcher called Dale back on the radio and informed him that the subject had no warrants for his arrest outstanding.

Dale said to Frank, "You being behind these closed businesses like this makes us cops a little suspicious."

"I understand sir," replied Frank respectfully. "I won't do it again."

"Where do you live?" asked Dale.

"Right now, I'm homeless sir," replied Frank. "I've been sleeping in the jungle."

Dale thought that was an odd thing to say. "Jungle?" What do you mean 'jungle?'" asked dale – his curiosity piqued.

"The hobo jungle," replied Frank. "It's in the woods under the overpass going toward Eagle Lake."

"Oh, OK," replied Dale, pretending to know the place Frank spoke of.

"Well listen," said Dale, "I'm out here most every night, so stay out from behind these closed businesses at night time, OK?"

"Yes sir," said Frank.

"Look, I know you're just out here looking for cans to make a little money, but other officers that catch you might not be as lenient or as accepting of your presence out here as I am and they might take you to jail for loitering and prowling," Dale said.

"Yes sir, I understand sir," said Frank.

"Alright, you're free to go," said Dale. "But keep in mind, I don't forget faces." Of course, Dale didn't mention to him the reason he would remember his face in particular was because he was a doppelganger of his deceased father.

"Yes sir," said the man picking up his trash bag partially full of aluminum cans he had collected and then he shuffled off into the night. Dale never saw Frank again after that one encounter.

As Dale drove away, he wondered what this "jungle" looked like and drove to the dirt access road that ran parallel to the Highway 17 overpass. He drove as far as he could and then got out with his flashlight and walked into the woods. He could smell smoke from a campfire and when he reached the clearing, he saw eight to twelve other street people sitting around the fire, talking, laughing, and drinking beers.

When the men and one woman saw Dale, they tensed up, fearing that he was there to run them out of their make-shift homes. Several tents and cardboard shacks surrounded the fire pit.

Dale greeted them in a friendly manner and reassured them that he was just there to take a look around. They relaxed after a few minutes as Dale joked and laughed with them and showed them a few magic tricks he carried with him.

Dale was hesitant to run their names for warrants because he wasn't sure that their camp was officially within his jurisdiction. It was very close to the city/county jurisdictional boundary. After some more chit-chat, Dale returned to patrolling his zone.

He thought about Frank and the street people he had met that night and how carefree they were. They were living rent free, enjoying life, and seemed happy. The more he got to know them however, Dale came to later understand that many of them were street people because of addictions or tragedies that happened to them at some point in their lifetime.

In the weeks and months that followed, Dale met lots of other street people and started being able to recognize them by face when he would see them and they started to recognize "Officer Dale."

Dale began keeping a notebook in his uniform shirt pocket with a comprehensive list of their names and dates of birth. That way, if he saw them and it had been a while since he encountered them, he could run their names for warrants without having to stop them and go through the process of getting their information again.

If they had a warrant, he would make contact with them, have a conversation and break the news to them gently that they had a warrant and 100% of the time, they would submit to the arrest without resisting.

If they didn't have a warrant and he wasn't busy on other calls, he would sometimes stop them and just have a pleasant conversation with them – asking them how they were doing and if they needed anything. Many times, he would buy them socks, t-shirts, or blankets using money out of his own pocket. He did have one very strict policy about cash. He would NEVER give them money because he knew that the money would be used to buy alcohol and further feed their addictions.

He began to form bonds with them. He would take the time to have conversations with them and listen to them and not just roust them like some of the other officers would. He would treat them like humans, but still arrest them when it became necessary. Dale quickly gained a reputation among the street people as being an officer that was fair but firm. An officer that they could trust. He was an ally to the homeless and they grew to respect him.

Winter Haven, Florida – December 23, 1989

A few days before Christmas, Dale was shopping with his wife Lynn at a large discount retailer. He noticed that tins of Christmas cookies were on sale for an astonishing low price of only $2.00 each. He had an idea. He bought all of them they had. About two dozen tins of Christmas cookies.

A few days later, Dale was working dayshift on Christmas day. As he came on duty, he waited for the officer who was getting off duty who he shared a car with to pull into the department's parking lot.

Once the officer arrived and off-loaded his equipment. Dale transferred his own briefcase which contained report forms and his duffle bag that contained his other police equipment from his personal vehicle to the patrol car. Then he put the two dozen tins of Christmas cookies in the trunk.

Christmas dayshift was always typically a slow day for law enforcement. Dale had plenty of time to drive around to the various homeless camps that he knew about and deliver the tins of cookies to the street people in the city. It was such a small gesture, but it made Dale feel like Santa Clause giving out gifts on Christmas morning. But then something he never expected to happen, happened. He cried.

He had delivered most of the tins of cookies and only had a few more stops to make. One of the stops was to deliver cookies to a street person named Freddy Robinson. Freddy was an older gentleman with a slim build. He was probably in his mid-60's. He had straight silver hair that came down about half-way over his ears and a scraggly, yet shortly cropped grey mustache and beard. If one was to stand in close proximity to Freddy, one could immediately tell that taking baths was not necessarily at the top of Freddy's daily itinerary.

Freddy slept in some bushes close to the big Department of Agriculture building in town. Dale parked near the building and walked through the bushes where Freddy usually slept. Sure enough, there was Freddy stretched out on his cardboard bed and using a dirty blanket that Dale had bought him for his cover.

Dale gently kicked Freddy's foot to roust him awake but he didn't move. Dale kicked his foot slightly harder and called out to him, "Freddy! Wake up!"

Finally, Freddy began to stir and rubbed the sleep out of his one good eye to wake up. Freddy was blind in his left eye and it always had a film and something that appeared like puss in it. He sat up and said, "Hey Officer Dale. Is there something wrong? Do I need to move along?"

"No Freddy, you're fine," Dale replied. "I just came by to visit you since it's Christmas morning and all."

"Today is Christmas?" asked Freddy.

"Yep, it sure is! Merry Christmas," replied Dale joyfully. "and I brought you a present!" Dale held the tin of Christmas cookies out toward Freddy and Freddy took them in his hands.

Holding the cookies Freddy bowed his head, looking at the ground. "I thought you might enjoy a little treat today," said Dale cheerfully.

For an awkward amount of time, Freddy didn't respond. He just continued to appear to look at the ground. Then, Dale noticed his shoulder's slightly bouncing up and down and heard a small whimper. Freddy was crying.

Finally, he looked up at Dale and with tears streaming down both of his cheeks and with his voice quivering said, "Nobody has given me a Christmas present since I was a little bitty boy."

Now fighting back his own tears, Dale replied, "Well, it's not much Freddy. It's just cookies." To Freddy, it might as well been a hundred million dollars in cash. He was so genuinely touched by Dale's gesture that he broke down in even more tears.

Dale had intended on visiting with Freddy for a longer amount of time, but decided he needed to excuse himself. Trying to lighten the mood a bit, he smiled and said, "Well, I need to go Freddy. I've got more cookies to hand out and crime to fight."

Freddy stood up on his feet using the building for support because of his painful arthritis. Dale reached out to shake Freddy's hand but was surprised as Freddy stepped toward him and wrapped his arms around him giving Dale a big bear hug and continuing to cry.

"I've gotta go Freddy," said Dale. Freddy released Dale from his hug and holding to the wall, slid back down to the ground to sit back down while dabbing at his eyes with his fingers.

Dale briskly walked to his patrol car and after closing the door, burst into tears himself. He never expected that giving someone a two-dollar tin of cookies would generate such an overwhelming amount of emotion – both from the recipient and from himself. In that moment, Dale's heart was filled with Christmas spirit.

Winter Haven, Florida - June 15, 1992

In the summer of 1992, the city of Winter Haven was being plagued by so-called "smash and grab" burglaries of businesses located within the south west side of town. Burglars would throw a rock through a glass door or a plate glass window, enter the business, grab electronics or other expensive items and be gone in seconds before the police would arrive.

There was never any evidence such as fingerprints left behind. Surveillance cameras weren't very prevalent but the grainy images captured by some that did exist were not of much evidentiary value to investigators.

The property crimes detectives were pulling their hair out because these types of burglaries were occurring almost every night and they just couldn't develop any leads or suspects in the case. The only thing they were fairly positive about was that they were being committed by the same person or persons because the modus operandi was the exact same in every burglary.

Midnight shift patrol officers were instructed to increase their presence around closed businesses during their shifts when not working other calls for service. Still, the burglaries continued and detectives were no closer to solving the cases.

At about 3:15 AM one Tuesday morning. An officer working the southwest zone was dispatched to an alarm call at the Radio Shack store in the Zayer's shopping plaza. Sure enough, when he arrived, he could see that the front glass door had been broken out. He stood by and waited for a key holder to show up and took another report on the stolen items that was sure to further exasperate the detectives working this string of burglaries.

At about 4:30 AM, the department received a call from a man who only identified himself to the dispatcher as "Kirkland." He wanted to meet with "Officer Dale" at the Burger King restaurant in the southwest area of town but he wouldn't tell the dispatcher why. He was also adamant that it had to be "Officer Dale" and not anyone else.

The dispatcher passed along the message over the radio and Dale who was working the northeast zone that night, received permission from his supervisor to leave his zone to meet with the man.

Dale recognized the name Kirkland and immediately thought to himself as he drove to the restaurant, "I bet this is Kirkland McFee. It has to be." McFee was a street person who Dale had many encounters with.

As Dale pulled into the parking lot of Burger King, he could see that sure enough, it was indeed Kirkland McFee. Kirkland was sitting down on a curb awaiting Dale's arrival. "Hey Kirkland! What are you up to ole buddy?" said Dale cheerfully.

Kirkland stood up quickly and walked over to Dale's patrol car and leaned against the driver's side door. He had a serious look on his face and for a change, actually seemed sober. "Hey Officer Dale!" said Kirkland with an excited nervousness. "I saw something earlier and thought you should know about it."

"OK, what did you see?" asked Dale.

Kirkland replied, "I was digging for cans in dumpsters and was walking through the parking lot over by Zayers. I saw a car pull up and two dudes jumped out and smashed the window out of the Radio Shack! They went in and carried out armloads of stuff! It happened fast!"

"Do you remember what the car looked like" asked Dale.

"I sure as hell do! It was a dark blue Chevy. I think it was a Camaro. Older model." said Kirkland.

"That's great!" said Dale. "What about the two guys? What did they look like?" asked Dale.

"I don't know really. About all I could tell was that they were white guys. Had on dark clothes," said Kirkland.

"Is that all you remember" asked Dale.

"Well, there was one other thing. I got their tag number if you want it. I memorized it," said Kirkland. Kirkland shared the tag number with Dale and Dale thanked him for the information.

Breaking his own self-imposed rule about giving street people cash, Dale reached back and took out his wallet. He opened it and removed a five-dollar bill and held it outstretched in his hand toward Kirkland. "Here ya go man. I appreciate the info," said Dale.

Kirkland raised his flattened palm toward Dale, refusing to take the cash. "I didn't tell you this for money Officer Dale. "I told you because you're my friend."

"Are you sure?" asked Dale, still holding the money toward Kirkland.

"I'm good man," replied Kirkland. "I better get back to my can hunting. It's gonna be daylight before long."

"Alright buddy. Thanks again for the info!" said Dale.

Dale passed the information along to the detective division and within a day, they were able to make two arrests and close out more than a dozen unsolved burglary cases. None of this would have happened had Dale not formed that relationship with Kirkland McFee.

Not too long after that. Kirkland was "running a sign" at the entrance to the K-Mart on the north side of town. "Running a sign" was the term that street people used for sitting on the side of a roadway with a cardboard sign with messages scrawled on them that said things like, "will work for food," "U.S. veteran, please help" or "hungry." It was a way of pan-handling without verbally asking people for money. Of course, the money they collected was almost always spent on liquor.

Dale was on dayshift and was patrolling through the parking lot of the store. As he started to exit the parking lot, he spotted Kirkland. Since there was no traffic behind him, Dale rolled down the window of his Crown Vic patrol car and said hello to Kirkland.

They chatted for a minute or two and it was obvious to Dale that on this day, Kirkland had a very significant level of intoxication going on. Then, glancing down at the cardboard sign Kirkland was holding, Dale burst out laughing.

Kirkland said, "What's so damn funny!?"

Pointing at Kirkland's sign he replied, "Kirkland, your sign says "will work for wood!"

Kirkland turned his sign around and looked at it and then cursed himself under his breath. In his drunken stupor, he had gotten too ambitious with the letter "W" and instead of "food" had written the word "wood!" With a car now behind him ready to exit the parking lot, Dale drove off still guffawing at Kirkland's unintended but outrageously hilarious spelling error.

A few minutes later, Dale rode back through the parking lot and rolled his window down when he was next to Kirkland again. Dale speaking to Kirkland said, "Here ya go buddy. Thought you could use this since you're asking people for it on your sign." Dale pitched Kirkland a piece of tree bark he had found shortly after he had left the first time. Dale drove off again as Kirkland threw the piece of bark into the bushes, mumbling and cursing to himself. Dale had a second good belly laugh at Kirkland's expense.

A few years later there was a house fire in the early morning hours at an abandoned, run-down house in Winter Haven. The fire department was able to recover a single male victim's body from the fire. Nobody knew who the man was as he had no identification on him.

The police officer who worked the call suspected that the dead man was homeless. He contacted Dale who was off-duty at home. He knew that Dale knew every transient in town and asked Dale if he could come to the scene of the fire and try to identify the body. Dale went right away.

When he arrived, he unzipped the body bag lying on the ground to look at the face of the deceased. It was badly charred, but Dale was immediately able to tell that it was Kirkland McFee. It was later determined by arson investigators that the fire had most likely started because of a candle that had overturned during the night. Kirkland was, as usual, highly intoxicated and had died of smoke inhalation.

Dale investigated many deaths over the years. He saw bodies in horrible states of decomposition and some that were mangled beyond recognition in car crashes. He saw the ghastly wounds to people's heads after they had committed suicide by shotgun. None of these scenarios bothered him that much. But the image of Kirkland McFee's burnt and charred face haunted him not only for the rest of his career, but for the rest of his life.

Winter Haven Florida - January 3, 1993

In early 1993, Dale went to work and before briefing, checked his interdepartmental mailbox like he did every day. On this particular day, there was a pink paper phone message to call a woman named Mrs. Hampton in Ohio. Curious as to what this stranger wanted, after briefing, Dale went into a quiet unused office and phoned the number.

"Hello?" said the woman on the other end of the line.

Dale said, "Hello Mrs. Hampton. This is Officer Dale Garrett with the Winter Haven Police Department. I received a message to call you."

The woman went on to explain to Dale that her brother lived on the street and was currently in the city of Winter Haven. She said, "I understand that you know him. His name is Freddy Robinson."

"Oh yes! I know Freddy very well!" Dale said.

"He talks about you every time I speak to him on the phone," said Mrs. Hamilton. "He thinks very highly of you."

"Well, Freddy's a good guy and stays out of trouble for the most part. I like him too," replied Dale.

Mrs. Hamilton went on to tell Dale that she was worried about Freddy's declining health and how she desperately wanted to get him back to Ohio so that she could make sure that he gets the medical attention that he needs. She said that she was afraid to wire him money for a bus ticket because she feared that he would instead just use the money for alcohol.

Dale thought to himself while listening to her, "You're probably 100 % right about that."

Then Mrs. Hamilton proposed that she send Dale the money and have him get Freddy the bus ticket home. Dale told her that she didn't need to send the money and that she could pay for the ticket in Ohio and the bus station in Winter Haven would have it in their system and could print the ticket out for Freddy.

Mrs. Hamilton was happy to hear this but still felt uneasy about Freddy actually getting the ticket and actually getting on the bus to come home – even though he promised to do so. She asked Dale for his help in making sure Freddy got on the bus if she arranged the ticket. Dale said to her, "I'd be more than happy to help out in any way I can."

They hung up and she called back the next day and left another message for Dale with the dispatcher. When Dale called her back, she told him that the ticket was purchased and the date and time Freddy needed to be there. Dale told her, "Don't worry. I'll make sure he gets on that bus!"

Two days later, on his day off, Dale's alarm clock went off at 4:00 AM. He talked his wife Lynn into going with him to put Freddy on the bus with the promise they would go out for breakfast after Freddy was on his way. After a quick shower and getting dressed, they left their apartment at 5:00 AM to go find Freddy.

Lynn waited in the car as Dale trudged through the bushes next to the Agriculture Building to Freddy's sleeping spot. Freddy wasn't there. They drove around a bit to Freddy's usual haunts. They checked the liquor store which of course, wasn't even open yet, the city park, and the benches outside the library. No Freddy.

Dale then reflected out loud to Lynn, "Well, maybe he actually went to the bus station on his own. He knew what day and time he had to be there." Dale drove to the bus station and there was Freddy sitting on the bench in front of the building.

Dale introduced Freddy to his wife and Freddy said to her, "Your husband's a fine man young lady. You hang on to him, you hear?"

Lynn smiled at Freddy and replied, "I think I will."

When the bus station office opened at 6:00 AM, the three of them went inside. Dale and Freddy went up to the window and told the clerk that Freddy should have a ticket waiting for him in their system. With a few keystrokes, the clerk found the information and printed out Freddy's ticket to Columbus, Ohio.

Dale and Lynn waited around the bus station with Freddy until he boarded the bus at 7:25 AM. They waved to Freddy and Freddy waved back at them from the window of the bus as it pulled out of the station.

Dale and Lynn went on to have breakfast at a small mom-and-pop diner in town and didn't really speak any more about Freddy. But Dale thought about him often during his career and well after retirement.

He oftentimes pondered on whether or not Freddy ever straightened out his life and lived to a ripe old age or if Freddy's story had a happy ending at all.

He wondered if Freddy had made it all the way to Columbus to his family. He wondered if he had ever kicked his powerful alcohol addiction and got the medical attention he needed. Dale liked to think he did.

CHAPTER 13
THE SWAYZEE JOB

Swayzee Indiana. December 8, 1972

On its welcome sign, the sleepy little town of Swayzee, Indiana claims to be "the only Swayzee in the world." The motto is based on an old story about a postcard sent by a military serviceman from overseas during World War II. It was addressed only to a lady in "Swayzee", with no mention of Indiana or any other information and was said to have still been successfully delivered to its intended recipient.

Not too far from that welcome sign, stood the branch bank that almost everyone in town used. The air in Swayzee was crisp and cool on the morning of Friday December 8, 1972.

Malcolm and Jimmy sat in the back seat of the stolen 1964 olive green, four door, Chevrolet Impala. Jimmy nervously checked to make sure that both barrels in his sawed-off shotgun were loaded with buckshot and ready to go. "Would you stop checking that damn gun!?" Malcolm said annoyed with Jimmy's nervousness. "That's the third fucking time you've checked it!"

Jimmy's upper lip covered in perspiration droplets replied, "I'm just making sure brother! I'm just making sure!"

"And why are you sweating dumb-ass!? It's 29 damn degrees out" asked Malcolm glancing up at the time and temperature sign in front of the Swayzee branch bank.

"I don't know man! I don't feel right about this one!" said Jimmy.

Malcolm replied, "Everything's going to be fine. In and out - just like we planned and just like we've done before, got it!?" Jimmy nodded his head.

Malcolm addressing Billy Ray in the driver's seat, "You're awfully quite up there Billy boy! You good?"

Billy, chomping at the bit to drive fast replied, "I'm ready-Freddie man! Let's do this!"

Malcolm replied, "hold your damn horses little brother."
Looking again at the time and temperature sign. "It's 9:59.
We go in at 10:00 just like we planned. We've gotta make
sure they've had time to stock all the teller drawers with our
money." Billy Ray grinned in response.

Looking back toward Billy Ray again, Malcom continued,
"Just keep it running and when we come out, you light outta
here like a cat with his goddamned tail on fire, you got it!?"

"I've got it, I've got it!" came Billy Ray's reply. "I know my
job!" Billy continued to scan the street for any sign of police
cars on their routine patrols while nervously drumming his
fingers on the steering wheel to CCR's 'Down On The Corner'
playing on the radio.

Jimmy spoke up and said, "How much do y'all reckon we'll
get on this one?"

"A shit-load," replied Billy Ray. "It's Friday! People are gonna
be cashing their checks later today so they're gonna be
loaded to the gills with dead Presidents!"

"Yeah!" grinned Jimmy, "and all we gotta do is go in and ask
real nice-like for it!" Jimmy and Billy Ray both chuckled.

Malcolm who had been staring at the time and temperature sign during their entire conversation said, "All right boys, y'all ready? It's time! C'mon brother, let's go!"

Malcolm and Jimmy took one last look around at their surroundings for cops, pulled their black ski masks down to cover their faces, and exited the Impala. It was only about twenty-five yards from the car to the front door of the bank. They covered the distance quickly, openly carrying their sawed-off shotguns in one hand and brand-new zippered yellow gym bags in the other. Malcolm was also carrying a blued Smith and Wesson Model 19, .38 caliber in his waistband just in case things went sideways.

Malcolm was first through the front glass door and immediately took charge of the room. "Hands in the air! All of you! Get your goddamn hands up!"

Jimmy called out to Malcolm, "Malcolm, watch this motherfucker!"

Looking toward the bank manager who was behind the counter assisting one of the tellers with her morning count, Malcolm said, "Fat boy, if you even think about pushing that alarm button, I swear to God, everybody in this room is gonna be able to see daylight through you! You understand me!?"

The manager with his hands shaking and raised in the air nodded and backed away from the counter to assure Malcolm that he wasn't pressing any buttons or signaling the police in any way.

Jimmy and Malcolm both threw their gym bags at two different tellers and told them to fill them up with cash. Nervously crying, one of the tellers, the dark haired one, pleaded with Malcolm, "Please, I have two children at home. They need their mother!"

"Fill the goddamn bag!" barked Malcolm.

Jimmy added, "And y'all don't even think about putting a dye pack in there! Because I swear to God, I'll come back and kill every damn one of you if this blows up with that dye shit! You hear me!?"

Both tellers managed to mumble out a subdued "yes sir" in response to Jimmy's demand.

Within four minutes, Jimmy and Malcolm burst through the front door of the bank running to the waiting Impala. It was gone! No sign of Billy Ray OR the car! "Where the fuck is Billy Ray!?" shouted Jimmy. "I told you this didn't feel right!"

They both started running through the parking lot of the bank toward the side street while trying to hide their shotguns under their jackets.

Now on the side street but walking briskly down the sidewalk instead of running so they wouldn't attract attention to themselves, they both heard the bank's alarm bell begin to ring behind them. They both knew it would be a matter of minutes until the cops got there.

"Shit! We've gotta get another car and fast!" said Malcolm. Just then, they heard the screeching of tires coming around the corner. It was Billy Ray! Billy Ray skidded to a stop in the street next to them and they jumped in the back seat. Billy Ray gunned it and they headed down Highway 13 toward State Road 35 and then left onto Interstate 69.

Jimmy asked, "What the hell was that back there Billy Ray!? You could have got us all pinched!"

Billy Ray responded, "Right after y'all went in, about a minute later, a fuckin' cop came driving by and was giving me the stink-eye like he was wondering what's this motherfucker doing parked in the front of the bank? So, I smiled at him and waved like 'no big deal, sir' and put it in drive. I went around the block, but one of the roads was a one-way so I had to go way the fuck outta my way and then got turned around and couldn't find the street the bank was on! But I got ya didn't I?"

Malcolm replied, "You almost fucked us all but you did the right thing Billy Boy – waving at that cop and playin' it cool and all. You did good!"

As they traveled down the Interstate, Malcolm looked over at Jimmy and said, "Hey, you did a good job in there too little brother. You did real good telling them no dye packs. I totally forgot that shit."

Jimmy smiled back at Malcolm and replied, "Thankya big brother. I learned from the best!" Malcolm replied, "I'm gonna make a bank robber outta you yet!" They both shared a chuckle and then stared out their respective windows at the passing scenery.

As he drove northbound on the Interstate, Billy Ray reached down and cranked the car's radio volume up just as 'Jumpin' Jack Flash' by the Rolling Stones began to play.

An hour and fifteen minutes later, they arrived at Connover's Court Motor Lodge in Fort Wayne, Indiana where they had spent the night before in a small one room cabin rental.

Once inside, they were all still enjoying their adrenaline high from the robbery and patting each other on the back. Jimmy, pulling an unopened beer can out of a mostly melted tub of ice and said, "This calls for a drink boys!"

"To Hell with a drink, let's see how much the take is!" replied Billy Ray. Malcolm was way ahead of Billy Ray and was already dumping the money from his gym bag onto the bed spread.

Once the money was all counted, the haul was $22,350. Billy Ray upon discovering the total said, "Damn! That's like seven grand each right?"

Malcolm finishing his calculations on a writing pad, put his pencil down and replied, "Actually, according to my ciphering, it's $7,450 each boys!" The three of them bear-hugged each other. Malcolm looked over at Jimmy and said, "I think I'll take that drink now!" Laughter all around.

CHAPTER 14
NELSON AND FOSTER, FBI

Indianapolis, Indiana – December 8, 1972

Agents Andrew Nelson and Daniel Foster were both glad it was Friday. They had a long week and were writing up the last of their reports on a kidnapping case out of Evansville they had been assigned to about three months ago.

As it turned out, the kidnapping of a wealthy banker in Evansville wasn't a kidnapping at all. The banker who was potentially facing some serious criminal charges for embezzlement, had faked his own kidnapping and had planned to remain missing until his wife could have him declared dead and collect the insurance money. Their plan was to then both live out their days on a beach somewhere in Mexico while sipping on margaritas and watching sunsets.

The case was pretty easy to crack for Nelson and Foster after the wiretap they had obtained on the wife's phone captured her chatting on multiple occasions with her "kidnapped" husband who was living in a condo in Puerto Vallarta, Mexico.

Nelson and Foster were not only partners at the FBI, they were best friends. They had a lot in common. Both of them were huge racing fans. When their schedules would permit, they would go to the speedway together to see the races.

Nelson was a thirty-one-year-old married man and had two little girls. Foster, only one year older, was also a married man with two daughters and one infant son. Their families would sometimes vacation together and at least once a month or so, one of them and his family would be at the other one's home for a cook-out or a pool party.

With December in full effect and temperatures during the day dipping down into the low 30's, the upcoming weekend was a bust for any outdoor activities. So, their plans were to spend the day indoors with their families on Saturday touring the Indianapolis Motor Speedway Museum.

They had both been to the museum before on a few occasions, but their exhibits were always changing. There was always something new to see. In fact, this weekend, they had a special exhibit on roadsters opening. Roadsters, popular in the 1960's, were front-engine vehicles that absolutely dominated the Indianapolis 500 for years, as the fastest car on the track.

Nelson and Foster were both beyond excited about attending the new exhibit. Unfortunately, their weekend plans were about to crash into the wall.

Right around 11:30 AM, just as they were starting to talk about where to go for lunch, Nelson's desk phone rang. It was their direct supervisor, Agent Richard Sullivan calling from his office on the 5th floor.

The purpose of his call was to tell them to get to Swayzee, Indiana ASAP! There had been a bank robbery there that morning only an hour ago. Nelson hung up the phone with Sullivan and turned to speak to his partner. "Well, there goes lunch!" said Dan. "Bank robbery in Swayzee," Dan continued.

"Oh well, we'll just grab McDonald's or something on the way," replied Andy.

"Grab your coat. Let's go!" said Dan.

The First National Bank branch in Swayzee was about an hour and a half away. An hour and forty-five minutes if you count the little detour through the McDonald's drive-thru.

Once they arrived, they found the bank closed and the doors locked which was standard procedure for banks that had been robbed. They both flashed their FBI badge and credentials to the Swayzee officer standing just outside the bank. He knocked on the door and a second officer inside unlocked the door so they could enter.

They made contact with the bank's manager, Arnold Feingold. Dan started interviewing Mr. Feingold and the tellers while Andy began looking at video footage in Feingold's office of the robbery.

The video didn't reveal too many clues on first watch. Dan could tell the robbers were white males wearing ski masks and each of them were carrying what appeared to be sawed off shotguns. Andy could also tell that the taller of the two robbers was carrying a revolver in his waistband.

The one thing that stuck out to Dan was the identical gym bags that the robbers had brought with them into the bank to use for carrying out the stolen money. The video was in black and white and was a bit grainy, but he could tell that the bags looked brand new. In fact, one of the bags still had a price tag or label attached to its handle.

Meanwhile, Andy was doing his initial interviews with the tellers. They confirmed that the guns the robbers pointed at them were double barrel shotguns by describing the size of the bores they were staring down as the two robbers pointed them at their faces.

One of the tellers told Andy that she remembered one of the suspects, the shorter one, called the other one's name during the heist. The teller said the shorter one said something like, "Malcolm, watch this motherf'er!" when he saw Mr. Feingold move closer to the counter than he wanted him to."

Andy asked the teller. "Did he say 'motherf'er' or did he actually say - and excuse my language ma'am – 'motherfucker?'"

The teller replied, "Oh he said the actual word!" Andy listened to the teller describe the rest of the encounter as he continued to write notes down in his notebook.

Dan came out of the back room carrying a tape with the video footage he had just watched that had been recorded by the bank's CCTV cameras during the hoist. Dan smiled and said to Andy, "You bring the popcorn this weekend. I've got us a movie!"

While they were doing their investigations, the FBI forensic team showed up. The FBI forensic team's job was to collect and compare latent fingerprints. They were also responsible for analysis, collection and examination of other physical evidence and trace evidence left at the crime scene.

Later, back at FBI headquarters in Washington DC, behavioral analysts, profilers, body language experts, and investigators would analyze the evidence collected and the behavior of the bank robbers to develop profiles of potential suspects.

In the coming days, FBI bank records experts would descend on the bank in the tiny town of Swayzee and would scrutinize bank records to trace the movements of financial transactions, account activity, and withdrawals.

All of these exhaustive and intense types of investigative techniques would be compiled for Andy and Dan and could cumulatively assist them in identifying patterns and potential motives which might in turn develop leads and suspects in the case.

Indianapolis, Indiana – February 15, 1973

Many of the leads and analysis' in the Swayzee robbery had come back from Washington. Their body language and the fact that one of the robbers had ordered the teller to not include a dye pack in with the money indicated that this was not the first time that these two had committed this type of crime.

Forensics had lifted a partial fingerprint and a palm print, but neither was complete enough to indicate they belonged to a specific person in the FBI database.

A Swayzee police officer had contacted the FBI a few days after the robbery and told Dan and Andy that on the day of the robbery while patrolling, he remembered seeing a man in a light green car with a Tennessee license plate parked on the street in front of the bank just before the robbery happened. He didn't get the plate number but specifically noticed that the tag was a Tennessee plate.

He told them that he just figured that the man was having car problems or had stopped briefly to look at a map. He unfortunately wasn't able to provide much of a detailed description of the car or of the man driving the car other than that he was a younger white male and had actually waved to the officer as he drove by.

The yellow and black gym bags the robbers used seemed to be their best leads. They were made by a company called, "Happy Sports" which was a subsidiary of a larger company called "Inoxto." The bags were imported from China, however they were imported in limited numbers and only sold through two specific retailers, TG&Y and McCroys.

Based on the vehicle's tag being from the state of Tennessee, on a hunch, Dan and Andy began an exhaustive search for a list of all of those two chain stores within the state of Tennessee. Twenty-eight stores were determined to exist scattered across the state of Tennessee.

Twelve were TG&Y stores and sixteen were McCroys. Working the phones and talking with managers, Andy and Dan determined that of those twenty-eight stores, only about thirteen of them carried the Happy Sports bag by Inoxto in yellow and black during the last year.

Eliminating all stores that had not sold any units of the bag within three days before the Swayzee robbery, only four stores remained on their radar. Two in Nashville, one in Maryville, and one in Sevierville.

Cross-referencing that information with vehicles that were light green in color that were reported stolen just prior to the robbery, they got a hit on a 1964 light green, four door, Chevrolet Impala that had been reported stolen on the morning of December 6, 1972 from in front of a bar in Alcoa, Tennessee. That same vehicle was found burned down to the rims alongside a dark country road in Fort Wayne, Indiana – only an hour and fifteen minutes from Swayzee.

If their hunches all proved to be correct, Andy and Dan thought that the robbers most likely lived in or near Alcoa, Tennessee. Of course, there was always a margin of error. There was a chance that one or more of their hunches could be wrong and they were on the wrong trail. But at this point, this was their leading hypothesis.

Now came the arduous and monumental task of checking with hotels, motels, motor courts, boarding houses, and campgrounds in the Fort Wayne area to inquire about any parties of three men who may have stayed over-night around the date of the Swayzee robbery.

CHAPTER 15

C.O.D.

Bartow, Florida - December 22, 1972

Malcolm was flush with his share of the Swayzee bank robbery money. Other than the little hiccup with Billy Ray not being where he was supposed to be when he and Jimmy exited the bank, everything had gone smooth as silk!

Malcolm decided that it was almost Christmas and since he was breathing free air, he would take a drive down to Florida to see his father Al and his uncle Hayden. Al lived in Lake Wales with his wife Delois. The only son they had still living at home was Dale. The older boys had all grown up and moved out. His uncle Hayden and his family had temporarily moved from Tennessee to Bartow, Florida, about a twenty-minute drive from Lake Wales.

Malcolm figured that as far as a place to stay, he could crash at uncle Hayden's place. Even though he wasn't escaped from jail at that time, his father's wife Delois, didn't approve of his criminal ways. She thought he was a bad influence on her kids and never allowed him to stay overnight at their house when he would come for a visit. She would allow a brief visit with Al for an hour or two, but after that, she wanted him gone.

There was an understanding between Delois and Malcolm that after his visits, she would always contact the sheriff's office to let them know he had been there. Of course, on this particular visit, it didn't really matter because he was a free man at the moment and wasn't wanted by the law.

Sure, he was violating his parole by leaving the state of Tennessee, but he didn't really consider that anything much to be concerned with. Still, Delois was insistent about limiting his visit with his father to only an hour or two.

When he showed up, Malcolm had brought a Christmas present for Dale. It was a small General Electric transistor radio. Dale was excited to receive it. It was about the size of a pack of cigarettes. He had never seen a radio so small. Dale thanked him for the radio and went to his bedroom to play with his new toy while Delois busied herself with washing dishes in the kitchen.

Malcolm and his father took their coffee out on the front patio overlooking the mature Oak trees adorned with Spanish Moss. With temperatures hovering in the high 70's, it didn't feel like the Christmases that Malcolm was used to in Tennessee, but it was comfortable.

Al asked Malcolm, "Well, how long are you planning to be in Florida son?"

Malcolm replied, "I don't rightly know. Figured I'd go see uncle Hayden. Maybe a week or two."

"Are you working anywhere?" asked Al, already knowing the real answer.

"Naw," said Malcolm. "I've got some leads on some jobs though when I get back up home."

"What kind of jobs?" probed Al.

"Awww, just this and that. First one thing then 'nother. You know how it is pop."

"Son, I wish you'd start livin' right. What makes you want to rob and steal from folks?" admonished Al.

"It's easy money pop. I could never bust my ass like you do working for other people. A foreman tellin' me to nail this board here and carry that bag of cement over there. It just ain't for me," said Malcolm, "Besides, I only take bank money. Not money from poor folks tryin' to get by. All them banks are insured anyhow. They ain't out nothin.'"

"It just ain't right," said Al. "I want to ask you something son, and I want you to answer me with the truth. Have you ever killed anybody?"

Malcom grinned a slight grin and paused – not immediately answering his father or saying anything. It was as though he was thinking to himself about just how much of his life of crime he really wanted to reveal to his father. He knew if he told him the truth, he would be angry and disappointed in him. But then, he didn't want to outright lie to his father either.

"Where do you reckon all that moss comes from anyway?" asked Malcolm, changing the subject and looking up into the branches of the Oak tree that stood closest to the house.

Their conversation continued for about an hour and a half about Al's brother Hayden and his wife and children and about other extended family members up in Tennessee. Neither Malcolm or Al ever circled back to the topic of Malcolm's crimes.

Once Malcolm left, Delois, true to form, waited about thirty minutes and called the sheriff's office to report that Malcolm had been there. Since he had no warrants showing on their system this time, they didn't bother to send a deputy to the house.

By Christmas morning, Dale was so excited about tearing into all his other gifts that he never even noticed that his mother had taken that transistor radio away and disposed of it.

He just thought that he had lost it. She knew that Malcolm had never had gainful employment and that the radio was either stolen or bought by Malcolm with stolen money. She didn't want her boy to have it in his possession or for it to even be in her house.

After Malcolm left his dad's house in Lake Wales, he drove twenty minutes to the town of Bartow. Malcolm's Uncle Hayden greeted him on the porch. They stood there chatting for a bit. Eventually, Malcolm got around to asking his Uncle

Hayden if it would be alright If he stayed there for a week or
so.

"Are you on the run from the law boy?" asked Hayden.

"Naw sir," replied Malcolm. "I just can't stay at pop's place.
You know how his ole lady is."

"Yep... Well, c'mon in," said Hayden. "Edith can put the kids
on the couch and you can sleep in their room."

"Are you sure?" asked Malcolm. "I have money for a motel
if it's a problem."

"Nah, no problem at all boy!" replied Hayden. "Stay as long
as you want."

"I appreciate it Uncle Hayden!" said Malcolm, stepping into
the living room. Edith, Hayden's wife, made Malcolm and
the family a big dinner. It was seldom that Malcolm was able
to enjoy a good home-cooked meal.

The next morning, Hayden had a package he needed to mail
to a cousin in Maryville. It was a small wooden horse he had

carved by hand. He asked Malcolm, "You wanna take a ride with me up to the post office?"

Malcolm responded, "Sure. You can show me the sights!"

Hayden replied, "Pfft! This is Bartow. Ain't many sights to see around here."

As Malcolm sat waiting in Hayden's pick-up truck in the post office parking lot while Hayden mailed his package, his eyes wandered to the business directly across the street. It was a gun shop. The wheels in Malcolm's criminal mind began turning. "I bet a post office rakes in the cash. Probably less than a bank, but still, I bet it'd be a good haul," he thought to himself.

Later that night around 10:00 PM, Malcolm told his aunt and uncle that he needed some smokes and was going to drive up town and find a convenience store. It wasn't a lie. Malcolm was low on cigarettes.

But after he bought them, he drove by that gun shop again. There wasn't much traffic out and about at that hour. If Malcolm was going to do a burglary, he usually preferred to do them in the wee hours of the morning but this time, he was making an exception.

He drove around to the back of the building and backed up his car to within about ten feet of the back door of the gun shop. He stomped the gas and the rear of his car smashed through the back door and part of the wall of the gun shop.

He pulled forward a bit, jumped out and collected a few .38 caliber pistols and a box of ammunition from the gun shop. And then, just like that, he vanished into the night and was almost back to Hayden's place before the police had even responded to the gun shop's alarm.

A few days later. He walked into the post office in broad daylight – not even bothering to conceal his face – and quietly robbed the clerk of all the money in his till. The take was just under $400.00. It wasn't much, but it was enough to provide him with some "walkin' around money" as Malcolm liked to call it.

He didn't have to rob the post office. He still had plenty of cash from the Swayzee robbery. But he felt compelled to. He was drawn to it like a moth to a flame. He had also buried a nice little nest egg in three mason jars under the barn on his grandmother's farm, but he had brought plenty of cash with him to Florida for hotels, food, cigarettes, and that little transistor radio he bought for Dale at a gas station on the way down.

On the Friday afternoon that Malcolm decided to leave to head back to Tennessee, he was pulled over by a Polk County Deputy Sheriff for a broken tail light not two miles from Hayden's house. The tail light was a casualty of backing through the gun shop door twelve days ago. Malcolm was arrested and taken to the Polk County Jail.

Ironically, it wasn't the tail light that got him arrested. It wasn't a warrant from back in Tennessee. It wasn't the burglary to the gun shop or the post office robbery either. The police still had no suspects in either one of those cases.

No, what got him put in jail that evening was the fact he didn't have a valid driver's license. Malcolm was too embarrassed to admit to the other county jail inmates what he had been arrested for. To Malcolm, a big-time bank robber, getting busted for a driver's license violation was penny ante and beneath him. So, Malcolm would just say, "I beat up a cop" when asked by the other inmates about why he was there.

It was Friday and Malcolm felt inconvenienced by being put in jail on such a petty charge. It would be Monday before he would be able to see a judge and get a bond issued. He decided that he didn't have time to wait around for that.

The next day. He complained of stomach pains and was taken to the jail's medical station. When they brought him in, Malcolm noticed that the medical area was close to the sally-port. He thought to himself, "If I can get down there that close to the door, maybe I can bolt out to the outside."

As fate would have it, while Malcolm was sitting in medical waiting to be seen by a nurse, he could see the week-enders gathering in the hallway. Week-enders were people convicted of minor offenses that had to report to the jail on weekends to serve their time – either in a cell or by working along the roadways picking up trash.

Seizing the opportunity, Malcolm stole a sweater out of a closet in the medical room, put it on over his jail uniform, and fell right in line behind the weekenders as they were buzzed out of the building. Before boarding the sheriff's office bus to take them out to pick up highway trash, Malcolm said to one of the guards, "Boss-man. You mind if I run to my car really quick? I forgot my hat." The guard, busy checking off names as the week-enders boarded the bus didn't even look down and notice Malcolm's jail uniform pants. He said, "Make it quick! We've gotta go!"

Malcolm walked out of the sally-port and around the corner of the building. Thirteen hours later, he was lying in his own bed back in Maryville, Tennessee.

He had successfully escaped from the Polk County Jail. Ironically, it was the same Polk County Sheriff's Office where his youngest half-brother, Dale, would be employed as a deputy sheriff a short eleven years later.

CHAPTER 16

THE AMBULANCE

Maryville, Tennessee, January 1, 1973

Malcolm took a sip of his coffee and said, "We're going to need some new wheels for the getaway. Something fast!"

"Oh, don't worry about that big brother!" said Billy Ray. I've already got that covered!"

Malcolm asked, "It's a four-door, right?"

Billy Ray replied, "Nope, it's a five door!"

"What the fuck are you talking about!?" asked Malcolm.

"It's an ambulance!" said Billy Ray.

With a quizzical look on his face, Malcolm responded, "I'm sorry, it sounded like you just said you got us a fucking ambulance for a getaway car."

Billy Ray grinned a big shit eating grin and said, "Yep! It's a '70 Cadillac, Miller-Meteor Life-liner Ambulance!"

"Are you outta your ever-loving mind?" asked Malcolm.

Jimmy interjected, "I don't know, it could work! Think about it! The cops ain't gonna stop no ambulance with its lights and siren goin' because they'll think it's on its way to an emergency or some shit!"

"BINGO!" exclaimed Billy Ray. "We'll be hiding in plain sight, right under their fucking noses! ...Clean getaway big brother!"

Malcolm pondered for a moment and said, "I hate to be the one to break the news to you, but they're going to be looking hard for a stolen damn ambulance. They probably already are!"

Billy Ray replied, "no they won't and no they ain't either! It ain't stolen! I bought it myself fair and square with cash money from the Swayzee job we did last year! Got it up there at the auction house in north Knoxville! It had a fucked-up fender, but I'm already working on that. I've gotta sand the Bondo down a little more and give it a shot coat of primer and a little paint and we'll be good to go!"

Malcolm thought a bit and rubbed his chin as though in deep thought. "Hmmm. Maybe. Just maybe," he said softly.

Charlie spoke up, "I think it's a great plan! So, are me and William in or what?"

Billy Ray replied, "I say you're in."

"I say you're in too," added Jimmy as he looked over toward Malcolm for his approval. "What say you brother?"

Malcolm paused for a second then smiled and replied, "Any friend of my baby brother is a friend of mine! You boys are in! We'll hit the bank on the 12th. That's a Friday," said Malcolm looking at the January 1973 page of the big calendar that was hanging on the wall beside him above the non-working black and white 13" TV set. "They're always ripe for the pickin' on Fridays!"

"Me and William is gonna need guns," remarked Charlie.

Malcolm replied, "I'll take care of that little detail myself!" Malcolm raised his coffee cup in the air in a final toast and continued, "we're gonna be rich boys!"

Billy Ray let out a loud whoop in excitement followed by a shout of "Hell yeah!" from Jimmy as he pumped his fist in the air.

Jimmy spoke up, "So you got a line on us some new hardware?"

Malcolm replied, "Sure do." Gesturing toward his front door, Malcolm continued, "Right over there across the street in that little strip mall is a gun shop. Their back door is literally right across the street from the front porch out there! I walked over there a few days ago and went in to look around. They've got two tommy guns hanging on the wall and they spoke to me while I was in there. They said, 'come steal us, Malcolm! You need us for your next bank job!'" Everyone in the room guffawed with laughter.

"Thompsons, huh? That's pretty fucking cool," said Charlie.

"You're damn right it is! Pistols and sawed-off shotguns will get the job done, but if you want total compliance by everybody in the fuckin' bank and from any cops that might wanna fuck with you, they ain't nothing like a Tommy!" said Malcolm.

Malcolm had a fascination with Thompson sub-machine guns ever since he had been a young man because that was the firearm of choice by all of the old-school gangsters from the past that he idolized so much. He saw himself as a modern day Al Capone, Clyde Barrow, Baby Face Nelson, or John Dillinger. He was especially enamored by the exploits of Dillinger.

"Hell yeah!" said Billy Ray excitedly. "I've always wanted to shoot one of those!"

"We'll take care of the hardware Billy Boy. You just concentrate on getting us the hell outta there fast when the time comes!" replied Malcolm.

"That's why I bought the ambulance brother!" replied Billy Ray.

"Oh lordy," commented Malcolm. "You and this damn ambulance. I reckon you ought to show me this thing. Where's it at?"

"Right now it's in granny's barn till I can get finished working on that fender and get it primed and painted," replied Billy Ray.

"Alright," Malcolm replied, gesturing toward William and Charlie. "Why don't you take these fellas on back home and meet me out at granny's house about 4:00 this afternoon?"

Speaking to everyone in general, Malcolm continued, "We'll all meet back here this weekend and go over all the details."

"Sounds good to me," said Charlie.

"Me too!" added William.

With that, the men all stood up, shook hands and shuffled out the door. Billy Ray took William and Charlie back to Jimmy's house where their cars were parked and they went home.

Billy Ray and Jimmy hung out on Jimmy's couch and watched the Rose Bowl Parade and drank a few beers. Malcolm, his head still pounding from his hangover, went back to bed and slept until it was time to go meet Billy Ray at granny's place.

When he arrived at the farm, Billy Ray was already there sanding away on the fender Bondo. Billy Ray's radio sat on the hood of the car blasting out 'Brown Sugar' by the Rolling Stones. "Look at you actually doing real work!" joked Malcolm as he entered the open doors of the barn.

"Hey big brother! Didn't even hear you drive up!" said Billy Ray

"That's because you're playing your hippy shit music too loud!" joked Malcolm, obviously feeling much recovered from his hangover.

"That's the Stone's, man! It's better than that shit-kicking country stuff you listen to!" responded Billy Ray.

"So this is it huh?" said Malcolm as he bent down, leaned in the window, and looked around at the ambulance's interior.

"Yep! She's a beauty ain't she!? She'll run like a scalded dog too!" said Billy Ray.

"I just hope your little crazy idea works. It's a little high-profile for knocking over banks," said Malcolm.

"It'll work! Trust me! We leave the bank in a borrowed ride, torch it, and jump into the ambulance. They won't even be looking for it when they start searching for the car that just left the bank!" explained Billy Ray.

"Well, you're the wheel-man. Guess you know best," smiled Malcolm.

"You wanna hear her run?" asked Billy Ray.

"Sure, crank her up!" replied Malcolm.

Billy Ray enthusiastically hopped into the driver's seat and turned on the ignition. He revved it up a few times and the powerful eight-cylinder engine roared with life. Without warning, Billy Ray flipped on the overhead red beacon light and sounded the ambulance's siren.

The siren was so loud inside the confines of the barn, Malcolm covered his ears to protect them from the piercing noise. After a few seconds, Billy Ray turned off the emergency light and siren and switched off the ignition.

"Goddamn! That thing is loud!" exclaimed Malcolm.

"Damn sure is!" said Billy Ray, exiting the ambulance and slamming the door shut.

"Hey you wanna a beer?" asked Billy Ray.

"Yeah, that sounds good," replied Malcolm.

The two of them sat down on old wooden crates in the barn next to the ambulance, enjoying their beers and marveling at the unique vehicle parked right in front of them.

Billy Ray spoke up, "Hey brother, there's something I've been meaning to talk to you about."

"Oh, shit! This sounds serious," chuckled Malcolm.

"Well, it sorta is," responded Billy Ray. "You know me and that girl Barbie have been seeing each other for a while now, right?"

"Yeah, so?" responded Malcolm.

"Well, we've been talkin' and... Well, we're thinking about gettin' hitched!"

"No shit!?" responded Malcolm. "You didn't go and knock her up did you?"

"Naw, nothin' like that," responded Billy Ray.

"Well, congratulations Billy Boy! That's great to hear!"

"Yeah, well, thing is, Barbie wants me to settle down. You know, get a real job and all," stated Billy Ray.

"Is that so?" came Malcolm's response.

Billy Ray turned up his Pabst Blue Ribbon beer can and finished off the last drop. "Yeah. She don't want me pullin'

jobs with you and Jimmy anymore. So, after Fairmount...
After Fairmount, I'm gonna be out."

"Well, if that's the way you want it, that's the way it's gonna
be," replied Malcolm.

"You ain't mad at me are ya?" asked Billy Ray.

"Shit no! I ain't mad at ya baby brother. I hate to lose the
best wheel-man I've ever had, but you gotta keep that girl of
yours happy," said Malcolm.

"I'm glad to hear you say that. I've been sweatin' tellin you
for a few weeks now," said Billy Ray.

"Ain't no big deal," replied Malcolm. "But I know one thing
for sure!"

"Yeah? What's that?" Billy Ray asked.

"That fender ain't gonna sand itself!" said Malcolm. Both
men chuckled.

With what remaining daylight he had left, Billy Ray got back to work on smoothing out the Bondo to get it ready for primer and paint.

As he watched his younger brother work, Malcolm thought to himself, "This whole ambulance thing is gonna work. I sure am gonna miss having Billy Ray on the crew though."

Malcolm went back to his place around 7:00 that evening. He sat at his dining room table and ate his hamburger from Burger King that he had picked up on the way home. Then, he made himself a nice hot cup of coffee. He took his cup out onto the front porch, wrapped the tattered quilt around himself and sat down in his rocking chair.

The longer he sat there sipping on his coffee, the more he thought that tonight needed to be the night he went across the street and got those Tommy guns. He ran several scenarios through his head on ways to get into the building to get the guns. He finally settled on one.

When he had drank about half of the cup of coffee, he got a crowbar, hammer, and a screwdriver out of the trunk of his '69 Dodge Charger and crossed the street on foot.

He pried the door open and with a couple whacks, removed the pins to the door's hinges. Leaving the door on the ground, he took his tools and the doors hinge pins back across the street to his house. He tossed the tools back in his trunk, stepped back up on his porch and wrapped himself in the blanket again.

Ten minutes later, the police responded to the alarm at the gun shop. Malcolm watched from his porch as two Maryville police officers searched the business' interior. One of the officers noticed Malcolm sitting on his porch and walked across the street to talk to him.

"Good evening, sir!" said the officer.

"How do?" replied Malcolm.

"It looks like we've had a burglary across the street over there. Did you see anybody around?" asked the officer.

"Naw sir. I heard the alarm going off while I was making my coffee, but when I walked out here and sat down, all I saw was the open door over there," explained Malcolm. "You know, come to think of it, I did see one of them hippy VW busses pulling out onto the road just as I came out here."

"Do you happen to remember what color it was?" asked the officer. "Did you see a tag?"

"Naw sir. I didn't really pay it no mind to be honest with ya," stated Malcolm.

"All right, If you can think of anything else that might help us out, give us a call at the Maryville PD." said the officer.

"Yes sir, I surely will!" replied Malcolm.

Malcolm watched the store's owner respond and nail up a piece of plywood over the gaping hole until he could have it fixed the next day. Since nothing was taken, the owner and the police figured that the person or people in the VW van had gotten spooked and just left before making entry into the building.

Malcolm now knew that it would take the police about ten minutes to respond to the alarm. The plywood would be easier to get into than the door was. About two hours later, he got the crowbar out of his trunk again, crossed the street, and pried off the plywood.

He grabbed the two Tommy guns, two drum magazines and two stick magazines to go with them. He also grabbed a couple .45 caliber 1911's and shoved them into his waistband. Carrying all that, plus all the .45 caliber ammo he could carry in the pillow case he had brought with him, he went back to his house, turned out all his lights and went to bed.

He had just sat down on the side of his bed when he saw the flashing blue and red lights across the street. As he lied back on the bed and pulled the cover up over him, he smiled to himself at how clever he had been to pull off the heist right across the street from his own house.

Not only that, he mentally patted himself on the back for having the balls to chat with the police officer and tell him that bullshit VW story. "Talk about shitting where you eat!" Malcolm laughed to himself as he closed his eyes and began to drift off to sleep.

CHAPTER 17
CAREFUL PLANNING

Maryville, Tennessee - January 7, 1973

It was noon on Sunday. Malcolm was expecting his house guests, William, Charlie, and his brothers Jimmy and Billy Ray. They all pulled up about five minutes late in two separate cars. Billy Ray and Jimmy were in Billy Ray's Gran Torino and William and Charlie were in William's bright yellow Mustang.

Malcolm stepped out on the porch as they were all exiting their cars. "Y'all are late!" exclaimed Malcolm. "I expect y'all to be punctual next Friday." he said.

"Quit your bitchin!'" said Jimmy. "we're here ain't we?"

"C'mon in," said Malcolm as he led the way into his house. "Anybody wanna drink or anything?" Everyone declined. They all filed into the kitchen. Some leaned against the sink and counter area and the rest sat around Malcolm's kitchen table. Malcolm remained standing.

"Well, let's get down to business then, shall we? Billy Ray, how's the ambulance comin' along?" asked Malcolm.

"It's ready to roll! Put the last coat of paint on it last night. I ain't no paint and body man, but it looks pretty dang good if I say so myself!" responded Billy Ray.

Billy Ray continued, "Wednesday or Thursday, I'm gonna boost us the other car we'll use to get to the ambulance in Fairmount. I've had my eye on one for a few days now."

Jimmy added, "I'm helping him get the wheels and then we'll hide it out in the barn over night with the ambulance. We'll pick them both up and swing by to get you Friday morning."

"OK, sounds good," said Malcolm.

"Exactly what time do we need to be leaving your house since we ain't staying overnight in Indiana this time?" asked Billy Ray.

"Well, let's see." said Malcolm. "It's about seven hours driving time to get there and we need to allow ourselves thirty minutes to find a good place outside of town to hide the ambulance. So, I figure to get us in front of the bank at 10:00 AM, we need to leave here right at 2:30 in the morning."

Jimmy joked, "2:30 in the damn mornin'! That don't sound like no banker's hours to ME!" Everyone chuckled.

Charlie spoke up and asked, "Hey, I have a question. I get the whole not shitting where you eat thing, but how come Indiana? What made you want to do jobs up there?"

Malcolm responded, "No real reason, I guess... When I was a boy, my pop would sometimes take me on construction jobs with him around that neck of the woods. I thought the people up there were all real nice, so I just decided one day to start robbing them!" Everyone chuckled.

Malcolm continued, "What about you Charlie? You all set for Friday?"

"Yeah, I'm good. I'm only gonna need a few tools to cut the power when I see you boys going in," replied Charlie.

Malcolm asked, "You ridin' over with William, I presume?"

"Yeah, if he'll let me get in his precious little car," replied Charlie glancing over at William and winking. "He almost didn't let me get in it a little earlier."

"Just don't bring no coffee in my car like you tried to do this mornin,' said William. "I don't need you spillin' shit in my ride!"

Charlie grinned and rolled his eyes. "I hate to be the one to break it to you, but your 'ride' looks like a fuckin' banana going down the road!" said Charlie.

"Fuck you," smiled William, taking Charlie's little jab in stride.

"Speaking of your fancy ride, you clear on everything?" asked Malcolm of William.

"Yep. I drop Charlie off at the bank and haul ass to the other side of town to get a cop to pull me over," said William.

"What if you can't find a cop?" asked Malcolm.

William replied, "Well hell, I guess I'll just go to the police department and cut donuts in their parking lot until one of'em pays attention to me!" Everyone laughed out loud.

"Oh, by the way, I know the perfect place y'all can hide the ambulance. There's a little dirt road outside of Fairmount just off of highway 26. It's an old logging road. Nobody's ever around there anymore." continued William.

"Alright," said Malcolm. "You can show us where it is that morning." Looking over at Charlie, Malcolm asked "After the job, are you riding back with us or William?"

"Don't matter to me," replied Charlie.

"There's a park behind the bank," said William, "if you want to ride back with me, I could pick you up there. Or, you could join up with these guys back at the car in front of the bank after you get the power cut."

"Either way. Doesn't matter to me," said Charlie.

Malcolm spoke up, "Well, y'all get that worked out amongst yourselves. Y'all wanna see the new toys?"

"First, I got us a set of these," Malcolm said, displaying a set of four walkie talkies. "If we need to talk to each other or anything, we'll have these. I don't wanna have to wonder where you are like I did in Swayzee last year Billy Boy," joked Malcolm.

"I'll have one for me and Jimmy. Billy Ray, you'll have one with you in the getaway car. William, you take one with you. And Charlie, here's yours," Malcom said, as he passed out the walkie talkies as if he was handing out Christmas gifts. "If anything goes wrong, we'll be able to communicate with each other."

"Billy Ray looked over his walkie talkie and said, "Look at us gettin' all high-tech and shit!"

"I've got y'all some more goodies," Malcolm said, as he dumped the contents of a pillowcase onto the table. It was three revolvers and two 1911 .45's. He picked up one of the .45's and said, "This one's mine, y'all can fight over the rest of'em."

Everyone leaned in and chose one of the firearms while Malcolm reached behind him to retrieve a box of .45 caliber and a box of .38 caliber ammunition from the kitchen counter. "Here ya go boys, load'em up!"

"I've got one more thing to show y'all. Well, two more things actually," Malcolm said, as he stepped just inside the doorway of his bedroom.

Malcolm emerged from his room and had two brand new Thompson sub-machine guns in his hands. He flexed his knees and posed with one in each hand while pointing them at the ceiling. He shook them. "Ratatatatatat!" he said, simulating the rifles quickly firing multiple rounds.

"That's what I'm fuckin' talkin' about!" exclaimed Jimmy excitedly as Malcolm handed him one of the iconic guns. "Just like the old-time gangsters used to carry back in the 30's!"

Jimmy looked the rifle over and passed it over to Billy Ray. "Damn! That son of a bitch is heavy!" said Billy Ray.

Malcolm joked, "That's why only us men should carry them."
Everybody guffawed as Malcolm handed the second Tommy
Gun to Charlie for him and William to look over.

"Those are some damn nice boom-sticks Malcolm!" said
William.

"So, who gets these?" asked Charlie.

"These are for the one's doin' all the heavy liftin' inside the
bank. These are for me and Jimmy," answered Malcolm.

"You got enough ammo for'em?" inquired Jimmy. "These
sumbitches can go through the bullets quick."

"Yeah, I've got enough for these two drum magazines and I
also have a couple stick mags as back-up in case the shit gets
deep," stated Malcolm as he reached back into his bedroom
to retrieve the stick magazines.

"I wanna shoot'em!" said Billy Ray.

"Well, I kinda figured one of y'all would say that. I got a
couple extra boxes of ammo just for that purpose. Load up

the drum on this one Jimmy." Malcolm said, as he took the rifle from Charlie and handed it over to Jimmy.

"Where are we gonna shoot it?" asked Billy Ray.

"Into that clay bank out yonder," said Malcolm, gesturing out his back window. "Where did you think we were gonna fuckin' shoot it!?"

"I don't know," answered Billy Ray. "You're kinda close to town here. You don't think the cops are gonna come do ya?"

"Shit, we'll have all this ammo shot up and be back in here having our second cup of coffee before Johnny Law can get the donut crumbs brushed off their shirts and drive over here!" laughed Malcolm. Everyone chuckled.

With that, the five of them went out Malcolm's back door and set up some beer bottles and cans in the patch of snow against the backdrop of the red clay bank behind Malcolm's house. They all took turns blasting the glass bottles into oblivion and thoroughly ventilating the beer cans.

After all the fun, they all went back inside and had a cup of coffee to warm up. They spent the next hour and a half socializing and gabbing about the Vietnam War, D.B. Cooper, robbing banks, prisons and jails they had served time in, the Apollo space missions, and a myriad of other topics before parting ways.

They were all brimming with anticipation and excitement for the upcoming event on Friday. Little did they know, in that moment, that the looming specter of danger and death was lurking just beyond the not-so-distant horizon, poised to engulf them all.

CHAPTER 18
THE FAIRMOUNT JOB

Fairmount Indiana – January 12, 1973

At 9:40 AM, three cars turned off of Highway 26 about two miles outside of the city of Fairmount, Indiana onto the old logging road. William and Charlie led the way in William's yellow Mustang followed by Billy Ray and Jimmy in the ambulance. Bringing up the rear was Malcolm in a stolen medium blue '68 Buick Skylark sedan.

At a wide place on the road which was starting to grow over with grass and become more of a trail than a road, William did a U-turn. Billy Ray and Malcolm followed suit.

Everyone got out of the vehicles to stretch their legs after the long seven-hour drive. "Man, I don't think I ate enough breakfast this morning," said Billy Ray. "I'm hungry!"

"You're ALWAYS hungry!" remarked Jimmy.

"Hey, what can I say, I'm a growing boy!" joked Billy Ray.

"You're thirty damn years old!" said Jimmy.

"I'm still young compared to your old ass!" teased Billy Ray.

"Well, we can all get some grub on the way home when we're through with the job," said Malcolm.

Malcolm continued, "William, we'll probably get separated after the job so if we don't see you back here or on the highway, just meet us at my house back in Maryville."

"Will do!" said William.

"Billy Ray, tell me you remembered the gas for torching this Buick when we get back here," said Malcolm.

Billy Ray looked shocked. "Oh no! I forgot the gas!"

"Goddammit!" shouted Malcolm, "I told you to get the fuckin' gas!"

"Calm down big brother! I was just fuckin' with you. It's in the trunk," said Billy Ray.

"Shit-head! Don't mess with me like that! I've got a lot on my damn mind! I don't need the additional stress!" said Malcolm, relieved that Billy Ray had indeed remembered the gasoline.

"Well, let's go ladies! Let's get this show on the road!" said Jimmy.

With that, Charlie and William got back in the Mustang and Malcolm, Jimmy, and Billy Ray piled into the Skylark with Billy Ray in the driver's seat of course. "Let's go!" said Malcolm as he signaled William that they were all ready to move out.

They couldn't have timed it much more perfectly. Billy Ray pulled up in front of the Fairmount Bank at 9:56 AM. Four minutes before the time they had planned to hit the bank.

William stopped briefly in front of them and Charlie got out of the passenger side. William drove on. Charlie walked to the side of the bank and continued walking down the sidewalk to the rear of the bank.

Charlie called Malcolm on the Walkie Talkie. "You're gonna have to let me know when to cut the power over the radio. The meter is on the back of the bank and not on the side," said Charlie.

"OK!" said Malcolm. "Give it about three minutes. I'll let you know just before we get out of the car to go in," he replied.

As Charlie stood behind the bank waiting for Malcolm's order to cut the power, he was being watched by an older man sitting on a park bench across the street from the back of the bank. The man was curious as to what Charlie was doing just standing there and thought that Charlie looked suspicious. The three minutes finally passed and Malcolm keyed his walkie talkie and said, "Go ahead and cut it Charlie!"

Charlie came back over the air with, "You got it!"

Malcolm keyed the button on the walkie talkie again and said, "Do your thing William! It's go time!" There was no response from William. Malcolm figured that he was probably out of range and too far away to hear him over the walkie talkies.

Jimmy and Malcolm pulled their black ski masks down concealing their faces and quickly exited the sedan with their yellow gym bags in one hand and their heavy, fully loaded Tommy guns held down at their sides in their other hands. They walked briskly toward the bank's front doors while glancing left and right.

Billy Ray drummed his thumbs nervously on the steering wheel in beat with 'Travelin' Band' by Creedence Clearwater Revival playing on the car radio - which he had cranked up as Malcolm and Jimmy had exited the car. He vigilantly kept a lookout all around and in his rearview mirror for any cops on patrol in the area.

Malcolm slammed the front doors open and raised his machine gun into view as he announced loudly, "This is a hold up! Everybody on the floor!"

The bank manager, three tellers and four customers who were in the bank initially just stood there in shock – motionless - not comprehending what was happening.

Suddenly from behind him, Malcolm heard a loud burst of gunfire. He jerked his head toward his shoulders as he turned around to see where it came from.

Jimmy had sprayed five or six rounds from his Tommy gun into the ceiling of the bank. Upon hearing and seeing this, everyone in the bank dropped on their bellies to the floor.

"Stand up!" Malcolm screamed at one of the tellers. "Fill the bags! No dye packs, you understand me!?" The teller nodded. He threw his bag at the teller. Jimmy tossed Malcolm his own bag while keeping an eye on everyone on the floor and the front door of the bank. Malcom threw the second bag at the teller. "Hurry up bitch!" he shouted.

The teller, scared and crying, stuffed money from her drawer with her trembling hands into the bag and moved down to the next drawer. She continued stuffing cash into the bag until it was full. She picked up the second bag from the counter and repeated the process with the third and fourth drawer.

While the teller was filling the bags, all the lights in the building went dark. "Good!" Malcolm thought to himself, "Charlie's got the power cut!" After the teller finished filling both bags, Malcolm ordered her to lay back down on the floor.

Within three minutes and thirty seconds, they were heading to the door. Malcolm was first out. Jimmy turned around before exiting and shouted to everyone. "Nobody moves for ten minutes or we'll kill you on the floor where you lay!" He turned again and exited the building. Jimmy and Malcolm ran to the waiting car and jumped in the Buick's backseat. Billy Ray punched it! And just like that, they were gone!

They got back to the old logging road so quickly it almost seemed like they had teleported there. Billy Ray had made an excellent choice in a fast getaway car and drove like part professional Hollywood stuntman and part racecar driver.

As Malcolm and Jimmy were transferring the Tommy guns and loot over to the ambulance, Billy Ray went to work on getting rid of the Buick.

He opened the trunk and took out a gallon glass jug ¾ full of gasoline. He removed the lid and poured some in the trunk and in the backseat of the car. He opened the front door and splashed plenty of it around on the front seat and dashboard too, tossing the empty jug on the front seat when he was done.

Even though he didn't smoke, Billy Ray had even remembered to bring the matches! He struck one of the matches against the back of the matchbook, lit the entire matchbook on fire, and then tossed it into the car. It made a loud WHOOSH sound as the car exploded into flames. The powerful concussion resulting from the sudden ignition of gasoline fumes hit Billy Ray, and he could feel its immense heat on his face, despite standing at a safe distance from the Buick.

"Let's get the fuck outta here!" shouted Malcolm.

The three of them piled into the ambulance. Jimmy threw a blanket over the Tommy guns and the gym bags in the back area of the ambulance that's meant for patients. Billy Ray drove down the logging road to the hardtop.

Once they hit the highway, Billy Ray flipped on the rotating red light on top and the ambulance's siren. He accelerated to speeds reaching 85 miles per hour. Any cars that were on the road, pulled over and yielded to the ambulance just as Billy Ray had predicted they would.

Within a very short while, they were forty miles away – well out of the range of any law enforcement roadblocks that might be set up. Billy Ray slowed down and killed the lights and siren.

Just south of Cincinnati, Ohio, traffic started getting pretty heavy. Billy Ray turned on the emergency red light again to get them around the wreck quicker. They went about three miles on the shoulder and could finally see what the problem was up ahead.

There had been a pretty serious car accident. An Ohio State Trooper was directing traffic around the crash and a second trooper was tending to those involved in the accident. Driving on the grass next to the roadway, Billy Ray breezed past them and continued driving south on the Interstate.

"Did y'all see how confused those fuckers were when we didn't stop at that wreck!?" They thought we were the real deal!" laughed Billy Ray.

Jimmy laughed at Billy Ray's comment.

Malcolm said, "I hope a real ambulance comes along soon for them. That one car was smashed all to hell! Did y'all see that!? Holy shit!"

They continued to drive straight through to Maryville with only one stop near Williamsburg, Kentucky for gas and to stretch their legs and take a much-needed bathroom break.

They also grabbed some gas station sandwiches, candy bars, and some sodas. They were all starving at this point.

They rolled up in the ambulance in front of Malcolm's house a little after 5:00 PM. The boys grabbed the two bags of cash and went inside. Malcolm dumped both bags out on his dining room table and they started counting the cash. The take was a staggering fifty-four thousand dollars.

Malcolm did some ciphering and said, "That comes to $10,800 each split five ways. But seeing how two of us ain't here at the moment while the cyphering is going on, we all get an extra two grand each and William and Charlie can have a total of..." Malcom did some more math on his pad of paper and finally finished his sentence, "$7,800 each."

They were all dividing up the stacks when Malcolm heard a car pull up in front of his house. "Shit! Go see who that is Jimmy!"

Jimmy walked into the living room and could see through the curtained window that it was William's yellow Mustang. "It's William!" said Jimmy.

"Go out there and stall him for a couple minutes till me and Billy Ray get this money straight!" said Malcolm.

Jimmy opened the front door and stepped out on the porch – closing the door shut behind him. He lit up a cigarette as he greeted William. Billy Ray and Malcolm hurriedly divided the money into five equal stacks of $7,800 each and hid the extra money in Malcolm's bedroom.

Malcolm started walking toward the door when Jimmy opened it and he and William came in. "We've got a problem!" said Jimmy.

"What's going on?" asked Malcolm. "Where's Charlie!?"

"That's the fuckin' problem! We thought he was coming back with William and William thought he had come back with us! He wasn't there when he went by the park to pick him up. Right now, he's MIA!" exclaimed Jimmy.

"Fuck!" said Malcolm, "I thought y'all had it all worked out who he was coming back with." said Malcolm.

William replied, "We had it all worked out. But I'm tellin' you man, he wasn't there! Cops were starting to swarm around the bank, so I beat feet! Maybe he's hitchhiking back now," suggested William. "I guess I'll just take my cut and head home. Maybe he'll call one of us."

Billy Ray brought William's stack in and handed it to him. "Your shares all there. $7,800," Billy Ray lied to William.

William gathered his loot in his arms and turned to leave. "I'll talk to y'all later," said William as he went out the door and left.

Malcolm, Jimmy, and Billy Ray all sat down in the living room. "What do y'all think happened?" asked Billy Ray.

"I don't know, but I bet Charlie's pretty pissed at all of us right now for leaving him high and dry," stated Malcolm.

"And rightly so!" added Jimmy. "You reckon we ought to go back to Fairmount and see if we can find him?"

"Hell no!" said Malcolm. "You know how many cats I did time with because they got caught when they returned to the scene of the crime!? We ain't going back!"

"He'll call right!? He's got your number doesn't he Jimmy?" asked Billy Ray.

"Yeah, he's got William's and mine. Guess I ought to go home too so I'm there in case he tries to call me," said Jimmy.

"Well, get your share off the table in there. Your other cash is under the pillow on my bed," said Malcolm.

Jimmy retrieved his bonus and his cut from the dining room table. "Alright boys. I'm gonna run. Hey, you got a paper sack laying around I can put this shit in?" asked Jimmy.

"Yeah, next to the stove over there," said Malcolm.

Jimmy looked around and didn't see the bags.

"Between the counter and the stove." directed Malcolm.

"Found'em!" said Jimmy, as he popped the A & P bag open and stuffed his cash in. "If I hear anything from Charlie, I'll give y'all a call and let you know what happened."

"Alright brother. Talk to you tomorrow if not sooner," said Malcolm.

"See ya man," said Billy Ray to Jimmy.

After Jimmy left, Billy Ray asked Malcolm, "I don't understand how this could have happened. Why do you reckon he wasn't in the park waiting for William like he was supposed to be?"

"I don't know Billy Boy. I just don't know." replied Malcolm.

Billy Ray continued, "You don't think maybe he got pinched by the cops do ya?"

"I hadn't even considered that as an option," replied Malcolm. "I certainly hope that's not the case."

"You don't think he would rat us out do you?" asked Billy Ray nervously.

"I don't know Billy Boy. Jimmy did time with him and he seemed to think he was a stand-up guy," said Malcolm.

"Shit!" said Billy Ray suddenly. "What time is it?"

Malcolm looked at his watch. "It's a little after 7:00 PM. Why?"

"I told Barbie I'd be back by 7 and take her out for dinner," said Billy Ray.

"Well, if you plan on getting any pussy for the rest of the week, you better get your ass in gear and not stand her up!" said Malcolm cracking a strained smile.

"You're right about that!" chuckled Billy Ray.

Billy Ray went into Malcolm's bedroom and got his bonus cash and grabbed his $7,800 off the kitchen table. Putting it all into one of the paper A&P sacks like Jimmy had done, he bid a good night to Malcolm and left to take Barbie out to dinner.

Neither Billy Ray, Jimmy, nor Malcolm would ever see Charlie again. Or would they?

CHAPTER 19
MAGNIFICENT MEL

Fairmount Indiana – January 12, 1973

Sixty-one-year-old Mel Saunders had lived in Fairmount pretty much his whole life - not counting his eight-year stint in the Army between 1932 and 1940. In the service, Mel served as a Military Policeman at Fort Benning in Georgia. Once he got out of the army, he and his new bride Helen moved back to his home town of Fairmount, Indiana.

She was a beautiful young lady. She had long auburn hair and the color of her eyes were like a mesmerizing pool. It was no wonder that Mel had fallen for her hard.

Mel had met Helen at the PX on the base where she worked. They both quickly fell in love and were married on the base by Mel's lieutenant - who just so happened to be an ordained minister. Their long-term plan was to grow old together as they enjoyed the small-town charm of living back in Fairmount. Unfortunately, that plan didn't work out.

In February of 1964, Helen was diagnosed with an aggressive brain cancer. She died only four weeks after the diagnosis. Mel was, needless to say, devastated. He retired from his job at the mill and spent most of his days puttering around in his garage making wooden toys which he would donate every year before Christmas to the local charities. Mornings however were his time of reflection.

About three or four times per week, no matter the weather, Mel would wake up, shower, eat breakfast alone in his kitchen, and walk six blocks from his home to the city park in Fairmount. He would always bring along a cup of coffee to sip on and a little bread or birdseed to pitch to the pigeons as he reminisced about the time he had spent with Helen in that very park having picnics or listening to concerts by local amateur bands in the gazebo in the center of the park.

Generally speaking, every visit to the park was the same for Mel. Except this particular day would prove to be anything but mundane. As he was just finishing feeding the last of the birdseed he had brought to the pigeons, Mel glanced up across the street. His favorite park bench faced the rear of the Fairmount Bank.

Mel saw a man standing there looking around nervously. He knew right away that he was out of place and Mel's experience as a MP told him that the man was up to no good. When Mel saw the man speak into a walkie talkie and then start removing the electrical meter on the bank, his suspicions were confirmed.

Mel casually stood up and walked across the street on the opposite side of the park to Mason's Furniture Store. Tom Mason, the owner, was an old schoolmate and friend of Mel's. "Tommy!" said Mel as he entered the store, "I need to use your phone! I think the bank is about to get robbed!"

Tom replied, "Sure, sure! No problem! It's right over there on the desk."

Mel quickly called the Fairmount police department. His neighbor, Perky, answered the phone. Perky was about Mel's age and had got her nickname honestly. She was a short spunky lady with wire rim glasses. She would light up any room when she would walk into it.

"Fairmount Police, how can I help you?" asked Perky.

"Perky, this is Mel Saunders! Listen! You need to send some cars down here to the bank. I think it's getting robbed! I just saw some stranger remove the meter and he ain't with the electric company!"

"Can you tell what the guy's wearing?" asked Perky.

"All I could see was dark pants and a dark jacket!" Mel said excitedly. "Get some guys down here!"

I will," replied Perky. "But I need information. Where's the man now?"

"Tom, can you see the guy!?" shouted Mel to Tom.

Peering out of the front window of his business, Tom replied, "Yeah, he just went over to the park and sat down!" Mel repeated what Tom had just said to Perky.

"OK," Perky said. "I've got a guy tied up on a traffic stop but I'll get Jake and the Chief out there to see what's going on."

"OK," said Mel, but tell'em to hurry. I don't know how long that guy is gonna sit there. It may not be anything, but it sure looked suspicious to me!"

"Alright Mel," said Perky, "Let me get off of here, I've got another call coming in."

The next call that Perky received was from the manager at the bank, Deke Langford, reporting that the bank had just been robbed. "Perky, this is Deke Langford! We just got robbed! Two guys in ski masks! They shot up the place too!" said Deke.

"Good Lord!" replied Perky. "Is anybody hurt!?"

"No, they shot up into the ceiling! Kathy, Diane, and Brenda are scared to death they're gonna come back!" said Deke. "Get somebody over here quick please!"

"I've already got them coming. Did the power go off by any chance?" asked Perky.

"Yeah!" replied Deke. "It went off right in the middle of the robbery. How did you know!?"

"I'll tell you later," said Perky. "Did anybody happen to see what they were driving or get a tag number?"

Holding the phone away from his face, Deke yelled to everyone in the bank, "Did anybody see what they were driving!?"

One of the customers who had been in the bank said. "I did! They were in a blue Buick!" said the man. "A four-door I think! They went up toward the Shell station!" Coming back on the phone, Deke relayed that information to Perky who in turn relayed it on the radio to the officer and the Chief who were already responding.

Chief Grady Wilson and his officer Jake Turner were racing to the area. Grady came across the radio and told Jake to not go directly to the bank, but instead, to start searching west of town for the car the witness in the bank had described to Perky. The Chief went straight to the city park behind the bank.

As the Chief came around the corner, Charlie Fagin saw the Chief's marked police car, jumped to his feet and started running. Chief Wilson's patrol car came to a screeching halt on the roadway right next to the park bench where Charlie had been sitting.

The Chief jumped out of his car and started chasing Charlie across the park. In high school, Chief Wilson had been the star of the track team. "There's no way this summbitch's gonna out run me!" he thought to himself as he chased after Charlie on foot.

Once across the street from the park, Grady chased Charlie down the sidewalk. Both men were running as fast as their feet would carry them past the storefronts. Suddenly, Charlie remembered that he had a revolver in his coat pocket. In a desperate attempt to get away, he reached in and wrapped his right hand around the grip of the gun and pulled it clear of the jacket. While still running, Charlie, looking back at his pursuer aimed the pistol in Grady's direction!

There was a good possibility that Charlie would have hit the Chief with a bullet had he had time to fire. But just as Charlie was pointing the gun, he ran in front of Mason's Furniture. Mel, who had been watching the chase the whole time, swung the glass door open and Charlie crashed into it. The glass shattered and although Charlie never lost consciousness, he fell to the ground dazed and seeing stars from his unexpected impact with the door.

The gun he had been carrying skittered across the sidewalk next to the curb. Charlie was bleeding from a large gash on the side of his head caused by his surprise collision with the door in front of the furniture store.

Grady covered ground quickly and got to him before Charlie even realized what had happened. Grady handcuffed him, jerked him up to his feet, and began walking him back to his police car. As they walked, both men were breathing heavily. He paused only briefly to retrieve the handgun that Charlie had been carrying. Once at the patrol car, Grady searched Charlie and found a screwdriver and a pair of wire cutters in his left jacket pocket.

Watching this all unfold; Tom wasn't even mad at Mel for the broken door. He was just happy that the bad guy had been captured. All the excitement was worth way more than it was going to cost to replace the glass door. They chuckled about helping the police bag the bad guy and patted each other on the back while watching the Chief search the suspect.

Meanwhile, Officer Jake Turner was coming up empty on his search for any blue Buicks in the area. Figuring that the suspects were already way out of his jurisdiction by now, Jake returned to the bank and started taking down information for his report and speaking with the witnesses. Another officer, Louis Mimms, who had been out on a traffic stop with a yellow Mustang heard all this activity going on over his radio and also responded to the bank.

Grady drove around the bank to the front door and left Charlie locked in the cage in the back seat. He went inside and directed Jake and Louis on a few details that they needed to take care of. "You and Louis be sure to get all the customers names and have them all write out statements," ordered Grady. "Be sure to keep everybody over there in the lobby's seating area too!" continued Grady. "Our perps may have left us some fingerprints behind."

"Is that one of the robbers you got out there in your car?" asked Louis.

"I ain't sure yet. Probably." said Grady. "He was definitely up to no good. He had a gun too! You boys get to work here on these witnesses. Don't let anybody come in here or leave. I'm gonna take this shithead down to the jail and let him cool his jets while I call the FBI. If y'all need anything or have any questions, gimme a call at the PD."

With that, Grady left and took Charlie down to the police department.

During the ride, Charlie said, "Hey!"

Grady ignored him.

"Hey!" Charlie repeated a little louder. "These cuffs are too tight and my damn head is bleeding!"

"Oh boo-hoo! I'm all broken up over that!" Grady said sarcastically.

Charlie asked, "What did I do anyway!? Why am I under arrest!?"

The Chief continued driving and responded, "Well, first of all you made me run. I don't like to run. I used to like to run. But I don't like to run anymore! Especially when I'm wearing cowboy boots!" said Grady. "You also aimed a damn gun at me and that thoroughly pissed me off!" He continued, "Plus, I'm pretty damn sure you had something to do with that bank robbery back there."

Charlie responded, "I didn't do nothing. I don't know nothing about no bank robbery! You ain't got shit on me!"

"Well, we'll see about that," responded Grady.

In just a few moments, Grady pulled up in the sally-port of the police department and led Charlie inside. They walked down the hallway to the holding cells. Grady opened one of the cell doors and un-handcuffed Charlie.

"Inside!" ordered Grady.

Charlie, rubbing the indentions on his wrists the tight handcuffs had caused, stepped inside the holding cell. As Grady turned the key securing the door, Charlie turned around and asked, "How long am I gonna be in here?"

"A while I would imagine," came Grady's response as he put his handcuffs back in their holster on his duty belt. "If I were you, I'd get comfortable." Grady grabbed a roll of paper towels off of the counter they used to fingerprint arrestees. Pushing the roll through the bars, Grady said, "Here. Use these to sop of some of that blood on your noggin! Don't be bleeding all over my clean holding cell!"

Grady left the prisoner to tend his own head wound and ponder the error of his ways. He went to his office and sat down in his well-worn dark coffee-brown leather desk chair. Pushing the intercom button, he said, "Perky, get me the number to the FBI up in Indianapolis please."

"You got it Chief!" responded Perky.

CHAPTER 20
A TALKING FISH ON ICE

Indianapolis Indiana – January 12, 1973

FBI Agent Richard Sullivan received Chief Grady Wilson's call around 11:20 AM. After speaking briefly with him on the phone, Sullivan called his two best men, Agents Andrew Nelson and Daniel Foster and told them, "Get on the road to Fairmount. They've had a bank robbery and sounds like they may have one of the perps in custody," said Sullivan.

Andy and Dan drove the seventy minutes to get there. Their drive seemed to go by quickly as they talked shop and NASCAR along the way.

Once at the bank, they met with Officer Jake Turner. Jake filled them in on what they had so far. He pointed out the tellers, bank manager, and customers who were still there waiting to be interviewed. He showed them an area at the

Teller's window where one of the robbers may have placed his hand and he pointed out the bullet holes in the ceiling of the bank.

"Our supervisor mentioned you guys have a suspect in custody?" inquired Dan.

"Yes!" replied Jake. "He's locked up in one of our holding cells down at the PD right now. He'll be there when you guys are ready to chat with him."

"Perfect!" said Andy.

Andy and Dan began interviewing the witnesses. A little later, Dan asked the bank manager, Deke Langford to show him where the surveillance video footage feeds to.

Dan and Deke went to Deke's office to retrieve the video footage of the robbery but as they entered, they both remembered that the entire building had no power. The video footage was going to have to wait. Dan asked Deke some questions about what happened and what he saw. Deke was able to supply quite a few details. Afterward, Dan asked Deke to write out his witness statement.

"I've already filled out a statement," said Deke.

"Yes sir, that was for the police department. If you don't mind, the FBI likes to get our own witness statements," responded Dan.

"Oh, OK," replied Deke as he went to work writing down what happened and what he saw.

While Deke worked on his statement, Dan contacted the power company to see if they could get a repairman out ASAP to get the electricity back on at the bank.

While Dan and Andy were conducting their investigation, the FBI's forensic team arrived for photographs and the collection of any evidence or fingerprints.

When Deke had finished writing his statement, he started to go back out to the lobby.

"Hey when you go back out there, can you ask my partner to step in here please?" asked Dan.

"Yeah, sure, no problem. said Deke. Deke went out to the lobby where he found Andy finishing up getting the witness statements from the tellers and the customers.

"Excuse me, Agent. Your partner asked me to have you come back to the office," Deke told Andy.

"OK, thanks," replied Andy who then turned and addressed the group. "If I've already talked to you and you've completed your statements, you're free to leave the bank if you need to."

Andy made his way back to Deke's office. "What's up partner?" asked Andy as he entered the room.

"Did your witnesses tell you about the bags the perps used for the money?" asked Dan.

"Yeah, yellow gym bags," replied Andy.

Dan said, "Yeah, that's what the manager told me too," Then Dan asked, "Remember that bank job we worked in Swayzee about a year ago? Yellow gym bags!"

Andy replied, "Shit! I had forgotten about that. Think it's the same guys?"

"Damn sure could be. Swayzee isn't more than thirty minutes from here. When we get back to the office, we need to pull that file!" said Dan.

"Definitely!" agreed Andy.

"Are you about finished out there?" asked Dan.

"Yeah, I think there's one lady still working on her statement. She's probably finished by now though. Did we get any decent footage?" asked Andy.

"Power's out" said Dan.

"Oh yeah, I guess it is." chuckled Andy.

"I've got the power company on the way, but who knows how long that's going to take," said Dan, "I say we go interview our guy they have down at the jail and just have forensics bring the video footage back to the office when they go back to Indy."

"Sounds like a plan to me!" said Andy.

Both Agents walked back out and collected the statements and other paperwork and drove the short drive to the Fairmount Police Department. As they arrived, they were greeted in the lobby by Chief Grady Wilson.

"Howdy boys! You fellas look like Feds to me!" joked Grady.

"Is it really that obvious?" laughed Dan.

Andy spoke up, "We hear you've got us a fish on ice down here."

"Yes sir, that's a fact!" Grady went on to fill in Andy and Dan on his interaction with the prisoner, Charlie Fagin, and about the electrical meter being removed from the service box on the back of the bank during the robbery.

After the briefing, the three men walked down the dark wood paneled walls and terrazzo floored hallway of the police department. "Here's our little interview room. If you fellas want to wait in here, I'll go get the guest of dis-honor," said Grady.

Dan and Andy chuckled. "Works for us!" replied Dan.

Dan and Andy waited in the interview room and discussed more with each other about what the witnesses had told them. Within just a few minutes, Grady led Charlie in in handcuffs and said, "Here he is fellas. This is Mr. Charles Fagin. If you guys need anything from me, just pick up the phone there in the hallway and hit 7-2-2. That rings straight to my office."

"OK," replied Dan. "We appreciate it!"

Andy pushed the tape recorder toward Charlie and hit the record button. "Mr. Fagin. My name is FBI Agent Andrew Nelson and sitting beside me is FBI Agent Daniel Foster. Before we get started, I need to read something to you here. You have the right to remain silent. Anything you say can and will be used against you in a court of law. You have a right to an attorney. If you cannot afford an attorney, one will be appointed for you. Do you understand these rights as I've read them to you?"

Charlie nodded yes.

"I need you to answer verbally for the tape recorder please. Do you understand your rights?"

Charlie responded, "Yeah, I understand."

Andy continued, "Having your rights in mind, would you like to answer some questions we have for you?"

"Depends on what you wanna know." said Charlie.

"What is your full name for the record?" asked Andy.

"Charles Edward Fagin." he replied.

"And what is your date of birth sir?" asked Andy.

"March 2nd 19 and 41." said Charlie.

"Charlie where do you live? asked Andy.

"Right now I live in Alcoa, Tennessee," replied Charlie.

"Alright," said Andy while jotting down notes on the legal pad in his clipboard. "And what brings you to our great state of Indiana today?"

"I'm just here visiting friends," lied Charlie.

"And what are your friend's names?" asked Andy.

Charlie, looking down at the desk, didn't immediately respond. Finally, he looked up and said, "John and James."

Andy asked, "and what are John and James' last names?"

"I don't know," responded Charlie, "I haven't known them long."

"Well, where do they live," asked Andy. "Do they live here in Fairmount?"

"Yeah, but I couldn't tell you where. Like I said, I'm from Tennessee. I don't know my way around here," explained Charlie.

"Tell us what happened this morning down at the park," requested Andy gently.

"Well, I was sitting in the park waiting for my friend, uh, John, to pick me up and that cop that brought me in here came driving up to me like a bat outta hell. I got scared and I ran away! He chased me down and slapped handcuffs on me and here I sit. That's pretty much it," stated Charlie.

"OK, what about the gun Mr. Fagin?" asked Andy. "Why were you carrying a gun?"

"That gun ain't mine. That's John's gun," Charlie explained. "We were doing some target shooting this morning and I guess I just stuck it in my pocket when we were through. I was trying to hand it to that cop when I ran into a door."

"What about the screwdriver and the wire cutters Mr. Fagin. Why did you have those with you in your pocket?" inquired Andy.

"I was helping my buddy switch out the stereo in his car last night. I guess I just stuck them in my pockets and forgot about them," shared Charlie.

"Mr. Fagin, were you at any time this morning around the back of the bank across the street from the park?"

"No sir," was Charlie's response.

"So you didn't mess with the electric meter on the back of the bank building at all then?" probed Andy.

Again, Charlie's response was, "No sir."

About that time, Dan suddenly and abruptly stood up and loudly slammed a clipboard he had been writing notes on onto the table. "You're full of shit Fagin! You know damn good and well you took that meter off the bank so the alarm wouldn't go off while your buddies were in there robbing the place!"

Dan continued shouting, "You're a convict and you and your little convict buddies robbed that goddamn bank this morning didn't you!" bluffed Dan who had not even looked up Fagin's criminal background yet.

Dan angrily continued, "You want to sit here and blow smoke up our asses and we already know the truth, you fucking scumbag! You better start soul searching and come up with the truth before we charge you with the whole damn robbery motherfucker!"

Charlie's eyes widened due to the intimidation.

Dan shoved the chair backwards he had been sitting in and it tipped over and clattered to its side. He shoved the wooden table hard! It made a squealing sound as the table legs slid across the terrazzo floor. The edge of the table now pressed up tightly against Charlie's chest. Then, Dan stormed out of the room, slamming the interview room door behind him, and walked down the hall a little way.

"I apologize Mr. Fagin. I truly do. My partner's a little high strung. You do need to understand however that this is pretty serious. Up until now, you've probably only dealt with the local authorities. You're playing on a whole other level when the FBI gets involved and my partner out there wants to bury you on this thing. I mean, he told me that himself before you even came into this room. Tell you what. Sit tight and I'll go out there and see if I can calm him down a little. Do you need some water or something? How about a soda or some coffee?" asked Andy.

Slightly trembling, Charlie said, "I could drink a soda please."

"Alright," said Andy. "I'll see if I can round you up one. Just hang out here and relax and I'll be back in a bit, OK?"

"OK," replied Charlie, gently pushing the desk off of him and resting his elbows on the table and his face in his hands.

Andy turned off the tape recorder and carried it with him as he exited the room. He walked down the hall and joined Dan who was staring out of the window of the police department overlooking the parking lot.

"How was my performance?" asked Dan without taking his gaze from the parking lot.

"Academy Award quality as usual!" smiled Andy.

"What do you think about this clown?" asked Dan, turning away from the window toward Andy.

"Oh, I think he's guilty as hell!" said Andy. "Did you see how his hands were shaking in there when you started huffing and puffing? He'll crack. I think we need to get him back to Indy though. Let the weight of being in FBI custody sink in a bit."

"I agree 100 percent!" said Dan. "Let's close up shop here and give Mr. Fagin a ride to the big city. I'm sure he'll have lots to tell us once we sweat him a little more."

"OK," replied Andy. "We've still got a couple more witnesses to talk to here in town though." Looking at his notes, he continued, "A Mel Saunders and a Thomas Mason. They're the ones that reported Fagin in the park."

"Let's come back on Monday and chat with them. We've got their contact info, right?" asked Dan.

"Yeah," replied Andy. "The Chief gave it to me."

Andy and Dan drove Charlie back to the FBI field headquarters in Indianapolis. After being threatened with being charged with master-minding the whole robbery and being told that they would talk to the judge about a lighter sentence if he cooperated with the investigation, Charlie relented.

He thought to himself, "Serving a year or two is way better than twenty to thirty years in a federal prison!" It only took about three hours for Charlie to give up everything he knew about William, Jimmy, Billy Ray, and Malcolm. He told Dan and Andy everything. About the Tommy guns, the ambulance, where Jimmy and Malcolm's houses were. Everything.

Andy and Dan took their case to their supervisor, Agent Richard Sullivan's office on the 5th floor. They laid out all the information they had. They explained all the details and Charlie Fagin's involvement and his statements about his cohorts in Tennessee.

"Do you think he's being honest?" asked Sullivan. "Do you think he's being straight-up about the accomplices?"

"Oh yeah, definitely!" replied Dan. "He rolled like a tire down the track at the Indy 500 on them!"

"OK then!" said Sullivan. "Sounds like you two are going on a trip! Get Dolly Parton's autograph for me while you're down there, will you!?" All three men chuckled.

Sullivan assigned several more agents to assist on the case and ordered Dan and Andy to get with the Knoxville, Tennessee field office to coordinate surveillance, wiretaps, and search warrants.

Six hours later, Dan and Andy's jet took off from the Indianapolis International Airport bound for the McGhee Tyson Airport in Knoxville Tennessee.

The three Garrett boys had no idea what would unfold in the coming days. But one thing was certain. Their careers as bank robbers were about to be over.

CHAPTER 21
CANDY AND JW

Knoxville, Tennessee – January 13, 1973

William, like the rest of the guys, had had a big day Friday in Fairmount. Today was Saturday. The neighborhood he lived in was quiet and William was enjoying sleeping in. His sleep was abruptly ended however about 9:30 AM when his phone rang. He was still groggy and only half awake and was just going to ignore it until it stopped ringing. Suddenly, he remembered that it might be Charlie calling. He sat up in bed and fumbled for the phone's receiver on his nightstand.

"Hello?" said William.

"Hello." said the female voice on the other end of the line. "Is this William?"

"Yeah, who is this?" asked William, while holding the phone with one hand and rubbing the sleep from his eyes with the other.

"Hi William. My name is Candace Maldonado. I'm the assistant director at the Grant County Medical Examiner's Office here in Grant County. Do you know a Charles Fagin by chance?"

"Yes, I know Charlie. What's going on?" asked a concerned William.

"Sir we found your name and phone number in Mr. Fagin's wallet. I was wondering if you are related to Mr. Fagin or if you might happen to know who his next of kin might be? inquired Miss Maldonado.

"Next of kin!? asked William. "Is Charlie dead!?"

"Sir, I'm really not at liberty to say until we have notified Mr. Fagin's next of Kin." said Miss Maldanado matter-of-factly.

"So, he is dead!" stated William.

Miss Maldanado sighed a heavy sigh. "Sir, I'm not really supposed to release any details, but yes, Mr. Fagin is deceased. He was unfortunately killed yesterday while walking down Interstate 26. It was a hit-and-run collision. We believe it may have been an eighteen-wheeler. Our office is assisting the Grant County Sheriff's Office with their investigation and we desperately need to speak with his family as soon as possible." stated Miss Maldonado.

"I was just a friend ma'am. I don't think Charlie had any family left. I know he told me once that his ma and pa were both dead. I've never even heard him mention any other family members to me." replied William.

"OK. That's unfortunate. Listen, if you happen to recall any family members, can you please give us a call back?" asked Miss Maldonado. She continued, "Actually, can you please call the Grant County Sheriff's Office. They'll be the one's handling the investigation from here forward."

"I really didn't know him that well ma'am, but if I do, I'll surely call and let them know." Charlie said – while thinking to himself, "There's no way in hell I'm gonna call the cops and tie myself to Charlie and possibly the bank robbery."

"OK sir. I certainly appreciate you taking my call. Thank you very much." said Miss Maldonado. Click.

FBI Agent, Candace Maldonado hung up the phone that was sitting on the conference table. "Well, do you think he bought it?" asked Candace.

"Do I think he bought it!? Hell, I think I bought it - and I'm the one who locked Fagin in a cell myself back in Indy!" laughed Dan.

"Yeah!" said Andy. "The eighteen-wheeler thing was a nice touch!"

"Well, you boys said you wanted Mooney to think Fagin was dead and I figured what would be better than a story about him getting smooshed by a semi-truck!" smiled Candy.

"Yeah, we just didn't want him and the others getting spooked thinking he might be in custody and might be talking," said Dan. "We needed to buy us some time."

"I don't think we have to worry about him thinking Fagin's in custody!" added Andy. "That was damn convincing Candy!"

"Thank you, gentlemen! I appreciate it!" replied Candy.

"So, should we lay the rest of the case out for you now, or wait for your partner?" asked Dan.

"Jerry should be back from Nashville just about any time now." said Candy. "Probably best to wait so you don't have to repeat yourself."

"What's he got going on in Nashville?" asked Andy.

"He's up there helping out on a joint case with the Secret Service on a counterfeiting thing they had. Their perp was a guy we have had on our radar for quite a while now." Glancing into the hallway through the glass wall that surrounded the conference room, Candy said, "Speak of the Devil! Here's Jerry now!"

Agent Jerry Franklin walked into the room. He was a tall, slender man, about 6' 04" in height and looked a little like the actor, Paul Newman.

Candy began to speak, "Gentlemen, allow me to introduce my partner. This is..." Candy was abruptly interrupted by Dan.

"I know who he is!" said Dan sharply as he stood to his feet and slammed a file folder that he was holding onto the conference table. "I can't believe the Bureau wants me to work with this lanky scumbag!" said Dan angrily.

"Likewise!" said Jerry, matching Dan's disgust. "This fucker's dumber than a box of rocks and I can't even believe they let him join the FBI!"

Dan stepped closer to Jerry and said, "Say that again cocksucker and I'll knock you on your goddamn ass right in front of these other agents!"

Jerry stepped closer to Dan. Their chests were now touching. "You wanna a piece of me you son-of-a-bitch!?" asked Jerry angrily and clenching his fists.

Candy and Andy glanced at each other. The tension in the room was now at a fever pitch. Andy reached out and touched Dan's elbow to guide him back away from Jerry. Dan jerked his elbow away from Andy's grasp.

Now face to face and nose to nose Jerry and Dan peered into each other's narrowed eyes.

"You don't know who you're fucking dealing with here!" said Jerry.

Dan gritting his teeth replied, "Well I do know one thing!"

"Yeah!? What's that bitch!?" shouted Jerry.

Dan paused for just a second and said, "Your mouthwash ain't making it!" Both men fell silent, still staring at each other and both were pursing their lips.

Suddenly, they erupted in the laughter they had both been suppressing the last couple seconds. They gave each other a huge bear hug and patted each other on their backs while they embraced.

Andy and Candace's panic and concern turned into confusion. Dan released Jerry and turned around toward Candace and Andy to explain.

"Andy, this big tall drink of water is JW Franklin. Me and this big ugly galoot graduated the academy at Quantico together!" explained Dan.

"Yeah," added JW, "You know how they do everything alphabetically up there? Since he's Foster and I'm Franklin, we sat next to each other in classes, had chow together, and stood side by side when we were on the range. We were even sparring partners when we took our self-defense block!"

"Yep!" added Dan. "Our rooms in the dorm were right next to each other!"

"We did a little drinking and hell raising in our down time too!" added JW. "But don't tell the bosses. We could probably still get fired for some of the shenanigans we pulled! Right Dan!?"

"You're right about that my friend!" said Dan. Both men chuckled.

Candace and Andy both had expressions of relief on their faces – now knowing that their partners were actually old friends and weren't really going to go to blows with each other.

"Candy said your name was Jerry Franklin and that threw me for a loop because I've always called you JW. I didn't even think about it being you! What's up with the name change anyway?" asked Dan.

"Ah, you know, 'Jerry' just sounded more professional on my FBI business cards so I just went with it!" explained a grinning JW.

Dan said, "I also didn't expect you in Knoxville. I thought they sent you to Atlanta?"

"Well, they did for a few months, but a position came open here in Tennessee and I jumped on it. It's a lot closer to my family up in Lexington," explained JW. "What about you? You still in Indianapolis?"

"Yep, yep," replied Dan. "Still loving it up there! I've got a great partner here in Andy too!"

"That's great, that's great!" said JW.

"So, I see you and Andy have already met my partner, Candy," said JW.

Andy spoke up, "Yes, we have! And she's already impressed us when she called one of our perps on the phone for us a few minutes ago."

"She's amazing, that's for sure!" stated JW.

"Boys, you're gonna make me blush now. Quit it!" said Candy.

"So the office called me in Nashville and said y'all had a bank robbery you're working on?" inquired JW.

Dan replied, "Yeah, they're doing all their jobs up in our neighborhood and then coming back to Tennessee to hide out. Guess they heard Agent Franklin in Tennessee ain't shit, let's live down there!" ribbed Dan. JW laughed.

"Well what can we do to help you fellas out?" asked JW.

"We're gonna need wiretaps on all four of our guys and search warrants too." said Andy.

"We're also going to need tails on them. You guys have the man power for that?" asked Dan.

"We can handle that. Don't you think so Candy?" asked JW.

"Sure. We can cover that," Candy replied.

Dan asked "How's your federal judges around here? Are they gonna hassle us about the wiretaps?"

JW responded, "Judge Deloach is my go-to. He'll grant them."

"You seem mighty sure of that." said Andy.

"If he doesn't. I'll sic his daughter on him." said JW.

"How's that?" asked Andy.

"His daughter, Sarah, is my wife," laughed JW. Everyone chuckled.

The four FBI agents sat down around the conference table. Dan and Andy brought Candy and JW up to speed on everything they had so far and the intelligence they were able to get out of Charles Fagin. With Candy and JW's supervisor's blessing, They started enlisting other Knoxville based agents in the investigation and working out their game plan.

Although it was unspoken, Dan and Andy had a feeling that they could get this case wrapped up pretty quickly. Six or seven days maximum. They went to work on the details that would eventually bring down the Garretts and put an end to their bank robbing and crime sprees for good.

CHAPTER 22
MIDLAND MALL MAYHEM

Maryville, Tennessee - January 15, 1973

With the news of Charlie's death from Jimmy via William, Malcolm was still shocked. But by the same token, he knew he had to move on. He needed groceries. Now flush with the cash from the Fairmount job, he set out to stock his pantry. He parked in a spot at the A & P close to the store and started to get out of his car when something caught his eye.

An armored truck pulled up in front of the grocery store. An armed guard got out and went into the store while the driver remained in the truck. When Malcolm saw the guard come out of the store carrying two heavy bags of money – one in each hand, he exited his car and walked toward the entrance to the store. He timed his stride just right so that when the guard opened the back doors of the armored truck, he could glance inside.

What he saw inside made him salivate. Bags and bags of money! As he pushed his shopping cart up and down the aisles of the store, he imagined what the take would be if he actually ripped off an armored truck. It wouldn't be easy though.

Unlike a bank teller, these guys were armed. It could get messy. If this was going to be something he would do, it would require planning and a crew of at least four.

With himself, Billy Ray, Jimmy, and William now onboard, this could work! The take would be so great that none of them would ever have to commit another crime the rest of their lives – unless they just wanted to.

Malcolm finished his grocery shopping and drove home. As he was approaching his driveway, he noticed that the workers with South Central Telephone and their panel van, were still there working on the phone junction box beside the street at the back of the strip mall across from his house. They had been there for two days already.

"I wish they would get through with whatever they're doing and get those stupid cones out of the edge of the road," Malcolm thought to himself as he turned into his driveway. He didn't even suspect that those were FBI agents watching his every move and listening to his every phone conversation.

After he got his groceries put away, he sat down in his blue wing back chair and called Jimmy to tell him what he had observed at the A & P and discuss the possibility of knocking it over. They mutually decided that they would approach William and Billy Ray with the plan over dinner.

He knew that William would probably be on board – no problem. But Billy Ray was the issue. He needed a reliable wheel man that he could trust. Malcolm remembered what Billy Ray had told him in the barn that day about Fairmount being his last job. But he knew if he laid out the plan and told him how much he could earn to set him and Barbie up for the rest of their lives, there was a good chance he would participate.

Since Jimmy was calling William later, Malcolm picked up his phone and called Billy Ray. "Listen, I have something I want to talk to you about. It's kinda urgent."

"What's going on?" asked Billy Ray.

"It's kinda detailed. It's a score that'll set us all up for life! Let me buy you supper this evening and I'll tell you all about it," said Malcolm.

"I don't know man. You know how Barb is." stated Billy Ray.

"I know, I know! I remember what you said!" explained Malcolm. "But this one is different! It's a can't miss thing! You'll make more money on this than you have ever imagined! I'll explain it to you and Barbie both if I have to. Trust me, she'll let you play!"

"Well, hell! Now you've got my curiosity up!" replied Billy Ray. "But I can't tonight. My car took a shit and I'm trying to get it fixed 'cause I told Barb I'd take her out to a movie this afternoon."

"What picture show are you going to see?" inquired Malcolm.

"It's that new Steve McQueen movie called 'The Getaway,'" answered Billy Ray.

"Aw, hell! I kinda wanted to see that one too! Sounds right up our alley!" laughed Malcolm. "Listen, why don't I call

Jimmy and we meet you at the picture show and then I'll take all of you out for a nice steak supper!" invited Malcolm.

"Sure! That sounds good to me! I ain't one to turn down a free steak! That is if I can get my car fixed by then," said Billy Ray.

"Have you still got the ambulance at your house?" asked Malcolm.

"Yeah, it's still here. I haven't had time to take it back out to granny's barn yet," stated Billy Ray.

"Well, just drive that then!" said Malcolm.

"Yeah, I guess I could do that." replied Billy Ray.

"What time is the show?" asked Malcolm.

"It starts at 5:00," replied Billy Ray.

"Alright," replied Malcolm. "which theater?"

"The one at the Midland Mall," replied Billy Ray.

"OK, I've got some errands to run first, but I'll meet you there," said Malcolm.

"Okie dokie," replied Billy Ray as he hung up the phone.

Malcolm immediately called Jimmy back and told him about the movie and dinner plans. He told Jimmy to call William back and see if he wanted to meet up at the theater and then have supper so that Malcolm could lay out the armored car job to everyone. Jimmy made the call to William and everything was set.

Meanwhile in the South-Central Telephone panel van parked just down the road twenty yards in front of Malcolm's house, FBI Agent Andy Nelson and Dan Foster listened to and recorded the entire conversation.

They already had a search warrant of Malcolm's house issued by the federal judge in Knoxville that his buddy and fellow FBI agent, JW, had expedited for them and were planning to execute it within the hour and start making arrests of all those involved at their various residences. But after listening to their phone conversations, they decided to execute the search warrant at Malcolm's house after he left and take the entire crew down all at once as they exited the theater later that evening.

Malcolm went out about 4:30 to meet Billy Ray and everyone at the theater. He had barely driven out of sight when Andy's lock pick entered the door knob's key hole of the front door of Malcolm's house.

They found everything. Guns, two yellow gym bags, plans for the Fairmount bank job drawn out on a piece of notebook paper. Everything. They even found most of Malcolm's share of the robbery in his freezer wrapped in white butcher paper and labeled, "greens" in magic marker. They found everything except the machine guns and ski masks that were used during the robbery.

Dan surmised that another member of the crew probably had those items in their possession and one of the other FBI teams would find them when they served the search warrants at their places after they left to go to the theater. The FBI forensics team was there in minutes and started collecting all of the evidence that would later be used at trial.

The movie, about a bank robber who made a clean getaway, was scheduled to let out about 7:15. Andy and Dan along with JW and Candy and several other FBI agents helping out with the case all assembled in the parking lot of Midland

Mall at 6:30 PM. They were joined by agents from the ATF, the Blount County Sheriff's Office and Maryville Police Department. Dan and Andy directed everyone on where to position themselves and were all provided mugshots of William, Billy Ray, Jimmy, and Malcolm.

Candy and JW along with two other FBI agents and three deputies covered the rear exit doors of the theater. Andy and Dan, three other FBI agents, the two ATF agents, and several Maryville city police officers covered the parking lot and the main exit where the crew was expected to exit. Tensions were high because they knew that Malcolm and Jimmy were known to regularly carry handguns concealed on them.

The clock ticked around to 7:15. People began exiting the theater. The plan was to take them down on the side walk all at one time. It was going to be difficult with so many innocent civilians also milling about and exiting at the same time.

Soon, William, Jimmy, Billy Ray, and Malcolm emerged. Barbie had to make a pit stop at the restroom after the show. On the sidewalk, the four of them, waiting for Barbie to join them, were quickly swarmed by Maryville PD and Andy and Dan. The four men were ordered to turn around and put their hands on the wall. They all complied.

But almost as soon as his hands touched the wall, Jimmy's right hand dropped down to his waistband and he drew his .45 semi-automatic. He spun around and fired two to three rounds. One of those rounds struck Dan in the chest. Chaos erupted! Police and civilians alike were running for cover and the crew ran for the closest vehicle, Billy Ray's ambulance! They piled into the car. And Billy Ray fired up the engine and punched the gas.

Jimmy leaned out the window on the passenger side and fired several more shots until his pistol ran dry. Meanwhile, Maryville police officers were unleashing a barrage of shots at the ambulance as it sped toward the exit of the parking lot.

Another Maryville officer, Patrolman Keith Larabee who was just arriving on scene saw what was happening and heard the calls of shots fired over the radio. He was the only officer in a vehicle at that moment and was in a perfect position to block the ambulance from leaving.

Unfortunately, it beat him to the exit and turned onto the roadway that ran next to the strip mall. Officer Larabee jumped the curb in his patrol car and rammed the ambulance broadside in an effort to stop it! The ambulance was a heavy vehicle and normally an impact like that wouldn't have had much effect. However, it hit it hard enough to knock it off the road and the ambulance tumbled and rolled over twice landing upright on its wheels at the bottom of the ten-foot drop-off.

The tumble down the hill broke one of the axles of the ambulance. It wasn't going anywhere else. The crew all exited the passenger side to seek cover by the ambulance as pursuing officers got to the edge of the roadway and were all firing their weapons downward at the men behind the ambulance.

Suddenly, William remembered that the Tommy guns were still in the back of the ambulance because one of them had hit him in the head as the ambulance tumbled down the hill. Malcolm provided cover fire with his .45 pistol as William opened the back passenger side door and was able to find both Tommy guns with the drum magazines attached and only one of the stick magazines. He handed one of the Tommy guns behind him to Jimmy and he kept the other one and the stick magazine for himself. Billy Ray was the only one that was unarmed.

After climbing back out of the ambulance, William charged the rifle and crouching behind the front fender, fired a burst of machine gun fire at the officers up at the top of the hill. Andy, the ATF agents, and the officers ducked down and retreated back to avoid being struck by the automatic gunfire.

There was massive chaos and confusion, but someone said over the radio to get a few vehicles up there on the hill to use for cover. There was a lull in the gunfire while they got vehicles positioned. During that brief cease fire, William noticed the wood line behind them. He suggested that they all make a break for the woods while shooting behind them at the growing number of law enforcement officers at the top of the hill.

Malcolm advised against it because he knew that the wooded area wasn't very big. On the other side of it lied more businesses and a roadway.

"Well stay here and get fucking shot up if you want to, but I'm out of here!" shouted William, as he stood up and made a break for the woods!

Running as fast as he could go while spraying rounds haphazardly behind him, William made it about twenty feet – about half-way to the edge of the woods when he fell to the ground.

An officer's bullet had found its mark. It entered his back, clipping his spinal cord and lodged in his right lung. William didn't die immediately. He was coughing up copious amounts of blood but managed to shout back toward the crew over the pops of gunfire, "Give'em hell boys!" as he laughed and then fell silent as life begun to leave his body His arms went limp and he lay sprawled out on the snowy ground, still clutching the grip of the machine gun in his hand as he died.

What happened next isn't fully understood or explainable. Billy Ray always maintained it was carelessness. But Malcolm always contended that it was just pure rage on Jimmy's part because Jimmy had just seen the police kill his former cellmate and best friend.

Jimmy saw William's life end and as if in slow motion, he stood up and started spraying bullets toward the cadre of law enforcement officers. It was an unwise amount of time that he stood there exposed and not using the vehicle for cover.

Perhaps if he had known that Maryville police officer, Rick Heinlin, a recently returned Vietnam veteran and trained sniper was in a prone position and had his scoped .308 rifle trained on the hood area of the ambulance waiting for a target to present itself, he would've never stood up like that. But he did.

The .308 bullet entered Jimmy's forehead and made an unusually large exit wound as it came out of the back of his head. Jimmy was killed instantly. Like a tree that had been chopped at its base, Jimmy's lifeless body fell backwards into the accumulated patch of snow on the ground. Blood poured from his head wound and soon the snow around his head was a crimson red.

Billy Ray screamed, "NOOOOO!" and moved over to cradle Jimmy's head in his lap while sobbing like a child. Malcolm also cried as he hung his head and stared at the ground. The gunfire from both sides ceased.

"We're done here Billy Ray. We've gotta give up," conceded Malcolm.

"Those bastards killed Jimmy!" sobbed Billy Ray.

"I know they did brother. I know they did," replied Malcolm. "But if we don't surrender, they're going to kill us too!"

Billy Ray couldn't speak. With tears streaming down his face, he managed a slight nod toward Malcolm. Malcolm took off his green pull-over hoodie and button up shirt and then his t-shirt. He put the shirt and pull-over back on and picked up the white tank-top t-shirt and asked Billy Ray, "You ready?" Again, Billy Ray nodded while gently moving his dead brother's head from his lap and onto the ground.

Malcolm waved the white t-shirt above his head and above the top of the bullet riddled ambulance. "Hold your fire gentlemen!" came the command from Andy. The command was repeated by several other officers so that they were all on the same page. "Somebody get me a bullhorn!" said Andy.

Andy got the bullhorn handed to him and instructed Malcolm and Billy Ray to step from behind the ambulance with their hands in the air and not to make any sudden movements.

As they did so, they were slowly approached by Andy and Maryville PD officers with their pistols trained on them in case they moved. They were handcuffed and taken into custody. The Garrett boy's reign of terror had come to an end – but not without a high price. One of the ATF agents was slightly wounded during the gunfire. He survived his injury - as did an innocent civilian that was wounded when the shooting first started.

FBI Agent Dan Foster, however, died at the scene. Jimmy's first bullet he had fired back on the sidewalk in front of the theater had entered Dan's upper chest, just missing his Kevlar vest by millimeters.

Billly Ray and Malcolm had lost their criminal associate and brother, but Andy had lost his best friend and partner. He was devastated. He also cried for his loss. He had no idea how he was going to break the dreadful news to Dan's wife and three children.

CHAPTER 23
DILLINGER'S DOMAIN

Pendleton, Indiana – June 29, 1973

As the prison bus rumbled through the gates of the Indiana State Reformatory in the hot summer of 1973, the mood Malcolm was feeling was a combination of tension and trepidation. The bright sunny sky did nothing to mitigate the somber atmosphere that hung over the sprawling prison grounds.

The physical presence of the Indiana State Reformatory was imposing. Tall, gray stone walls surrounded the complex, topped with coils of razor wire that glinted ominously in the bright sunlight. The main entrance was a set of heavy iron gates, creaking as they swung open to allow the bus to pass through. The architecture, a blend of Gothic and Victorian styles, spoke to the institution's history and the severity of its purpose.

Inside the bus, Malcolm felt a knot of anxiety tightening in his stomach. As he peered out through the small, barred windows, the imposing structure of the prison loomed larger with each passing moment. Thoughts raced through his mind – the mistakes that led him here, the uncertainty of what awaited him behind those imposing walls, the fear of the unknown, and of course the death of his brother Jimmy.

But other thoughts were also racing through his mind as well as he took in his surroundings and surveyed the high walls and even higher guard towers. He thought to himself, "How can I escape this place? There's gotta be a way."

The bus came to a halt with a jolt. The bus's air brakes released a gust of air, and the heavy doors swung open. The clanging of the gates closing behind the bus echoed loudly like a final verdict, sealing Malcolm within the confines of his new reality. Uniformed guards with stern expressions ushered him and the other new arrivals off the bus.

The gravel crunched beneath their feet as each one of them stepped off the bus and onto the unforgiving grounds of the reformatory. They were marched in a single-file line toward the building – each prisoner wearing handcuffs secured by a belly chain and shackles around their ankles that limited the length of their strides.

Inside the prison, the sounds of clanging doors, distant voices, and the occasional shouts from prison inmates that had come before them added to the surreal atmosphere.

As Malcolm was led further into the heart of the reformatory, he couldn't shake the feeling that he was entering a world where time seemed to stand still, and the walls held many stories and regrets of those who had come before him. Yet, he smiled. He smiled because he was now walking in the same footsteps where his idol, John Dillinger, once tread.

John Dillinger, a notorious gangster during the Great Depression who commanded the Dillinger Gang, was well known for robbing 24 banks. Maybe more! Dillinger had been a prisoner in this very same prison between 1924 and 1933. The irony that Dillinger was also confronted by the police as he was leaving a movie theater just as Malcolm had been, was not lost on him.

After processing, and being issued his new prison clothes, Malcolm was led by two guards to his new "home." He thought to himself how cool it would be if he was assigned to the cell Dillinger once stayed in. But that wasn't meant to be.

Malcolm stepped inside the cell he was being assigned to and the guards closed the door behind him with a loud clang. The echo of the heavy metal cell door closing seemed to reverberate throughout Cell Block C.

Malcolm's new cellmate was a thin bookish looking man named, Oliver James. He sported a thin mustache like the one Clarke Gable used to wear. His short cropped dark hair was slicked down, also much like Clarke Gable. Malcolm's first encounter with him was a moment steeped in both tension and curiosity.

Malcolm measured up his new cellmate. He was a slender man sitting on the top bunk with his glasses perched on the bridge of his nose. The soft glow of the overhead light in the cell caught a glint of intelligence in his eyes as he looked up from his book. He extended a hand in greeting toward Malcolm. His demeanor was friendly and disarming.

"Hey there, I'm Oliver James," he said, his voice calm and measured.

Malcolm hesitated for a moment, the weight of the prison atmosphere still hanging heavily around him. He tentatively accepted the handshake, nodding in acknowledgment. "Malcolm," he replied, "Malcolm Garrett." Malcolm began to lower his guard a bit because of the genuine warmth in Oliver's eyes.

The cell itself was small and compact, the bare essentials of two bunks, a small desk, and a combination toilet/sink. The starkness of the surroundings contrasted sharply with the openness of Oliver's deportment. Books were neatly arranged on the desk. It was obviously Oliver's small oasis of intellect in the confined and sometimes chaotic prison.

Noticing Malcolm's glance at the books, Oliver gestured toward them and with genuine enthusiasm said, "I'm a bit of a reader. Helps pass the time, you know? Got a few good ones here if you're interested."

"Maybe later," Malcolm replied as he sat down on the bottom bunk in the cell.

"The prison's library has a nice selection as well!" added Oliver.

Malcolm's tension began to ease as they discussed life at the reformatory and what Malcolm could expect and people he should avoid. The two of them chatted for hours about their backgrounds and the decisions they made that led to them sharing a cell in Indiana together. As it turned out, Oliver was serving time for a white-collar crime, a sharp contrast to Malcolm's more turbulent background.

"So, what are you in for?" asked Malcolm.

"Well, the prosecution accused me of counterfeiting and the jury agreed and here I sit," replied Oliver.

"So, did you do it?" inquired Malcolm.

"Well," explained Oliver, "I worked for a while at a newspaper in Fort Wayne as their typesetter and graphics man. My father always said I should get into the newspaper business because I could make big money. So, I did. And he was right! I made big money. No doubt about it. It was about 1/16th of an inch too big!" Both men laughed for an extended amount of time at Oliver's joke.

"And what about you?" asked Oliver, as their laughter died down. "What did they accuse YOU of?"

"Bank robbery," replied Malcolm, "two of them!"

"Wow, two banks huh?" said Oliver, raising both eyebrows.

"Well," smiled Malcolm. "They only knew about two of them!" Both men laughed out loud again.

As they talked, Malcolm couldn't help but appreciate the irony of the situation—the contrast between the harsh exterior of the prison and the intellectual and friendly demeanor of Oliver. In the midst of confinement, a connection was forming—one that transcended the prison's walls and hinted at the possibility of friendship, understanding, and camaraderie in the unlikeliest of places.

Weeks passed and then months. It was a chilly day in mid-November on the exercise yard when Malcolm struck up a conversation with another inmate, Bobby Wellington, a recent transfer from D Block. During that conversation Malcolm was telling Bobby about how he got caught and about the big shoot out at the shopping mall.

"It was the perfect job too!" said Malcolm with pride. "We had a guy running interference for us with the cops on the other side of town and another guy cutting the power to the bank for us while me and my brothers knocked it over. It was beautiful! If it hadn't been for the one in the crew that cut the power ratting us out, my brother, Jimmy would still be alive," lamented Malcolm.

"Bet you'd like to get your hands on that mothertucker huh?" asked Bobby.

"Damn straight! We had heard the son of a bitch got himself ran over and killed by a truck!" said Malcolm. "But then, he shows up alive and well at my trial and turns state evidence on me and my brother Billy Ray!"

"Wait a minute!" said Bobby as if a lightbulb had just lit up over his head. "Where did you say this bank job was?"

"In Fairmount. Here in Indiana. Why?" inquired Malcolm.

"I knew a guy in D Block that told me he worked on a crew robbing a bank in Fairmount. Said he cut the power to the bank while his buddies did the stick-up." said Bobby.

"Can't be the same guy." said Malcolm.

"What was his name?" asked Bobby.

"Charlie, Charlie Fagin." replied Malcolm.

"THAT'S THE GUY! That's the guy over in D Block!" said Bobby. "He was like four cells down from me!

"You've gotta be shitting me!" said Malcolm in disbelief.

Malcolm couldn't believe what he was hearing! He was surprised they would put Fagin in the same prison with him, the man he had snitched on. Especially since him running his mouth to the feds got his brother Jimmy killed.

It dawned on Malcolm that the feds had intentionally put Charlie in Cell Block D while Malcolm was housed in Cell Block C. It had been done on purpose to keep them separated. Malcolm was seething.

Unfortunately Charlie being housed in an entirely separate area of the prison created a problem for Malcolm. That cell block had their own chow hall and their own recreation yard. The inmates from one building never had occasion to interact with the inmates of the other building.

Malcolm now had two goals on his mind. One was to eventually escape and the other was to teach Charlie a much-needed lesson on why one doesn't break the "Criminal Code" by ratting on an associate.

Escape was going to have to wait. First, Malcolm had to figure out a way to get to Charlie. The only shared facility that both Malcolm's cell block and Charlie's cell block used, was the infirmary.

For many nights after lights out, Malcolm laid there in the dark and ran possible scenarios through his mind. He had found out through his contact on the recreation yard that Charlie was only doing a two-year stretch for his role in the Fairmount job. Meanwhile, Malcolm was doing thirty. With Charlie scheduled for two years, he was already six months through his time. Malcolm knew he needed to act soon in case Charlie got early release for some reason.

As fate would have it, two weeks later, before Malcolm could ever get a plan together, news of a murder in the prison spread like wildfire. Ultimately, it was one of the prison guards who gave Malcolm and a few other inmates the news that the identity of the murdered prisoner was none other than Charlie Fagin.

Apparently, a disagreement about food occurred in the chow line over in Charlie's cell block. The other prisoner, a large burly man from Muncie, Indiana who was doing three life sentences for murder, had nothing to lose. He beat Charlie to death with a hammer in the woodworking shop a day after the food disagreement.

Upon hearing the news, Malcolm smiled broadly in the knowledge that the problem he had with Charlie had resolved itself - thanks to the guy, who before he was incarcerated, was nicknamed by the media, "The Muncie Maniac." Malcolm's only regret was that he wished it could have been him to swing that hammer.

Now it was time for Malcolm to turn his full attention toward the other problem at hand; successfully escaping from the confines of the maximum-security facility that is The Indiana State Reformatory.

CHAPTER 24
REDEMPTION

Indianapolis, Indiana – May 16, 1973

In the imposing federal courthouse in Indianapolis, Indiana, the trial of Billy Ray Garrett unfolded against the backdrop of a cityscape known for its towering structures and bustling urban life.

Charged with two counts of bank robbery, Billy Ray found himself at the center of a high-stakes legal battle that would test the limits of both his sanity and the justice system.

The courtroom, adorned with mahogany accents and bathed in the cold light of legal scrutiny, set the stage for the trial that would expose the intricacies of Billy Ray's criminal collaboration. Billy Ray, flanked by his defense team, faced the federal charges accusing him of being the wheel-man in the heists that rocked the small towns of Swayzee and Fairmount, Indiana.

The prosecution, armed with federal resources and a zealous determination, portrayed Billy Ray as an integral part of a criminal crew. Assistant U.S. Attorney Mary Mariotti built a case around the assertion that Billy Ray's role as the getaway driver made him a knowing and willing participant in the bank robberies orchestrated by his brothers, Jimmy Lee and Malcolm.

The courtroom drama unfolded as the prosecution presented a meticulously crafted narrative, blending surveillance footage, physical and forensic evidence, and witness testimonies from bank tellers, witnesses, and of course Charlie Fagin – the former member of Billy Ray's crew that made a sweetheart deal with the prosecution to testify against his associates in exchange for a much lighter sentence. The alleged precision with which the Garrett brothers executed their crimes became a focal point, captivating the attention of jurors and spectators alike.

The media circus surrounding the case was intense. Just as it would be at Malcolm's trial a month later. Journalists from local, national, and even some international outlets descended upon the courthouse, seeking to capture every nuance of the high-profile proceedings.

Newspapers, television stations, and radio channels provided extensive coverage, turning the trial into daily headlines that were voraciously consumed by the public. Reporters who attended court sessions, offered detailed accounts of the arguments presented by both the prosecution and the defense.

Editorial pieces in local newspapers explored the impact of the Garrett brothers' alleged crimes on the communities of Swayzee and Fairmount. Opinions varied, with some emphasizing the need for tough justice and others expressing sympathy for the Garrett family, portraying them as poor, abused, and uneducated country boys who had faced many challenges during their upbringing. Everyone seemed to have an opinion.

Billy Ray's defense team, led by the tenacious defense attorney Roger Douglas, fought to dismantle the prosecution's narrative. Douglas argued that his client, while present during the robberies, was coerced into participating by familial ties and an environment of intimidation. He painted a vivid picture of Billy Ray as a reluctant participant caught in the shadows of his brothers' criminal ambitions.

As the trial progressed, the tension in the courtroom reached its zenith. Witnesses offered conflicting perspectives on Billy Ray's level of involvement, and the federal prosecutor sought to demonstrate that the accused played a more conscious and calculated role than the defense suggested.

The jury, a diverse group of twelve individuals from the Indianapolis area, listened intently as both sides made their closing arguments. The fate of Billy Ray hung in the balance, and the echoes of shouting people from the small towns of Swayzee and Fairmount reverberated through the hallowed halls and front lawn of the federal courthouse.

The trial's conclusion would not only determine Billy Ray's future but also leave an indelible mark on the legal landscape of Indianapolis, shaping perceptions of justice, loyalty, and the thin line that separates compliance from coercion in the world of criminal alliances.

After their lengthy deliberations, the jury members took their seats in the jury box. The hushed murmurs in the courtroom subsided as all eyes turned toward them. Judge JJ Staton, the strait-laced figure of authority presiding over the case, observed the proceedings with a stoic demeanor.

Billy Ray, flanked by his court appointed defense team and surrounded by the tension in the air, awaited the moment that would determine his future.

"Ladies and gentlemen of the jury, have you reached a verdict?" asked Judge Staton.

"Yes we have your honor," replied the foreman.

"Please stand sir for the reading of the verdict to the court," instructed Judge Staton.

The jury foreman, a metered and well composed individual chosen to represent the group, stood up. The weight of responsibility was evident in his expression as he addressed the court. The room fell silent as the foreman read the verdict, each word echoing with significance.

"Regarding Federal indictment case number 237466, on count one of armed robbery, we, the jury, find the defendant, Billy Ray Garrett, guilty."

A loud murmur circulated around the courtroom. Judge

Staton irritated by the interruption banged his gavel and demanded silence from the spectators and order in the courtroom. "Please continue with the verdict Mr. foreman," requested Judge Staton.

The foreman continued, "On federal indictment case number 237467, count two of armed robbery, we, the jury, find the defendant, Billy Ray Garrett, guilty."

The pronouncement hung in the air, and the entire courtroom seemed to collectively exhale as the gravity of the verdict sunk in. Billy Ray's expression remained stoic, but the emotions in the room were palpable. Supporters of the Garrett family slowly shook their heads in disbelief, while those seeking justice felt a sense of victory and a measure of closure.

The judge acknowledged the verdict and thanked the jury for their service. As the jury filed out, the impact of their decision rippled through the courtroom. Billy Ray Garrett, now a federal convict, faced an uncertain future. The families of those affected by the bank robberies celebrated with a sense of justice served.

Billy Ray, once the central figure in a notorious double bank robbery trial, found himself shackled, his hands cuffed as a sobering symbol of his conviction. The echoes of the guilty verdict still resonated as he was led from the courtroom by stern-faced federal marshals. The gravity of the situation weighed heavily on him. He cast his gaze downward as he was escorted from the courtroom.

The courtroom's somber atmosphere extended to the sentencing a few months later, as Judge Staton, with a stern voice, articulated the consequences of his actions. Sentenced to 25 years for his role as the wheel-man in the bank robberies, Billy Ray faced the harsh reality of a federal penitentiary.

He was transported to the Oakdale Federal Prison in Allen Parish, Louisiana where Billy Ray encountered a stark and challenging environment. Over the years behind the prison walls, he began a personal journey of introspection and redemption. It was within the confines of the Oakdale Federal Prison that he found solace in religion, embracing Christianity and discovering a newfound sense of purpose.

Over the course of two decades, Billy Ray transformed his life. He proudly completed his education while in the confines of the prison, obtaining his high school equivalency certificate and even went on to take some college courses.

His commitment to faith became a guiding light, a source of strength that allowed him to navigate the complexities of prison life. It gave him a more cheerful outlook on life. Even when his case came up for appeal and he lost, he accepted it with aplomb.

Billy Ray's journey to finding Jesus within the confines of the prison was a transformation sparked by a series of profound events, one of which was a particularly harrowing incident that shook him to his core.

It was a normal day in the prison when Billy Ray witnessed a violent altercation. In the stark and cold tiled walls of the prison showers, he saw another inmate fall victim to a brutal shanking, a stark reminder of the perilous nature of prison life.

That gruesome scene along with seeing his brother Jimmy killed in front of him left an indelible mark on Billy Ray's psyche. It prompted him to finally confront the harsh realities of the world he had become a part of. The incident that day in the showers became yet another catalyst for his soul-searching and a turning point in his life.

As he delved deeper into the teachings of Christianity, Billy

Ray found a source of hope and redemption that transcended the confines of his cell. The message of transformation resonated with him, offering a glimmer of light in the darkness that had defined much of his life.

In the quiet moments of introspection, Billy Ray began to pray earnestly, seeking guidance and forgiveness. The process of coming to Jesus became a personal and spiritual journey, one that offered him a path to redemption and a chance to reconcile with his troubled past.

The prison chapel became a sanctuary where Billy Ray often sought spiritual refuge from the depressing surroundings of the paint chipped prison walls. He immersed himself in the Bible, finding comfort in its teachings and drawing strength from the idea that even in the depths of despair, one could find salvation.

This profound shift in perspective ultimately shaped the remainder of Billy Ray's life. His commitment to living a righteous and purposeful existence was deeply intertwined with his faith, and the memory of that fateful day in the prison showers served as a constant reminder of the purpose of his path. He became a respected figure within the prison population, known for his transformation and the unwavering faith that sustained him.

His release, after only seventeen years of his twenty-five-year sentence, marked the culmination of his remarkable journey. Billy Ray emerged from prison with a determination to live a life of purpose and rectitude.

Settling in Lafayette, Louisiana upon his release, Billy Ray secured a legitimate job with Arwine Enterprises, a major road and bridge construction company. Operating heavy machinery, he embraced the opportunity to contribute positively to society. Billy Ray always loved to drive anything with wheels. The big road machinery wasn't much different. A bit slower, but it had wheels none the less.

As he continued to work hard and prove his value to the company, he reconnected with his true love, Barbie, who had stood by him throughout his trial and entire period of incarceration.

They got married and their union flourished, resulting in a family that brought joy and fulfillment to Billy Ray's later years. Four children and eight grandchildren became the bedrock of his reformed life. Through the lens of his faith, he navigated the challenges of reintegration into society with both grace and resilience.

Remarkably, Billy Ray remained true to his commitment to never commit another crime for the rest of his life. His career at Arwine Enterprises spanned 26 years and he climbed the ranks within the company to retire as a supervisor. It was a testament to his work ethic and determination to lead an honest life.

In his golden years, he regretted not ever seeing his brother Malcolm again. He could have made an effort to visit him, but he didn't. They did however exchange a few letters over the years. Perhaps in the back of his mind, he thought that if he ever connected with Malcolm face to face, he would be drug away from the new life he had built and plunged back into the criminal chaos that Malcolm seemed to generate his entire life.

Upon retirement, he reflected on the journey that had taken him from a life of crime to one of purpose and contribution. Tragically, in 2021, Billy Ray Garrett suddenly passed away from heart failure at the age of seventy-eight while fishing with one of his grandsons on the banks of Spanish Lake.

His story serves as a testament to the power of redemption, transformation, and a meaningful and righteous existence.

CHAPTER 25
THE COVERED WAGON ESCAPE

Pendleton, Indiana – December 2, 1975

It had been three years since Malcolm first set foot on the grounds of the Indiana State Reformatory.

Violence was commonplace among inmates. If you were a snitch or ran your mouth too much or to the wrong person, eventually, somebody was going to get to you and either beat the hell out of you or murder you with a prison shank. Like all typical prisoners, Malcolm wanted out of this environment.

With escaping the facility a daily thought that crossed his mind, he had almost resigned himself to the idea that he was never going to be able to break out. He had examined all of the exits accessible to him as an inmate. None of them presented themselves as a weakness to him.

If there was one thing for certain, it was that the warden and the guards at the prison ran an incredibly tight ship and they did everything by the book!

Then, on this day, December 2nd, 1975, the thought occurred to Malcolm that them doing everything "by the book" could possibly be the weak link in the chain that he had been seeking all this time.

The fact that the guards blindly followed directions and orders, could well be his ticket out of there!

He began to form his plan. Malcolm noticed how the staff at the reformatory would mindlessly obey orders as they came down from higher ups. On this day while in his capacity as a trustee inmate, Malcolm was emptying the trash and sweeping the floor in one of the administrative offices. He noticed an official-looking form on one of the desks and that sparked his idea to use the soul-crushing weight of the prison bureaucracy in his own favor.

Since escaping by going over the wall, tunneling under the wall, or escaping in a delivery truck was as cliché as it was unlikely, he decided the best way to get out was to walk out the front door – similar to what he had done at the Brushy Mountain Prison back in Tennessee. His plan was to create some impressive documents ordering his immediate release from custody, and hope that like all orders, those orders would be promptly obeyed and executed.

Having a limited education though presented a problem with this plan. If the document was going to be worded professionally and look official, he was going to need help to make that happen. And he had the most perfect helper in mind. Oliver James, his counterfeiting, well read, intelligent friend and cellmate!

That night, Malcolm explained his plan to Oliver. He even suggested that Oliver forge a second document and they BOTH walk out of there.

"I appreciate you thinking about me Malcolm, I really do," said Oliver. "But I've only got three more years in here. If I get caught, they'll add twenty more."

"Well, the whole idea is to not get caught," said Malcolm.

"I understand that," replied Oliver, "but eventually, they're going to realize that the document isn't official and they'll hunt us down. They'll search hither and yon for us."

"So, are you going to do it or not?" asked Malcolm a bit more forcefully.

"Malcolm, you have been a great friend to me in here. I couldn't have asked for a better cellmate to spend my sentence with. I'll tell you what, I'll help you, but I'm not going to go with you. Fair enough?" asked Oliver.

"Well, I wish you would reconsider, but if you want to stay and serve out your time, I understand," said Malcolm.

"One more thing," said Oliver, "if you happen to get caught, you made the document yourself without my help. OK?"

"Of course!" said Malcolm. "That goes without saying!"

The document that Malcolm needed forged was a judge's order to release him on a trial technicality. It's often referred to as an "Order of Release" or "Release Order." This is something that occurs when a judge – after a trial - determines that there was a procedural or legal error during the trial that impacts the defendant's rights and, as a result, the judge orders the release of the prisoner.

Considering their rather limited access to materials they were allowed to have; Malcolm and Oliver's arts and craft project was to be all the more impressive. The official looking "Immediate Order of Release" document had to have signatures that matched those of an Indianapolis federal court judge and the state attorney as well. The most difficult part of the document for Oliver to forge was going to be by far, the gold foil seal of the court.

A week went by. Oliver had researched in the law books section of the prison library the exact wording of the documents he needed. He carefully crafted and typed the cover letter, the release order, and the envelope but was stymied by the reproduction of a legitimate looking gold foil court seal for the bottom of the order. He voiced his concern and an idea to resolve it to Malcolm that night in their cell.

"The seal is the trickiest part," said Oliver. "I think I've figured out how to do it though using some aluminum foil from the kitchen. I know a guy that works in there and he can get me a sheet. I read in a science book in the prison library about a method for putting a gold color on aluminum material. It will require us to place the aluminum material on which an anode oxidation film is prepared in a specific modified solution for dipping to enable the porous surface of the oxidation film to be absorbed with a layer of substances which can then realize the chemical reaction and can promote an electrochemical reaction.

And then we dip our conducting electrolytic treated metal into an acidic solution of coloring additive to obtain the gold-colored film layer to produce a pure and even color. Of course, after the aluminum is prepared, I'll have to figure out a way to emboss it with the court seal." Oliver's comments trailed off as he was in deep thought about the details of the process that was ahead of him.

Malcolm sat blankly staring at Oliver and finally spoke up and said, "I have no idea what the fuck you just said. The only part I got was that you need to duplicate the court's seal. Is that right?" asked Malcolm.

"Well, yes, in a nutshell," said Oliver.

"Why don't we just steal one from a real document?" asked Malcolm. "Couldn't you just glue it on to our document?"

"Well, yes, I suppose that would work equally as well," said Oliver.

"Then don't worry about it. I'll take care of that part." said Malcolm.

With Malcolm in the position as a prison trustee, he had weekly access to the administrative offices and of course, their filing cabinets when he would go in to clean.

The approaching occasion of his next cleaning assignment fueled Malcolm's determination to pilfer the crucial document from the filing cabinet containing the requisite court seal. Yet, the path to his illicit goal lay strewn with obstacles. In the confined space of the office, a constant presence loomed — be it a vigilant guard, an observant secretary, or, more often than not, both. The act of opening the filing cabinets and rifling through their contents risked exposure. A distraction, a well-choreographed diversion, became an imperative necessity in this intricate dance of subterfuge.

Two days elapsed, and the decisive moment arrived! With purposeful determination, Malcolm maneuvered his cleaning supply cart into the office, mirroring the routine of weeks past.

If a guard had been present, he would have spun a tale of an imminent inmate brawl in the common area, orchestrating a strategic diversion. Fortunately, destiny favored him on this particular day — no guard stood sentinel in the office. Instead, one lingered down the hall, engaged in a flirtatious exchange with a secretary who had captured his affections.

Meanwhile, the secretary within Malcolm's purview remained engrossed in her work, the rhythmic clatter of her typewriter served as the auditory backdrop to Malcolm's unfolding clandestine operation.

Malcolm embarked on the charade of dusting, weaving through the office until he reached her desk. Executing his plan with calculated precision, he purposely sent her coffee cup tumbling into her lap with a deft sweep of the feather duster.

Her response unfolded exactly as Malcolm had anticipated. Leaping to her feet, she hastened to the ladies' room in an attempt to salvage her skirt from the coffee stain. Meanwhile, Malcolm, feigning remorse, uttered multiple apologies for his seemingly careless actions, his contrition a carefully crafted facade concealing the true intent behind his orchestrated disturbance.

As soon as the restroom door clicked shut behind her, Malcolm sprang into action. Swift and calculated, he opened the filing cabinet drawer. He navigated through the labyrinth of documents until he laid eyes on one adorned with the court's seal. Doubt crept in, and to make up for his uncertainty, Malcolm snatched three additional documents, each bearing a seal, concealing them beneath his T-shirt, discreetly tucked into the front of his pants.

The filing cabinet closed with a muted click just as the secretary reemerged. Oblivious to the covert maneuvering, she resumed her place at the desk, reprimanding Malcolm for his apparent carelessness, all while the stolen documents lay concealed beneath his outwardly contrite exterior.

"Good!" Malcolm thought to himself. "She has no clue that I just lifted the documents!"

Malcolm finished his work for the day and returned to his cell. He made sure that no guards were in the vicinity before removing the documents from the front of his pants and showing them to Oliver.

"Perfect!" Oliver said. He continued, "We need to get some scissors to cut the seal out."

"Scissors are going to be hard to get. What about a razor blade?" asked Malcolm.

"Yes, that would be even better!" responded Oliver.

"OK. Hide these and I'll make us a razor shank tonight. It'll probably be the first shank ever made in a prison that wasn't built with the intent of cutting a motherfucker," smiled

Malcolm as he handed the documents with the gold seals to Oliver.

Oliver put the documents inside one of his books and later that night, Malcolm went to work constructing a modern-day hobby knife using fire from a match to melt together a toothbrush and the blade from a disposable shaving razor. The result was ideal and worked perfectly for Oliver's needs.

By December 15th, everything was ready to go. But there were two other hurdles to overcome. All outgoing mail was rubber stamped "Mailed From The Indiana State Reformatory" somewhere on the envelope. Plus, the post office cancellation on the stamp would say Pendleton Indiana instead of Indianapolis, Indiana where the federal court was located.

Even if the staff stamped it in the out-going mail with that stamp and overlooked the fact it was addressed to the warden, when it arrived, it would have that rubber stamp on it and the stamp would be cancelled locally. Someone would surely notice and the jig would be up. They had to figure out a way to smuggle the letter out and have someone mail it to the reformatory from the outside – preferably, from Indianapolis.

That task would be difficult. Unlike other jails and prisons Malcolm had stayed in, this facility didn't allow inmates and visitors to come into contact with each other. Visitation was facilitated at a row of booth windows and there were phones on the booth walls so visitors and inmates could hear each other.

Nestled in the stillness of the prison night, Malcolm found solace in the contemplative cocoon of his bunk. Here was the place and time he unraveled the threads of his thoughts, weaving intricate solutions to the problems that burdened his mind.

On this particular night, Malcolm birthed a diabolical plan, a solution to the quandary of mailing the crucial document. "Why stop at forging the cover letter and document?" his mind whispered, urging him to extend the deceit to the cancelled stamp on the envelope itself. A wicked notion took shape. He would need to slip the manipulated letter into the warden's office amidst his incoming mail.

As the first light of morning pierced the prison's gloom, Malcolm eagerly shared his Machiavellian brainchild with his cellmate. Oliver, equally captivated by the sinister brilliance of the idea, swiftly transformed the envelope to resemble a dispatch from an Indianapolis post office, completing the transformation within a mere two hours.

The following day, Malcolm came up with an even better plan. Instead of mixing the letter in with the warden's mail, his thought was to put it beside a desk or in a crevice, a place in the mailroom where when someone found it, they would believe it had accidentally been misplaced by someone and put it in the warden's incoming mail themselves. That way, they wouldn't have to go anywhere near the warden's office.

The scheme worked perfectly. The next day, the warden's secretary opened the letter herself. Because of the importance of the letter and document enclosed, instead of putting it in the warden's inbox, she walked it directly into his office and hand delivered the letter and its contents to him.

The warden, peering over his glasses read the letter intently and immediately summoned the captain of the guards. He instructed the captain to immediately prepare inmate Malcolm Garrett for release under an order from the federal judge in Indianapolis.

On the afternoon of December 18th, a guard came to Malcolm's cell with good news. "Garrett!" said the guard to get Malcolm's attention. "I've got some good news for you! You're being released first thing tomorrow morning."

Malcolm, feigning surprise said "WHAT! You're kidding me, right!?"

The guard replied, "Nope! The order just came down from the warden's office. Apparently, there was some sort of technical error at your trial and they're letting you go."

"That's great!" Malcolm said with a broad smile on his face.

Oliver and Malcolm hugged each other and reveled in the happy, yet expected good news. After the guard walked away, worry begun to set-in. Malcolm said to Oliver, "What if by tomorrow morning, they figure out this is all a scam!"

Oliver replied, "Well, what are they going to do to you? Put you in jail!?" The two men laughed out loud at Oliver's humor.

Malcolm spent the most sleepless night he ever had since coming to the Indiana State Reformatory. He worried that the truth would be discovered and that all of his efforts to escape would have been in vain.

The next morning, a guard brought a cardboard box to Malcolm's cell. He opened the cell door and handed the box containing a complete set of civilian clothing to Malcolm. "Put on these clothes and if you've got any stuff you want to take with you, put it in the box," said the guard. "You're out of here in one hour."

Malcolm quickly got out of his reformatory uniform and put on the ill-fitting civilian clothes and jacket he was given. He put a few books Oliver had given him in the box along with a wooden lamp shaped like a Conestoga covered wagon he had painstakingly made in the prison wood shop for his father Al and his wife Delois.

The minutes in the hour ticked away quickly. With every passing second, Malcolm thought that his ruse would be discovered and instead of walking out the front door of the prison to freedom, he would be thrown in "the hole" by the guards. It had now been an hour and a half.

"Surely they've discovered the deception," Malcolm thought to himself.

But just then, the guard delayed by his other duties returned to Malcolm's cell and opened it up.

"Time to go Malcolm!" said the guard.

Malcolm and Oliver said their final goodbyes to each other and gave each other a manly embrace. As he stepped out of the cell, Malcolm turned back around and said to Oliver with a wink, "Thanks my friend. Thanks for everything!" Oliver a bit choked up could only manage a smile and a nod in Malcolm's direction.

With that, Malcolm was led through the reformatory and buzzed through several doors until finally, when the last door opened, Malcolm was almost blinded by the bright sun. He stepped through the door carrying his cardboard box and breathed in the smell of sweet freedom.

With the $40 given to him upon his release, Malcolm had a nice lunch and bought a bus ticket south bound. The Greyhound bus eventually opened its doors in Lake Wales, Florida, the town where his father, step-mother and some of his step-brothers lived.

Aware of the statistical reality that most escapees face apprehension within 24-48 hours of discovery, Malcolm discerned the predictable patterns of capture. He considered that most often, an escaped inmate was captured at a relative's house or behind the wheel of a stolen vehicle. Uncertain about the timeline of the revelation of his cunning forged release document, Malcolm foresaw the relentless pursuit by the FBI and federal marshals once his ruse was exposed. Determined to tilt the odds in his favor, he decided to eliminate a common vulnerability: the risk of being nabbed in a stolen vehicle.

Opting for a less conspicuous mode of transportation, Malcolm brazenly stole a bicycle. He strapped the cardboard box containing the wagon lamp in a paper bag, and pedaling along the road that passed directly in front of the Lake Wales Police Department, he orchestrated a bold move. As he cycled past the building, an officer emerged from his patrol car, strolling through the parking lot toward the building.

In a seemingly innocent gesture, Malcolm lifted his hand and waved at the officer and said, "good mornin' officer! Beautiful day isn't it!?"

The reciprocal wave from the unsuspecting officer sealed the facade of normalcy. Malcolm pedaled on, unhindered and unquestioned. The gamble seemed to pay off, and in the delicate dance of evasion, his continuing steps of freedom were taken without a shadow of suspicion. So far, his charade had unfolded flawlessly.

He rode the bicycle through town down highway 60 to Martin Road South. It was only a 12-minute bike ride. His father's home was at the end of that dead-end street. Delois Garrett was sweeping off the front porch when Malcolm came riding up.

"Hey Delois!" Malcolm said in a friendly manner.

It took her a second to recognize Malcolm. She replied with surprise "Lord have mercy! Malcolm Garrett as I live and breathe!"

"How you doin' ma'am?" asked Malcolm.

"I'm doing just fine. How are you getting along?" Before Malcolm could respond to that question, Delois fired another one at him, "Are you on the run from the law?"

"No ma'am," Malcolm lied. "They turned me loose."

"Are you sure about that?" asked Delois.

"My hand to God!" replied Malcolm while raising up his right hand. "Is Pop around?"

"Yeah, he's in the house. Come on in. But you know the rules, Malcolm. One hour and then you've gotta go," stated Delois sternly.

"Oh yes ma'am, I know, I know," replied Malcolm.

As they walked into the house, Delois said, "I heard about Jimmy. I'm sorry for your loss. It was a little hard on your daddy losing a son and all."

"Yes ma'am. I appreciate it. I sure 'nuff miss him somethin' terrible."

"I know you do," replied Delois.

They entered the living room and Al looked up from his easy chair and smiled, "Well, I'll be! Look what the cat dragged in!" said Al. Malcolm walked over and shook Al's hand and took a seat on the couch next to Al's chair.

"What brings you around?" asked Al. "You ain't on the lam are you?" he asked.

"No sir, no sir, I was just telling Delois they let me go up in Indiana. Some sort of trial mix-up or something," Malcolm said, purposely trying to be as vague as possible about the details of his release.

"Is that so?" said Al.

"Yes sir. Hey, I brought you and Delois a little early Christmas gift!" Malcolm said changing the subject and producing the paper bag containing the covered wagon lamp he had hand-made in prison.

Al and Delois examined the lamp and admired Malcolm's workmanship.

"You made this yourself?" asked Delois.

"Yes ma'am, I sure did. Made it in the woodworking shop in prison," came Malcolm's reply.

"Well, you're very talented Malcolm. It's too bad you don't put your talents to work outside of prison," sniped Delois.

"Delois!" scolded Al.

"Well, I'll leave y'all to visit. I've got things I need to do," stated Delois.

Delois went on in the kitchen to wash some dishes and do some "busy work" but mainly so she could eavesdrop on Malcolm's conversation with his father.

About an hour or so later, she re-entered the room and Malcolm knew what that meant. It was time for him to go. His relationship with his step-mother was strained.

She allowed him time to visit with his father, but at the same time, she didn't approve of Malcolm coming around her own children. He was a bad influence and she always thought his presence could present a danger to her family if the police showed up looking for him while he was at her house. Still, he somehow strangely admired that quality in her and respected her a great deal for being so diligent in protecting her children.

Malcolm said his goodbyes and left the house on Martin Road on the same bicycle that carried him there. Delois suspected he was lying about being released from prison. She knew about all of the other times Malcolm had successfully escaped prisons and jails during his lifetime.

As she had done countless times before, she waited for thirty minutes and called the sheriff's office to report that he had been there at the house. This time however, the sheriff's office didn't respond. According to their teletype, Malcolm was not listed in the system as a wanted man. At least not yet.

CHAPTER 26
THE KEYS TO INCARCERATION

Maryville, Tennessee – December 29, 1975

Gary, Carl, and Dale's two twin brothers, Ronnie and Roger had stopped in at Barkley's Barbershop for a haircut before returning to the Airforce base they were both assigned to. Both wearing their Airforce uniforms, they were due back from their Christmas break on Wednesday and wanted to look sharp. Happy with their fresh new cuts, they tipped Barkley, told him to say hello to Dottie for them, and went on their merry way.

Just after they left, two men in nice suits came in for haircuts. It was right at the end of Barkley's day so these two gentlemen were going to be Barkley's last clients for the day.

One of the men sat down in the waiting area and the other sat down in Barkley's barber's chair. The men were pleasant and while cutting the first man's hair, Barkley struck up a friendly conversation with them.

"You boys from here in Maryville?" asked Barkley. "I don't think I've ever seen you here in the shop before."

"No sir, we're both from Knoxville," replied the man getting his hair cut.

"Knoxville!? Wow! Maryville is a long drive just to get a haircut. Are y'all in town for the holidays?" asked Barkley.

"No," said the one waiting for a haircut. "We're actually here on business."

"Oh is that so?" responded Barkley. "What sorta business are you fellas in?"

The man waiting paused and glanced at the other man sitting in the barber's chair. The man in the barber's chair gave him a nod as if to say, "It's OK to tell him."

The man waiting said, "actually were both special agents with the FBI."

"FBI!" Barkley exclaimed with surprise. "So, you fellas are here in little ole Maryville workin' on a big case huh!?"

The agent getting his haircut spoke up and said, "Actually we're here looking for an escaped convict. A bank robber." We've been tailing those two boys that were in here all day."

Barkley surprised replied, "Are you talking about those two servicemen that just left?"

"Yep," said the agent waiting for his turn in the barber's chair. "Their half-brother is the convict and we were hoping maybe they might lead us to him, but it looks like it's a dead end."

"So, when we saw them come in here, we decided to terminate the tail and get us some haircuts too!" laughed the agent getting his hair cut.

Barkley continued to chat with the agents about sports, the weather, and a few other topics while finishing up both of the men's haircuts. He closed up his barbershop for the evening and drove home.

When Barkley walked in the door, his perky wife, Dottie, greeted him. "Hey honey! How was your day!?" she asked.

"It was ok until the last two customers came in," he responded, "then it was just strange."

"Strange how?" Dottie asked.

"The last two fellas that came in the shop were FBI agents," said Barkley. "They were looking for an escaped convict and had been following your cousins, Ronnie and Roger Garrett. Said they were hoping they would lead them to their convict."

"Wow!" responded Dottie. "Why were they at your shop looking for them?"

"Roger and Ronnie had just left before they came in. They said they were following them and thought it was a dead end and then just decided on a whim I guess to get haircuts themselves," said Barkley.

"So, they didn't know you were married to Roger and Ronnie's cousin?" asked Dottie.

"Apparently not. And I didn't volunteer that information either," replied Barkley.

Naturally word got back to the twins that they had been followed. It wasn't the FBI agent's fault that the twins heard about it – not that it even mattered to the twins. The agents didn't know the town was filled with Garretts. One couldn't swing a dead cat by the tail in the Maryville area without hitting a Garrett or a relative of a Garrett.

Meanwhile, in Auburndale Florida, Gary Garrett was on patrol at his new agency, The Auburndale Police Department. He had left the small department in Frostproof for the larger town.

Gary's dispatcher called him on the radio and told him to return to the station to meet with some visitors. When Gary arrived, he was met by two more FBI agents who worked out of the Tampa, Florida office.

"Is there a private place we can speak?" one of the agents asked.

"Sure," said Gary as he led them to the PD's interview room.

The agents questioned Gary for about twenty minutes. They asked if he had had any contact with Malcolm. They asked if he had heard from Malcolm on the phone. They asked if Gary had any idea where they should look for Malcolm. Their questioning was friendly and they didn't use an accusatory tone, but unfortunately, Gary wasn't of much help to them.

He did tell them that Malcolm had stopped in at his parent's house in Lake Wales a week and a half or two weeks ago with a wooden covered wagon lamp he had made in prison as a gift. But that he didn't stay long and that his mother, Delois had called the sheriff's office on Malcolm shortly after he had left.

"Yep, we're aware of all that," said one of the agents. "Is there anything else you can think of that might help us find him?"

"I'm sorry," replied Gary. "I can't think of anything. But if I do, I'll definitely give you guys a call. And if he shows up here in Auburndale, I'll arrest him myself!"

The three men chuckled and one of the agents handed Gary his business card and thanked him for his time. The agents then left the police department to continue their work.

Those same agents had stopped by Al and Delois' house in Lake Wales before going to see Gary in Auburndale. They heard basically the same story that Gary had shared with them. Still, a surveillance team from the U.S. Marshal's Office watched the parent's house 24 hours per day where Dale still lived with his parents.

Carl Garrett, living on his own and working on construction sites as an electrician was also surveilled and questioned by federal agents on one of his job sites in the nationwide man-hunt for Malcolm.

Malcolm, now a notorious felon with a penchant for being consistently armed and dangerous, was one of America's most wanted fugitives. He had successfully escaped and evaded authorities in Indiana using his cunning "fake documents" method that had infuriated authorities and they were determined to return him to custody. The urgency to apprehend him permeated the air all the way from Indiana to Tennessee to Florida, as officials craved his capture with an insatiable intensity.

Key West, Florida – December 31, 1975

Malcolm knew that federal agents would be looking for him and that staying around his father's place in Lake Wales was just asking to be nabbed and sent back to prison. He decided that he needed to get away from the area. His motives were selfish ones. He didn't seem to care about the danger his mere presence posed to his father and his family. His reason for leaving was purely for self-preservation.

But where to go? He thought about returning to Tennessee but he knew the heat there would also be intense. The nation's bicentennial celebration was taking place and if he couldn't be with family or in the hills of his beloved Tennessee, he decided to ring in the new year in a tropical paradise – Key West, Florida.

He pulled into town about 4:00 PM and was lucky enough to rent himself a motel room right on the beach close to Mallory Square that had had a last-minute cancelation. He used money to pay for it that he got on the way there when he robbed a convenience store in Fort Lauderdale. The whole town was buzzing with excitement about the special new year that was arriving at midnight!

American flags waved from every building on Duval Street. Red white and blue patriotic buntings adorned just about every deck facing the street. People were everywhere! This was definitely out of Malcolm's normal comfort zone, but what better place to hide out from authorities than a sun-soaked beach in Key West sipping on tropical rum drinks, watching the sun set, and joining the big crowds on Duval Street later that night in welcoming in 1976?

By the time Malcolm woke from his long rum-induced nap on the beach and walked to his motel room for a quick shower, it was already 9:00 PM. He walked out on Duval Street which was heavily crowded with revelers. People were drinking and dancing in the street, setting off fireworks, and some of the women were walking around bare breasted! "This is my kind of town!" Malcolm thought to himself.

Malcolm landed himself a stool in the iconic Key West bar, Sloppy Joes. He spent hours there meeting new friends, laughing, and drinking alcohol. A lot of alcohol. Shortly after midnight, the police announced that they were closing up all of the bars early in the interest of crowd safety. The crowd strongly disagreed with the police's plan and began to protest the decision. Malcolm, caught up in the moment and emboldened by much too much alcohol joined the protest.

The clash between revelers and police continued to grow into a massive melee that newspapers in the coming days would call a full-on riot! Police attempted to clear the streets using tear gas and high-pressure fire hoses to pummel the crowd.

Eight people were injured and 114 were arrested during the chaos. The incident was such major news that several days later, Florida Governor Reubin Askew ordered an inquiry into the incident by the state Department of Criminal Law Enforcement.

In the roundup that ensnared 114 individuals charged with drunk and disorderly conduct, one conspicuous figure that stood out was Malcolm. Upon being apprehended and processed, Malcolm carrying no physical identification, resorted to verbally providing a false identity in a feeble attempt to conceal his true self.

However, fate intervened when a vigilant police book-in clerk, endowed with a great memory and a keen eye for detail, discerned a striking resemblance between Malcolm and the photograph disseminated by the FBI to law enforcement agencies across the nation.

In a pivotal moment, the cloak of anonymity that Malcolm sought to drape himself in was forcibly stripped away, marking an abrupt termination of his fugitive odyssey. The seemingly routine arrest during the riot unfolded as a turning point, bringing an end to Malcolm's audacious evasion of the law and setting the stage for his inevitable return to Indiana and his eventual reckoning with justice.

CHAPTER 27
PAYING THE PIPER

Pendleton, Indiana – January 10, 1976

The Justice Prisoner and Alien Transportation System (JPATS), nicknamed "Con Air," is a United States Marshals Service airline charged with the transportation of persons in legal custody to and from prisons, detention centers, courthouses, and other locations. It is the largest prison transport network in the world. Unfortunately, it wasn't created until 1995.

The air transport of federal inmates over long distances during Malcolm's time was much more complicated. The process required an escort by two U.S. Marshals, accompanying him on a regular passenger jet. This posed numerous problems, including danger to civilians, a backlog of marshals needed to perform such escorts, and a high taxpayer expense. Still, in 1976, it was the most efficient way to get Malcolm from South Florida back to Indiana to answer for the charge of escape.

Malcolm, shackled and led through the airport by two U.S. Marshals garnered stares and generated uneasiness from the other air travelers, especially the ones sharing the flight to Indiana. Even though the agents covered Malcolms hands with a jacket to conceal the handcuffs, his leg shackles were still very obvious.

The flight was uneventful. However, thoughts of escape and hijacking ran through Malcolm's head during the flight. It was a fun fantasy for him, but Malcolm knew that an attempt like that would be futile. He sat next to the window staring at the ground thousands of feet below him and thinking to himself that this would probably be his final opportunity to see the United States from this unique vantage point.

When he returned to the Indiana State Reformatory, he was given a hero's welcome by the other inmates. They had all been following news reports on the television and in the newspapers about his daring escape from prison and the resulting man-hunt. They were all eager to get a chance to talk to him one-on-one and find out what adventures he had experienced during his brief odyssey of freedom.

But that would have to wait a while. Instead of being locked up with his former cellmate, Oliver, Malcolm was placed in a separate portion of the facility in solitary confinement. The warden and the administration were none too happy about Malcolm making them look like fools in the press. They were fully committed to not allowing Malcolm an opportunity to escape custody again. He was given meals in his cell, not allowed to be on the exercise yard with other inmates, had an absolutely NO VISITORS rule imposed upon him, and was subjected to cell shake-downs on a regular basis.

He eventually went to trial on his escape charge and was found guilty. He was sentenced to an additional 30 years in prison, the maximum sentence allowed by law. He also got another plane ride back to Florida where he was charged and convicted on the armed robbery and grand theft auto that he committed while on the run in Florida. With time off for good behavior and gain time, Malcolm wouldn't be eligible for release until the year 2022.

The years behind prison bars rolled by. In 2001, Malcolm now 66 years old was considered "institutionalized." He had over the years gradually become less and less able to think and act independently, because of having lived for such a long time under the rules of prison life. By this time, he had spent more of his lifetime behind bars than he had as a free man. He learned to not only accept the regimented life of an inmate, but he came to depend on it.

Needless to say, at his age, Malcolm didn't like change and had become as comfortable behind the grey stone walls of the Indiana State Reformatory as most people are in their own living room. But change was coming, and it was coming soon.

The Indiana Reformatory now renamed and known as The Pendleton Correctional Facility, was sued in federal court in 2001 for cruel and unusual punishment of inmates. Alleged abuses included the restricting of food as punishment for rule infractions, excessive force by correctional officers, and the most egregious charge, over-crowding. Inmates in some cases were assigned four men to a cell meant to only house two.

The judge in the case found merit in some of the complaints and issued an order that some inmates were to be sent to other facilities to get the Pendleton Correctional Facility's inmate population under control. Malcolm was one of the inmates chosen to be sent to a new facility. Perhaps it was random or perhaps they saw it as an opportunity to get rid of an escape risk. Even at age 66, Malcolm was strong both in mind and body. Administrators always thought that even though he seemed "institutionalized," he still posed the threat of escape.

Malcolm and 19 other inmates found themselves relocated to the recently established Coleman Correctional Institute, a brand-new prison facility that had opened just the year before. Interestingly, this facility was situated in central

Florida, the very place Malcolm had always sought refuge when he would escape.

Coleman is a key component of the Federal Correctional Complex (FCC). Coleman, positioned near Sumterville in central Florida, is an expansive federal prison complex recognized as one of the largest in the United States. Comprising various facilities tailored to different security levels, FCC Coleman accommodates a diverse inmate population.

Given Malcolm's reputation as a flight risk, he was assigned to the maximum-security section of the complex. The security measures in place there highlighted the danger of those housed within.

In the maximum-security portion of the Coleman Correctional Facility, life unfolds within an environment marked by strict regulations, heightened security measures, and a palpable atmosphere of tension. The towering fences and formidable structures emphasize the presence of total control. High, reinforced walls and electronic surveillance systems underscore the facility's commitment to preventing escapes and maintaining order.

Malcolm's cell became a microcosm of his existence, a space where he grappled with isolation and introspection. Daily routines were punctuated by regimented schedules, with meals, recreation, and any permitted activities tightly controlled. Life in maximum security often meant limited privileges. Malcolm and the other inmates had restricted access to educational and vocational programs, visitation rights, and communal activities. Personal freedoms were curtailed in the interest of maintaining a secure environment.

On the morning of August 7th, 2010, Malcolm was abruptly awakened by a correctional officer with a stern directive: "It's time to go."

Accompanying the officer were three other correctional officers, the warden, and a minister. Malcolm found himself shackled and guided through unfamiliar hallways, each buzzing door signaling his journey toward Florida's infamous electric chair, known as "Ole Sparky." As the ominous chair came into view, Malcolm tensed up, requiring the correctional officers to coerce him closer.

Despite Malcolm's resistance, the younger, stronger officers secured him to the wooden chair with restraints on his wrists, ankles, and chest. A wet sponge placed atop his head let streams of water cascade down his face and neck, followed by the fastening of a metal and leather cap. The minister, a constant presence since Malcolm's departure from his cell, offered words of comfort, prayers, and reflections on forgiveness and repentance from a bible.

The warden, wearing a stoic expression, formally pronounced Malcolm Lee Garrett's fate for crimes of robbery and murder, as he carried out his duty in putting Malcolm to death. With a nod, the warden signaled to the individual next to an electrical panel. Malcolm, breathing heavily and his eyes widened by fear, observed as the switch was thrown.

As the execution unfolded, Malcolm suddenly jolted awake in his cell, his body covered in sweat, breathing heavily. The execution had been nothing more than a haunting nightmare.

Attempting to shake off the vivid imagery, Malcolm reclined back onto his bunk in an attempt to resume sleep. This recurring dream, coupled with others involving suicide and the fear of being murdered by fellow inmates, underscored the toll a lifetime in prison takes on the human psyche.

Despite the unsettling dream, Malcolm's spirits lifted later on this particular day when a correctional officer approached his cell and announced, "Garrett, you've got a letter!" Excited about the unexpected correspondence, Malcolm eagerly accepted the letter - which had already been opened by prison staff - and read the letter from his half-brother, Gary Garrett.

In it, Gary conveyed the somber news of Delois Garrett's passing. Malcolm felt a pang of sadness upon learning about Delois's death. Despite her stern approach to his visits, he held admiration for her protective nature, akin to a mother hen watching over her chicks.

Reflecting, Malcolm couldn't help but acknowledge the impact a strong maternal presence might have had on his own life during his formative years, perhaps wishing for a better path shaped by such influence. He expressed those feelings when he wrote back to Gary.

The two of them exchanged letters a handful of times. In one correspondence, Gary told Malcolm how he, Carl, and Dale had all become police officers and had all worked for the same law enforcement agency, The Winter Haven Police Department. Considering his life-long confrontations with the law, Gary was unsure how Malcolm might receive the news that three out of five of his half-brothers had pursued law enforcement as a career path.

Upon receiving a response, Gary was taken aback by Malcolm's unexpected sentiments.

"I realize that we haven't been particularly close over these many years, and I'm truly and sincerely sorry about that," Malcolm expressed in his letter. "But I want you to understand that the three of you made the right decision becoming cops. I'm proud of you. I've spent almost my entire life behind prison bars, and if there's one regret that weighs on me the most, it's not having the chance to be with my family. You and Carl and Dale's commitment to upholding the law and becoming policemen defines who you are and shows what remarkable men you've become. In some small way, I like to believe that your righteousness makes up for mine, Jimmy's and Billy Ray's life of crime. At least, that's my hope anyway."

Gary, astonished by Malcolm's reply, eagerly shared their correspondence with Carl and Dale. Subsequent to that exchange of letters, the frequency of communication between Gary and Malcolm dwindled, eventually leading to a cessation of contact.

Retired from his law enforcement career and now residing in Tennessee, Gary entertained the thought of paying Malcolm a personal visit at Coleman Correctional while in Florida. The allure of exchanging stories about their contrasting experiences as a police officer and as a former bank robber fueled Gary's interest. Regrettably, this envisioned meeting never came to fruition.

CHAPTER 28
HOOCH

Sumterville, Florida – October 22, 2005

On this fall day, Malcolm celebrated his 70th birthday in prison. It hardly felt like fall since the Coleman Correctional Facility is situated in central Florida. The temperature on this day was 84 degrees. Malcolm never got used to the constant heat in Florida. In Tennessee, by October, temperatures were usually already starting to dip down into the 60's. And forget about snow. He hadn't seen any of that since he had left Indiana.

In the scorching temperatures of Florida, an unconventional form of "snow" was a clandestine source of pleasure for inmates. Within the facility's walls, a smorgasbord of illegal substances awaited those who sought solace from their confined reality. Marijuana prevailed as the most commonplace, but the menu extended far beyond, featuring the likes of cocaine, ecstasy, heroin, molly, meth, and an array of other forbidden poisons.

While corrupt corrections officers were often the conduits for smuggling in illegal drugs, some inmates resorted to ingenuity to bypass the system. One particularly resourceful individual devised an inventive method involving his wife.

She meticulously packed minuscule condom tips tightly with cocaine or heroin and discreetly carried them into the facility, cleverly concealed within a re-sealed M&M bag identical to those available in the vending machine of the visiting room.

During his visitation, the wife would switch the bags and the inmate would swallow the balls of illicit drugs in the condom tips. After visitation, the inmate was strip searched and of course, the guards wouldn't find any contraband on him because the contraband was IN him. Later in his cell, the inmate would crap out the packages of drugs, rinse them off, and for as long as the supply lasted, he would be The King of Coleman.

The influx of marijuana followed a similar route. A minute quantity, akin to the size of a Chapstick lid, could be procured for a mere dollar on the outside. However, within the prison's confines, where the challenges and risks of smuggling were heightened, that same amount of marijuana would command a staggering price tag of around $25.00.

Upon the arrival of a fresh drug shipment within the facility, inmates seemingly emerged from the shadows. In a matter of hours, the entire yard was abuzz with knowledge of the newfound stash and its proprietor. This marked the commencement of a complex bartering dance. Deals ranged from promises to meticulously clean the dealer's cell to trading precious cigarettes, offering surplus food from the chow hall, and, indeed, even engaging in transactions involving intimate sexual favors, as inmates resorted to unconventional currencies to secure their coveted doses of drugs.

Throughout his life-time in prisons, Malcolm bore witness to a myriad of drug-related activities. While he occasionally partook in the recreational use of marijuana, he steered clear of the harder substances. For Malcolm, the allure lay in alcohol, a commodity more challenging to obtain within the facility, as it typically required collaboration with a corrupt guard. Undeterred, Malcolm turned to a resourceful alternative: crafting his own brew.

The journey into the world of makeshift alcohol began with prison wine. Armed with fruit from the commissary, sugar pilfered from the kitchen by fellow inmates working there, and the elusive yeast, Malcolm embarked on his clandestine brewing endeavors. Given the scarcity of yeast, torn-up pieces of white bread often served as a pragmatic substitute.

Mixing these ingredients covertly in a garbage bag became the initial step in Malcolm's intricate procedure.

To facilitate the fermentation process, Malcolm discreetly stashed the bag in an ideal location, the prison showers. Behind a panel, a hole in the wall provided the perfect warm enclave for the hooch to rest for approximately five days, transforming into the notorious potion known as "prison wine." While it might not rival the taste of a Napa Valley vintage, it reliably achieved its primary goal of inducing a potent buzz.

Malcolm evolved into a seasoned distiller. However, there were days when mere wine didn't suffice, particularly after enduring a challenging day on the yard or celebrating a special occasion. This was when the clandestine production of "White Lightning" took center stage. Drawing on insights from his cousins in Tennessee, who were still involved in the art of crafting moonshine, Malcolm possessed a solid education in the alchemical process.

First, he needed to make what was commonly called a "stinger." A stinger is an object built to boil water. It was simple to make. All one needed was two shower drain covers, four or five rubber pencil erasers sandwiched in between the shower drain covers, and a few rubber bands to hold everything together.

The last item needed to build a stinger was an electrical cord. Those were easily stolen from administrative offices by trustees while cleaning. A cord from coffee makers, typewriters, or computer power cords worked perfectly. After attaching the stripped ends of the cord – one to each shower drain cover – being careful that the bare wires didn't touch each other – and you were done!

The only thing left to do was pour your prison wine into a plastic bucket which was inside a garbage bag. The stinger's cord ran out of the mouth of the bag and the bag was tied shut with a shoe lace. Once the stinger was plugged into an outlet, the wine would reach a rolling boil quickly. The bag would capture the steam and the resulting droplets of liquid ran down the inside of the bag and collected at the bottom. That liquid at the bottom of the bag was pure prison made White Lightning and would make you drunk faster than a bat out of hell.

Malcolm separated his batches into the corners of garbage bags and tied them off. Each little bag contained about a quart of liquor. He could sell his White Lightning to other inmates for about $50.00 per quart. Everyone in Coleman knew that if it was wine or moonshine you wanted, Malcolm was the old-timer to talk to. During his entire incarceration in the Coleman facility, he was never caught making or possessing alcohol. An amazing feat when you consider that this operation was conducted right under the noses and watchful eyes of correctional officers.

Where ever you find controlled substances, or in this case, contraband liquor, violence isn't far behind. An inmate client of Malcolm's had a dispute with him about money owed on a previous batch. Malcolm cut him off and refused to supply him any more liquor until he had brought his account current. The other inmate, 28-year-old Glenn Hesteni, argued that nothing was owed and so their beef begun.

In prison, elderly inmates are not afforded any special treatment by other inmates. They are just as likely to get into a fight with an elderly inmate as they were inmates their own age. In prison, it's all about respect. If someone feels like you disrespected them, how they responded wasn't dependent on your age.

Hesteni made a prison shank by melting three plastic butter knives together and then sharpened them on the concrete floor of his cell. Then, using tape, he fashioned a handle that insured a positive grip on the weapon.

While in the yard on November 11, 2008, Hesteni walked up behind Malcolm and using the shank, stabbed Malcolm eight times in the middle and lower right of his back puncturing Malcolm's kidney before guards could intervene. Malcolm found himself in the infirmary and Hesteni was charged for the crime and put in the hole – or as it was also called, "The Shoe."

A weaker man may have died from the blood loss alone, but because Malcolm stayed in great shape into his golden years and was strong, he survived. He eventually made a full recovery and resumed his position of dominance as the premier alcohol supplier to the prison population at Coleman Correctional Institute until he was well into his eighties.

His title and good health didn't last forever though. In the confines of Coleman Correctional, Malcolm, a once vibrant and defiant man, found himself caught in the cold tentacles of fate. The yearning for freedom that burned within him for most of his life was now replaced by a mysterious ailment that silently crept through his body, only to reveal its devastating presence a bit too late.

It all began with a persistent, gnawing pain in Malcolm's abdomen, an ache that intensified over weeks. Ignored at first as a consequence of the harsh prison environment, the pain eventually became unbearable. Malcolm, with his characteristic stoicism, tried to mask his suffering, but his fellow inmates noticed the subtle changes in his demeanor.

As the pain persisted, Malcolm's physical condition deteriorated. He began to experience unexplained weight loss, a telltale sign that something was gravely wrong. His once robust frame withered away, leaving behind a mere shadow of the criminal mastermind he used to be. His energy levels plummeted, and even routine tasks became exhausting. The prison infirmary, equipped with basic medical facilities, couldn't provide the sophisticated diagnostic tools needed to uncover the mystery lurking within Malcolm.

The prison medical staff, initially dismissive of Malcolm's complaints, eventually recognized the severity of his condition. Concerned for potential contagion within the prison, they reluctantly arranged for him to be transported to a nearby hospital for more thorough examination. It was during this process that the truth revealed itself: Malcolm had advanced pancreatic cancer.

The hospital staff, now tasked with managing a terminally ill prisoner, faced ethical dilemmas and logistical challenges. Malcolm's treatment became a complex dance between security measures and providing humane care. In the confines of a high-security ward, he underwent surgery to relieve the immediate threats to his health, followed by a grueling regimen of chemotherapy.

As the now 85-year-old Malcolm battled the physical and emotional toll of his illness, a peculiar camaraderie developed between him and some of the hospital staff. His indomitable spirit and the stark contrast of his past life with his present situation struck a chord with those who saw beyond his prison uniform. Nurses, doctors, and orderlies became unexpected allies in Malcolm's fight against a relentless adversary as he regularly regaled them with tales of bank robberies and shoot-outs.

One nurse even made a failed effort to track down his next of kin. She however never contacted Gary, Carl, or Dale. Perhaps it was because Malcolm never even mentioned that he had half-brothers.

Malcolm's journey through illness and the unlikely friendships that emerged in the sterile corridors of the hospital wove a narrative that transcended the boundaries of confinement, leaving an indelible mark on those who witnessed his final struggle.

Meanwhile, in Winter Haven, Florida, the law-and-order part of the Garrett family gradually embarked on new chapters in their lives. Lynn, Dale's wife, took the lead in this transition, choosing to bid farewell to the high-stress role of a police dispatcher. Opting to leverage her college degree, she redirected her career into the insurance industry.

Gary's wife, Lindy, faced a tumultuous emotional period that led to her retirement. Gary, in a show of support, retired as well to become her primary caretaker. They relocated to a substantial farm in Tennessee. Despite the idyllic setting, their journey took an unexpected turn, and years later, they found themselves navigating the path of divorce.

Carl, the family's sole motorcycle officer, encountered a life-altering event when he was broadsided by a civilian while on patrol on his police motorcycle, resulting in irreparable back injuries. Initially, he transitioned to light duty and eventually moved to a desk job within the detective division. Concurrently, his marriage to Kelly unraveled, and she too departed from the department.

As the winds of change swept through the family, Dale Garrett remained dedicated to serving the Winter Haven community, instructing the DARE program to thousands of children.

However, even he eventually and reluctantly pivoted away from law enforcement, drawn to pursue his passion for performing theatrical magic on a national stage.

Dale and Lynn, committed partners, chose not to have children early in their marriage. Instead, they found their hands full, raising three lively Labrador Retrievers, as they continue to reside in Winter Haven, Florida to this day.

EPILOGUE

Knoxville, Tennessee - March 8, 2021

Mike De Luca stared at the stolen jewels on his coffee table that once brought him a sense of accomplishment. But now, he felt an overwhelming emptiness. The glittering diamond gems now seemed to reflect the void in his life.

The sudden loss of his father and grandparents in a tragic car crash shattered the only sense of normal in Mike's life. The grief and emptiness he felt were compounded by the revelation that his supposed grandfather wasn't biologically related to him at all. It was an unexpected twist in the narrative of Mike's life, and it left him reeling with questions about his identity and the secrets that his family had kept from him.

Amidst the funeral preparations and condolences from well-meaning friends and relatives, Mike found himself drawn to the memories of his grandmother, Ruby. Mike was close to his grandmother and he sought solace in her presence, hoping she could offer some explanation for the shocking revelation that had come to light a few weeks before.

One evening, before the accident, in the quiet solitude of Ruby's living room, Mike broached the subject again with a mix of trepidation and curiosity. The room, adorned with family photographs that now seemed like fragments of a shattered false past, became the backdrop for a conversation that would change Mike's perception of his family forever.

As they sat together, Ruby, a woman weathered by time and burdened by secrets, began to share a story that had long been confined to the recesses of her memory. Feeling that it was time that Mike knew the truth, she spoke of her youth, a time when she fell in love with a charismatic yet troubled man named Malcolm Garrett, a notorious bank robber serving time in The Brushy Mountain Prison.

With a hesitant yet determined voice, Ruby recounted the daring escape plan he had hatched to liberate himself from prison and the details about how he had enlisted her help. In a clandestine operation filled with risk and danger, Ruby explained to Mike how she helped Malcolm Garrett break free by smuggling in women's clothing for him during visiting day. She went on to explain how the two of them embarked on a fleeting journey together.

She explained to Mike that she had fallen in love with Malcolm and how they had made plans to live out their lives together. However, the romance was short-lived, and they went their separate ways the morning after a passion-filled evening they had shared together on that night the escape happened.

The revelation hit Mike like a tidal wave of conflicting emotions. The man he had known as his grandfather was now a stranger, and his biological grandfather was an inmate with a lengthy criminal past.

Ruby, with tears in her eyes, explained that Malcolm Garrett had left her the following morning, and she never saw him again. The consequence of that brief encounter was Mike's father, the product of the one-night stand that marked the intersection of Ruby's youthful rebellion and Malcolm's criminal life.

Faced with this revelation, Mike felt a complex mix of anger, confusion, and sorrow. The foundations of his identity were shaken. Ruby, sensing the turmoil within her grandson, suggested that he seek the guidance of a therapist to help navigate the emotional maze that lay ahead.

She apologized to Mike for revealing all this to him and told him that she had thought about just taking this secret to her grave. "But," she said, "something just told me that you needed to know."

Perhaps Ruby chose to tell Mike the truth because she had a premonition of her own death and knew that if there was ever a right time to tell him, it was now. And she was right. Because shortly after this revelation to Mike, Ruby, her husband and Mike's father were leaving a movie theater when a drunk driver crossed the centerline and hit their car head-on. All three of them were killed instantly.

After the funerals, Mike contemplated his grandma Ruby's advice. Mike, burdened by grief, loss, and the weight of family secrets, took the courageous step to see Dr. Evelyn Turner, a therapist who specialized in grief and identity issues.

Dr. Turner, a middle-aged woman with a warm demeanor, welcomed Mike and invited him to take a seat. The room was decorated with calming colors and filled with soft lighting, aimed to create an atmosphere of comfort and security. Framed watercolor pieces of art depicting serene scenes of beaches and boats moored in harbors hung on the walls.

As they began the session, Dr. Turner allowed Mike to lead the conversation. At first, he spoke about the recent loss of his family members, emphasizing the pain and emptiness he felt. As the therapist skillfully guided the discussion, Mike gradually started to open up about the darker aspects of his life—the hidden world of jewelry theft, deception, and the constant evasion of law enforcement.

Dr. Turner listened attentively, withholding judgment and offering empathy. Mike, perhaps for the first time, found himself articulating the reasons behind his criminal pursuits—the need for control, the thrill of the heist, and the false sense of accomplishment it provided. He spoke about the growing realization that the jewels he stole were poor substitutes for the genuine connections he had lost.

As the session unfolded, Mike's confession of his criminal background became intertwined with the grief over his family's death. Dr. Turner skillfully navigated the delicate balance between addressing the immediate pain of loss and exploring the deeper issues that led Mike down the path of crime.

The first session ended with a tentative sense of relief for Mike, as he began to see the possibility of healing and transformation through the therapeutic process. But did that mean the end of his criminal escapades? The answer was an emphatic no. Not by a long-shot.

Mike's mother had passed away during his birth 35 years
ago, so he never even knew her. But now, with his father
and grandparents gone, he was feeling especially alone in
the world. After a number of sessions with Dr. Turner, he
decided to seek out his real grandfather, Malcolm Garrett, in
hopes that he could help him process his grief and learn if his
own criminal tendencies may have been passed down to him
genetically.

As he researched old newspaper articles about Malcolm and
his brothers' daring bank robberies, he began to come to
know his grandpa Malcolm as one of America's most
notorious and famous bank robbers. As he read about the
shoot-outs, bank-jobs, and ingenious escapes, he started
feeling a strange respect and connection to this man he had
never met. He had a misplaced sense of pride in being the
grandson of such a criminal mastermind.

Mike wondered to himself if he too could ever achieve that
same level of notoriety in jewelry heists as Malcom had done
with bank robberies. If a possibility existed, it would need to
be a very high-profile heist – not his normal, more
commonplace jewelry store jobs.

After much research, he discovered that Malcolm was
incarcerated in Maximum Security of the Coleman
Correctional Facility in Florida. Unfortunately, by the time he
tracked down where Malcolm was imprisoned, it was too

late. He discovered that Malcolm had passed away from pancreatic cancer almost exactly one year before.

Discouraged by his inability to have the opportunity to meet Malcolm in person, Mike grabbed a beer from his fridge and flopped down in his favorite spot in his living room, a blue winged-back chair, and flipped on his 77" flat-screen television to unwind.

Just at that moment, a news story was on about a new special exhibit at The Metropolitan Museum of Art in New York City that would be on display through April. The name of the exhibition was called, "Jewelry for America" and featured "300 years of American jewelry design and innovation on display." After the story aired, Mike continued to watch several other shows until it was time for him to go to bed.

As he mindlessly watched the other shows, his focus was internal. Mike finished his beer and sat the bottle down. With an ink pen and a pad of paper he kept on the table next to his chair, he scribbled a three-word reminder down on the pad.

On his way to his bedroom, he tossed the pen and pad of paper on his desk next to the keyboard of his computer. He paused at the hallway and glanced back at the pad of paper as he slightly smiled and then switched off the living room light.

Those three cryptic words hinted at Mike's new agenda. Those three words would reshape the narrative of Mike's future, making "Research The Met" a phrase laden with unforeseen significance, risk, and intrigue.

PHOTOGRAPHS

The enigmatic Malcolm Garrett. Malcolm led the criminal trio of Garretts on their trail of mayhem as he plunged the mid-west and the south into chaos. This FBI book-in photo was taken following his arrest at the Midland Mall in Maryville, Tennessee on January 15, 1973.

Jimmy Lee Garrett. The second oldest of the Garrett gang. Jimmy Lee was shot and killed by a police sniper at the Midland Mall on January 15, 1973. File photo from previous arrest by the Blount County, Tennessee Sheriff's Office.

Billy Ray Garrett. The youngest of the three criminal Garrett brothers. Although incarcerated for his role as the wheelman in two bank robberies, Billy Ray eventually found redemption in Christ and lived out the rest of his life earning an honest living and raising a big family.

Gary Garrett. The eldest of the three brothers who became police officers. Gary's law enforcement career spanned multiple agencies in Polk County Florida. Gary is now retired and lives in Decatur, Tennessee.

*Carl Garrett. Assigned to the motorcycle division, Carl served
a traffic homicide investigator and later, after injuries
received on duty, as a detective with the department. Carl is
now retired and resides in Philadelphia, Tennessee.
(photo credit: Carl Garrett)*

Dale Garrett. The youngest of the three Garrett brothers who became law enforcement officers. Dale moonlighted as a professional stage magician during his career and continued to perform shows after retiring from police work. Dale is also the author of this book and resides with his wife, Lynn in Winter Haven, Florida.
(photo credit: Dale Garrett)

The Garrett family.
Back row, left to right: Carl, the twins, Roger, Ronnie
Middle row, left to right: Delois and Al Garrett
Front: Dale Garrett (photo credit: Dale Garrett)

The three law enforcement Garrett brothers together. Gary,
Carl, and Dale.
(photo credit: Dale Garrett)

The actual covered wagon lamp that Malcolm built while serving time in the Indiana State Reformatory. He gifted it to his father, Al, while on the run from the law. Over the years, the cloth covering the wagon (the lamp shade) deteriorated and the supporting ribs have been lost.
(photo credit: Gary Garrett)

The fortress-like Brushy Mountain Prison in Petros, Tennessee where Malcolm escaped dressed as a woman and was assisted by Ruby Alexander, a young, impressionable girl who Malcolm cajoled into helping him pull off the escape.
(photo credit: George Deal)

Delois Garrett. The mother of the three Garrett boys who became police officers. Each of them credits her as the driving force behind their disciplined up-bringing and for her voracious protection from negative influences. Especially their outlaw half-brothers.
(photo credit Gary Garrett)

FBI Agent, Andrew Nelson.

Instrumental in bringing the Criminal Garretts to justice. Agent Nelson worked tirelessly on the multi-state crime spree that paralyzed the region in fear.

FBI Agent, Daniel Foster (R.I.P.)

The lead FBI agent assigned to the Bank robberies in Swayzee and Fairmount, Indiana.
Agent Foster was shot and killed by one of the Garretts' accomplices while attempting to take them into custody in Maryville, Tennessee on January 15, 1973

Author Dale O. Garrett's retirement badge.
(photo credit: Dale Garrett. Special thanks to Glenn Hester)

-ABOUT THE AUTHOR-

Dale O. Garrett has been an author since 2014. Dale is also a retired Winter Haven, Florida police officer and taught the D.A.R.E. Program to thousands of children in his community during his career in law enforcement. Dale is married and lives with his wife and three Labradors in central Florida.

www.ingramcontent.com/pod-product-compliance
Lightning Source LLC
Chambersburg PA
CBHW071641260626
47170CB00001B/185